CW00858244

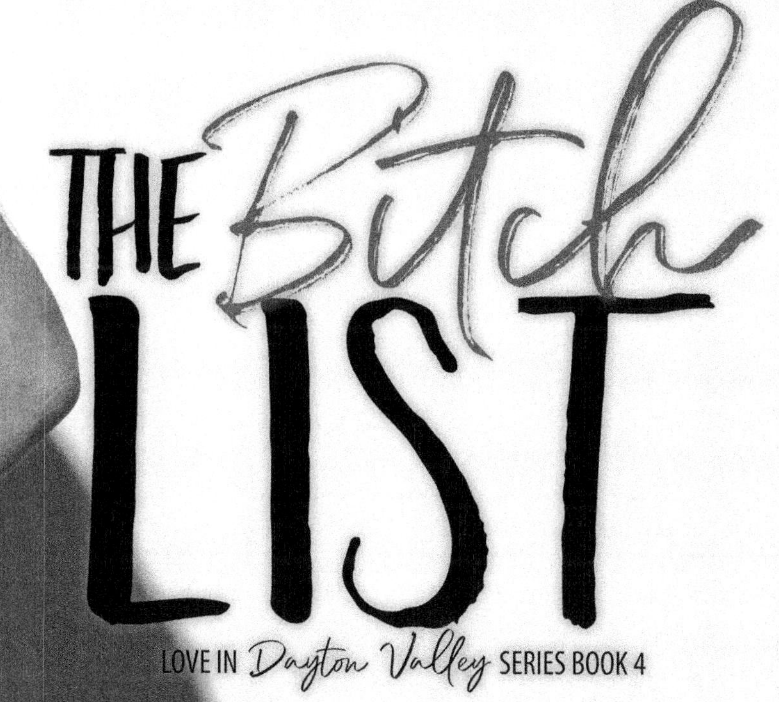

NIKKI ASHTON

The Bitch List

Published by Bubble Books Ltd

The Bitch List

First published September 2022 All Rights Reserved ©

Cover design – LJ Stock of LJ Designs

Edited by – Anna Bloom

Proofread by - Flora Burgos

Formatted by – LJ Stock of LJ Designs

WARNING

This book contains a hot man who is funny, bright, can hold a tune and is good with kids.
Please be aware this amount of awesomeness is not normal in one man.

ACKNOWLEDGMENTS

Does anyone actually read these acknowledgments? If you do here's some oldies but goodies for you.

What's the difference between a G-spot and a golf ball?

A guy will actually search for a golf ball.

What does the sign on an out-of-business brothel say?

Beat it. We're closed.

What's the difference between a tire and 365 used condoms?

One's a Goodyear. The other's a *great* year.

What's the difference between a hooker and a drug dealer?

A hooker can wash her crack and resell it.

What do the Mafia and pussies have in common?

One slip of the tongue, and you're in deep shit.

A huge thank you to you for reading this book and losing yourself in the crazy world of Dayton Valley

Love ya millions,

n i k k i

DEDICATION

To my gorgeous niece Nancy.
Your sensitivity and kindness are just two of the things
that make you beautiful.
Don't ever change

CHAPTER 1

Nancy

Late by three weeks, Aunt Flo had finally arrived, thank the lord. She'd never been one for being on time, a week or so late for a visit wasn't unusual, but three was pretty scary. Particularly as I hated the man who may well have put a bun in my oven. Imagine that—me having a baby with Shaw Jackson, the biggest dick on the planet. Despite him being such a douche, it was the second time I'd had sex with him. The first time had been almost a year ago at our friend's wedding.

While Ellie and Hunter were dancing the night away with their guests, Shaw was giving me a big O behind the the Delaney's barn. And I mean a *real big* O. Obviously I didn't tell him how good it was, his ego was already more inflated than a bouncy house. Instead, we'd done the deed and then walked away from each other, never to speak of it, or to each other again—at least we wouldn't have. Sadly for me, we mixed in the same circles. While Shaw had been away at Harvard, it had been easy. I barely saw him except for when he was home on college breaks. Now though, he'd transferred to Texas Tech law school and was working part-time for Tate Hallahan, the town's new lawyer, which meant if he was at school all week, he was then home most weekends.

Seeing him all the time hadn't changed my opinion of him. There was no doubt he was good looking, gorgeous in fact, with his blond hair and bright blue eyes, but he wasn't so gorgeous on the inside—not in my experience anyway. We'd clashed in senior year at high school, and it had gradually grown worse since then. All that pent up hate had led to some hot sex though. Plus, he had a really nice penis—and I mean a *really* nice penis. Not too big, not too small, nice and smooth with wonderfully manicured balls—his sister was a beauty therapist so maybe that accounted for that, but getting his sister to do that for him was weird!

Nice pecker aside, I didn't like *him*, and I blamed our last round of sex on alcohol. The first time I'd been nursing a bruised and broken heart, the second time I'd been nursing a bottle of fizzy wine and felt the need to share it. We'd both been at Bronte and Carter's housewarming party, and we'd both gotten drunker than skunks. At the end of the night as we'd waited outside for a couple of Ubers, one shared bottle of warm wine had led to us kissing. As my Uber had turned up first, we decided why not share and have more kissing in the rear seat.

"Seems a shame for me not to come back and finish that wine with you," Shaw had said.

"Driver," I'd cried, pointing the bottle in the direction we were travelling. "We're both going to my place, so step on it. ."

Two hours, forty minutes, and two rounds of awesome sex, some mutual giving of oral, and one finger banging session later, I'd kicked Shaw out. By then we were both starting to sober and lying naked next to each other and feeling a little weird. Now, three weeks later I was more than glad to be sitting on my couch with stomach cramps.

Bemoaning my sexual choices, I held a hot water bottle against my stomach and looked down at my ringing phone. It was my friend Lily which made me groan. I loved her, even though we'd only really been friends for a short time, since Ellie and Hunter's bachelor and bachelorette party, but we'd bonded over cornering and killing Shaw and my then boyfriend, Minnesota, at paintballing. From then on, we'd become close. She'd helped me come to terms with the fact that Minnesota had dumped me because he hadn't wanted me to go traveling with him, and I'd helped her to fit into Dayton Valley life. The groan therefore was because I knew she was going to try and persuade me to help out with the birthday party of JJ, the little kid she helped to look after. Okay, so I was a kindergarten teacher's aide, but I really didn't want to be near kids when I had stomach cramps. She was also the only person who knew about me and Shaw. I'd felt safe telling her, because at three years younger than me, she didn't mix with the older ones in my group of friends. She knew them obviously, Hunter was practically her stepbrother after all, but she wasn't around them on many social occasions. Plus, she wasn't officially old enough to drink so she was less likely to get drunk and blurt out my secret. The groan therefore was also because I knew she would want to grill me about my missing period, which, even though it had arrived, would lead to talk of Shaw and I really wasn't in the mood.

I knew however, she'd keep calling until I picked up. "Hey, you."

"You sound sad," she gasped. "Oh my God, did Shaw get you pregnant. Damn, Nancy, what're you going to do?"

"Take a breath." I sighed. "And no, he didn't. I got my period."

"Shit. I was like going like crazy for you."

After a year in Dayton Valley, she was losing her SoCal accent but from time to time, when she was excitable it slipped in—now was one of those occasions.

"I said you should have taken the morning after pill."

"I knew deep down I wasn't. I have the implant and we used a condom, both times."

"Wait. You did it with him twice?" she asked, her voice rising to a high a pitch.

"Three if you count the wedding sex," I mused.

"You really do like his penis, don't you? No matter how much you try to deny it." She started to make a clicking noise.

"What are you doing?" I asked, shifting on the couch to get a little comfier.

"Thinking."

"What about?" I shrugged even though she couldn't see me.

"How we're going to distract you from the peen in future. It's quite a dilemma."

"Seriously, Lily. You don't need to worry. I won't be going near it again."

"Yeah, that's what you've said before. I'm sure they were your first thoughts as you pulled your panties up. Why do you hate him so much anyway?" she asked. "You've never said."

I dropped my head back against the couch and closed my eyes. Good question. Trust Lily to remind me of the night that made me shudder.

"Prom," I responded, feeling a familiar spike of anger. "He asked me but didn't turn up. Left me standing like an idiot on our porch while wearing a hideous yellow dress that if I had my time again, I would never have let my mom buy." Thoughts of my mom made my chest ache and I felt bad at dissing her sense of style. I'd lost my folks in a fire when I was eighteen, not long after that hideous prom night, so as an only child I'd been left alone. My Uncle Raymond called from time to time, but he lived in Boston with his husband Mario. It'd been just me for almost five years.

Lily gasped, pushing my sadness to one side. "Woah. Burn."

"Yeah, exactly. And he has the nerve to hate me!"

"I mean I never wanted to go to prom, but I could imagine if you did and a guy like Shaw asked you, well that must have hurt." She whistled and I had to move the phone from my ear.

"What do you mean a guy like Shaw. What sort of guy is he?" If she said '*a good guy'* we could no longer be friends. He was a dick, no two ways about it.

"Hot," she exclaimed. "Because, you have to admit he is. He looks a lot like Charlie Hunnam."

And wasn't that the truth. Okay, so she was right, Shaw was most definitely hot but what was the point of that if you were an argumentative, egotistical idiot.

"Did I ever tell you I met him?"

"Who? Shaw?"

"No, stupid." Lily sighed. "Charlie Hunnam. My dad was kind of seeing one of the actresses on the show. I say seeing her, he was having sex with her in between her scenes."

"Was she a main character?" I asked, my interest piqued.

"Hmm, kind of." She huffed. "The point is I met him, and he was like real nice. He's English you know and to be honest Shaw has much bluer eyes."

I felt grumpy all of a sudden. I wanted her to think he was an argumentative egotistical idiot with pale uninteresting eyes, the color of twenty-year old washed-out denim, not the damn South Pacific.

"Okay, whatever." I sighed heavily. "Now you know I'm not having the spawn of Satan, you can go. I'm sure you have better things to do."

"Well, it is family night tonight. I do need to prepare my game face."

I giggled knowing she would be rolling her eyes. Her mom, Kitty, and Jefferson Delaney, Hunter's dad, were dating. Lily knew they were gearing up to tell her that she and Kitty were moving to the ranch.

It was obvious to everyone they were madly in love and would be taking the next step soon. Kitty and Jefferson however, had been arranging lots of family dinners and activities. All, that Lily was sure, were to prepare her for the big news and to get her used them becoming a family.

"You should just tell them that you know," I replied. "Then tell them how you want your room decorated."

"No way," she scoffed. "It's far more fun this way. Jefferson buys me so much bribery ice cream he pretty much has shares in the dairy."

"Up to you," I winced as a cramp hit. "But I'm going to eat chocolate, drink wine and watch Netflix. So g'night, Lily."

"No, no, no," she cried. "Don't go yet. I have a favor I need to ask."

I knew I should never have answered the damn phone.

CHAPTER 2

Shaw

"Honey, can't you take just a few days off before working for Tate?" Mom asked as she placed a mug of coffee in front of me. "You've just finished a real hard year of law school."

"I want the experience, Mom, and this project that Tate is setting up is important."

Tate Hallahan had moved to Dayton Valley a little less than a year ago and was already doing great things. Including setting up a specialized arm of his firm that specifically helped single moms, abused women and divorced women—basically any woman that had been wronged by a man. His dad trying to cheat his mom out of millions in their divorce had given him the idea.

"Tate's got a huge case load as well as interviewing a couple of other lawyers and he needs me to contact a ton of support groups to see if they want to partner with us."

Mom rubbed my head and sighed. "It's all amazing what he's doing, but I just wish you'd been able to take a few days off first. Austen was hoping that you'd go go-karting with him."

I gave her the side eye. "No, *you* were hoping I'd go karting with Austen. He's too busy doing what Austen does and you want *me* to find out exactly what that is. And if what Austen does is sex you want *me* to make sure he's being careful."

Her sigh was heavier this time. "I think I know the answer but he's sixteen. I'm worried that we'll have another grandchild on the way. Do you know he went out with *three* different girls last month? Three, Shaw. I'd bet money on the fact that he had sex with all of them."

"How the hell do you know that?" I laughed and reached for a piece of buttered toast and took a bite.

"He got a hicky on consecutive nights and the third night he came in with his shirt on backward."

"That doesn't mean he's having sex, Mom. He might just be making out with them. Admittedly that sounds like pretty hot making out, but that might be all it is."

She flopped down onto a chair next to me and hugged her own coffee mug to her chest. "At least when he was dating Peggy I knew where he was and that he had no idea that he could do more than pee from his wiener."

That made me burst out laughing—my mom was so naïve it was unbelievable. Austen had asked me all about sex when he was fifteen. Apparently, I was a much better source of information than Hunter and Carter, who both sucked. So, of course, I'd had to do the big brother thing and explain that they were both underage and maybe they should wait. Then I'd bought him a jumbo box of condoms and given him my copy of 'How to Please your Woman in bed'.

"Take good care of it," I'd said as I held out the delicate paperback. "Read the notes in the margins. They're mine, Hunters, Carters and Alaska's. They'll serve you well." It was a real fucking Obi Wan moment.

Austen however, had screwed up his nose at the mention of the other three men using the book, but I'd slapped his back and smiled. "Think about it Aust'. The three biggest studs of Dayton Valley High, now married to really hot women."

"Ugh, one of them is our sister," he'd replied. "That's gross."

"Yeah." I'd sighed. "But one is also Ellie Maples."

He'd gone bright red, snatched the book, and marched away, his hand already down his shorts—he'd had a huge crush on Ellie since he was eleven years old.

"The point is," Mom said, regaining my attention. "I need to know he's being safe. One of those girls that called him sounded older, like a college girl, not a high school girl."

I mentally high-fived my little brother if that were true.

"Mom, he's good. He's not stupid and he has condoms." I knew he was using them because I'd spotted him buying more only the week before. Fair play to my little brother, that'd been a fucking big box I'd bought him.

She gasped and almost fell off her chair. "So, he *is* having sex?"

And that was my cue to leave. I could not get into a debate with her about my sixteen-year-old brother having sex, I'd be there all day. That would also potentially move onto my love life where'd she'd question and bully me into admitting the only person I'd had sex with recently was Nancy Andrews, a girl it was common knowledge that I hated.

Well, hated might be a strong word, seeing I was pretty sure I was in lust with her pussy. It was just so damn good. Pity it was attached to Nancy.

"Mom, if you want to know just ask him." I swallowed back the rest of my coffee, took one more bite of my toast and then stood and kissed her cheek. "But be prepared for him to tell you to mind your own business."

"I don't remember being half this worried about you and Bronte," she replied, looking up at me with worry in her eyes.

"Well, maybe that's because Bronte and I were sneakier. She taught me everything I know about creeping out of the house when you thought I was studying."

Mom's eyes went wide as she gasped and I knew then that it was most definitely time to leave.

*

Tate had set up his law firm in the old fire house, right at the end of Main Street. While it was a pretty old building, his mom had given him a huge sum of money to renovate it. That meant while it looked all of its red-bricked one-hundred-and three years old on the outside with huge double doors and two-story arch windows, inside it was pretty state of the art. We had the best of everything. Our meeting room was more like mission control with all the high-tech video conferencing equipment. This all meant that Tate could still run a top law firm in a small town. To be truthful though, he was all about helping those who didn't have much, and I knew Tate was exactly the kind of attorney that I eventually wanted to be one day.

When I let myself in, Evie our receptionist had her head down and was looking at her phone. She'd worked for the local realtor Bobby Patrick but had got pretty pissed with having to make excuses for him when he let clients down. Kitty, Tate's mom, had been the one who'd suggested she work for Tate, and she was doing a great job.

"Morning, Evie," I said, tapping with my knuckles on her desk.

She jumped and slapped a hand to her chest before quickly throwing her phone to one side.

"Oh hey, morning."

"You okay?" I asked, seeing as she was frowning and looked pale.

She glanced down at her phone and then back up to me. "Yeah, yep. All good. You okay?"

I studied her for a second and then nodded. "Yeah, great thanks. Tate in his office?"

"Yes," she breathed out. "He's going over some things with Robyn and then he has Hank Danvers coming in."

Robyn was the firm's secretary and she and her husband, Miguel, lived in nearby Middleton Ridge with their three-year-old, Macy.

"Shit," I replied. "The Danvers thing still going on. I thought Wes had come to an agreement."

"Apparently not."

The Danvers brothers had been fighting over their father's land since he'd died and left everything to Hank. Hank had agreed to give his brother half but that wasn't enough for Wes. He'd been the one to help his dad work the land in the first place. Hank however, had been the one who'd bailed his dad out of debt ten years before, meaning he still had land to work. He'd never asked for the money back and was just glad the land stayed in the family.

"I'll leave him to it then," I replied.

"You want coffee?" Evie asked as I walked along the corridor to the main office. "I'm going to Delphine's in ten."

I started to walk backward and called. "The usual with a Danish would be amazing. I skipped the food part of breakfast at home." Come on, two bites of toast weren't breakfast.

"What do I tell you about it being the most important meal of the day." Evie rolled her eyes and jotted something down on her notepad.

"Yeah, well, when it's accompanied with talk of my baby brother's sex life it's not so important."

"Okay then." Her eyebrows rose and I laughed, turning back around to make my way to my desk. When I lifted my head up, I was surprised to see Antonia, Tate's legal assistant sitting at my desk. She was usually found in her own office pouring through documents and past cases that might help Tate.

Antonia was around my folk's age and had just seen her youngest son go off to high school. First, she'd applied for the position Evie now had, but when Tate realized she was a trained paralegal, he'd offered her the legal assistant role instead. She was amazing too. Nothing got passed her and she was a devil for the detail.

"Morning, Shaw." She smiled brightly and ran a hand over her close-cropped afro.

"Hey, don't often see you out of your office," I joked as I sat down to face her.

"I know, right." She leaned her forearms on my desk and grinned. "I feel a little lightheaded got to say."

I really liked Antonia as she never made me feel like the stupid college kid who knew nothing. She'd even asked my advice on a case, knowing I'd done Mock Court at college, on something similar only the month before.

"How can I help you?" I asked, turning on my Mac.

"Tate asked if you could do him a huge favor. I offered but I need to go over the documents for the unfair dismissal case he's going to court with next week. He said you might have time before you start calling the support groups." Her eyes were pleading. "If you don't have time, just say so. I can work late. I'll put John off bringing the kids to meet me from work for an early dinner at Delphine's."

"God no." I objected and frowned. "It's fine. I have plenty of time to get through my list. So, what is it he needs me to do?"

She sat back in the chair and steepled her fingers under her chin. "The custody case for Meghan Ranger, the lady whose husband took the kids from school one day and now won't let her see them? He's going for full custody."

I nodded.

"Tate wants to know if you could go and talk to the kindergarten teacher. She was the one who noticed how anxious the little boy was when his dad would pick him up. We need to see if she's changed her mind about testifying."

"She won't testify?" I asked, amazed.

Antonia winced. "She's feeling a little jumpy about it. Turns out Brad Ranger is her husband's brother's boss at the Chevrolet dealership in Lubbock."

"She has a duty of care to the kids though, right?" I couldn't believe the teacher wouldn't go to court. "And if he sacks the brother-in-law he sues for unfair dismissal."

"I agree, but she says she might have been seeing things that weren't there. You know, because she knew Mom and Dad were divorcing." Antonia sighed heavily and looked out of the office window to Main Street. "The boy shows no sign of injury and says his dad never hit him. When he wasn't ignoring them, he just hollered a lot at the boy and his sister."

I couldn't imagine being scared of my dad just from him yelling at us. I'd rarely heard him raise his voice, unless it was during Friday night football games. Mom had been the one who scolded us when we were kids, while Dad just gave us that 'I'm so disappointed with you' look that worked far better.

"But the teacher's testimony would help?" I asked.

Antonia nodded. "Sure would. But if she won't, well maybe talk to the teacher's aide."

My blood went cold, and my stomach dropped. Really? Did the world hate me that fucking much?

"The teacher's aide?"

"That's right. Tate thinks if we can't get the teacher but still got her it would be a huge help. Okay," she said and pushed up from the chair giving me a huge smile. "I'm going back to employment law cases, see if I can't find something we can use as precedent. Although being fired for posting your boss's bad taste in bathroom tiles on social media is kind of a new thing to me. See you later, honey and thanks again. Oh, and their addresses are on the file."

As she wandered back to her own office, I couldn't help but wish I'd known the favor before I'd said yes. Although to be honest, there was no way I could have said no. I was only a part-time Associate. And, if Mrs. Baker said no, then I was going to be making a visit to the person I wanted to see the least—Nancy-fucking-Andrews with the magical pussy.

CHAPTER 3

Nancy

Bang, bang, bang.

"Fuck off," I groaned under my breath, pulling my knees to my chest.

Bang, bang, bang.

That was the third time whoever was on the other side had decided to piss me off. The first time when I didn't get up, throw the door open and greet them with a smile, they should have got the message. The message being, as I said, 'fuck off'.

I never cussed. When working with little kids it was a real bad idea. You have any idea how often those kids repeat stuff? Imagine them going home, they bang their toe and shout out 'shit that fucking hurts'. What their parents say in front of them was one thing, but I was not going to be the one to sully those sweet innocent lips.

Bang, bang, bang.

"Nancy, I know you're in there. I can smell your breath."

Damn it. What the hell had I done to deserve this? I must have been a real bad person in a past life to have landed myself with Shaw Jackson. Lily was right, I really needed a distraction from his penis. I was kind of obsessed with it, even though I couldn't stand the sight of him. Just hearing his voice on the other side of the door made my cooch sit up and beg.

Shaw Jackson was most definitely a Grandmaster of the Cooch. In fact, I was going to rename his penis and balls Grandmaster Schlong and the Furious Two. I bet they did an amazing cover of The Message!

Laughing quietly at my own stupidity, I dropped my feet to the floor and with a sigh pushed up from the couch. Catching a glimpse of myself in the mirror, I second guessed my thought process of answering the door. I had a bird's nest on my head, coffee down my t-shirt, a huge spot on my chin while wearing the baggiest pair of sweats known to man. It was day two of my period and it was no better than day one.

"Doesn't matter," I hissed, as I turned the lock on the door. "Not like I care what he thinks of me anyway."

"Shit," Shaw groaned as I flung the door open. "Don't you look pretty."

"Not that I care what you think of me, Shaw, but I have my period."

He visibly winced and then broke into a grin. "That means…"

I rolled my eyes. "Correct. You haven't left me with the worst souvenir possible of the worst experience ever."

"Bullshit," he said as he pushed past me. "You loved every damn second of it."

He was right, I had. Didn't make me like him as a person any better though. The egotistical numbnut.

"Come in why don't you," I grumbled and pushed the door closed behind him.

"Official business not a booty call." He turned and flashed me what I hated to admit was a sexy grin. He was actually sexy full stop with his tight ass, ripped stomach and eyes that sparkled like the most beautiful ocean. He even walked sexily. He was the blond-haired, blue-eyed boy every girl would want if he wasn't such a… well, there weren't any words bad enough to describe him. I think I'd exhausted every insult I could think of, and I liked to be innovative whenever possible. Maybe I'd spend the evening thinking up new ones.

"What official business could you have with me?" I asked, my attention back on Shaw as I watched him bend to take a chocolate from the box on my coffee table. "Please help yourself."

He turned and shrugged, popping the chocolate into his mouth, and then opened his mouth to speak with it full—so disgusting. "Annie Baker has decided not to testify in the Ranger custody case."

"She said she would." I folded my arms over my coffee-stained chest, feeling a little pissed at the teacher I was the aide for. "She was the one who first mentioned to me that Eddie seemed uneasy when his dad picked him up from school. It was because of her that I kept an eye out."

"Yeah well." He sighed. "She's decided her brother-in-law's job with Brad Ranger is more important."

I gasped. "She can't do that. Her duty is to Eddie as his teacher."

"My thoughts exactly, but we can't force her to testify."

"And now you want me to?" I asked, already knowing the answer.

"That's about the size of it, yeah."

I shrugged. "Sure. Whatever I can do to help. I mean all I will be able to say is how excited he was when his mom picked him up, opposed to how he could get emotional and nervous when it was his dad. I don't think he was being abused or anything like that," I stressed. "I don't want those words being put into my mouth."

"No, we know that. There's nothing to say he ever has been. We just know he prefers to be with his mom." Shaw pushed his hands into the pockets of his charcoal-colored dress pants. I couldn't help but gaze at his corded, tanned forearms which were on show under rolled back shirtsleeves. "Tate will just want you to say what you saw, nothing more nothing less."

"I can do that."

We watched each other in silence for a beat until I started to feel a little uncomfortable and cleared my throat.

"So, is that it?"

"Yep." He flashed me a tight smile and then made for the door, pausing with his hand on the knob. . "You going to Kitty's birthday party?"

Jefferson had arranged a forty-ninth birthday party for Kitty because, according to Lily, her mom was absolutely dreading being fifty the following year. Jefferson therefore wanted her to have a huge party this year so she could let her fiftieth cruise by without any fuss.

"Supposed to be, why?"

He raised his brows. "Thought you might want to know I'm taking a date."

Ignoring the tiny little jump my heart made, I curled my lip. "And?"

"Don't want you walking in and seeing me with Ruthie."

"And I would care because?"

Shaw chuckled and opened the door. "Whatever, Nancy, whatever."

He disappeared through the door and didn't even close it behind him.

"Close the door," I yelled.

"Damn, sorry." I heard him call back. "I'm already at the elevator."

Stomping across my wooden floor, I put my hand on the doorframe and looked out into the hallway where Shaw was leaning against the wall. He was looking down at his phone as he absentmindedly pressed the call button for the elevator.

There was no doubt he was handsome, and he definitely had skills in the bedroom department, but all that aside he made my piss boil.

"You could have closed it behind you."

He looked up. "Thought you might change your mind about me leaving."

"Are you crazy?" I asked. "Why the hell would I do that? I told you, it won't be happening again. You're a despicable person and I can't believe I let you…" I looked around the hallway to check we were alone, "put your penis inside of me."

"Honestly," he said, pushing away from the wall. "I can't believe I actually wanted to."

"And I can't believe you even have the nerve to dislike me," I cried, taking a step outside my front door.

"You have a big opinion of yourself, Nancy," he said with a sigh as the elevator door whooshed open. "Anyone would think your shit don't stink."

He stepped inside and turned to give me a tight-lipped smile and I felt my insides twist with distaste for him.

"It doesn't as much as yours, you stupid asshole."

Yep, I really needed to make a new list of insults. That was just damn lazy.

"Says the Queen of Assholes," he called back, waving with a smirk as the doors closed on him.

"Ugh," I groaned, slamming back inside my apartment. "What a motherfucker."

Growling to myself, I went over to my desk, snatched up a pen and pad and wrote at the top of the paper.

Nancy's Bitch List for Shaw

- [ ] Maximus Douchimus

CHAPTER 4

Shaw

When I got back to the office, Tate was talking to Evie who looked like she'd been crying.

I had a sister and had learned when to keep my nose out of it, so I nodded and walked on by, hearing a sniff from Evie as I did.

"You sure you don't want to go home?" I heard Tate ask. I assumed Evie shook her head because then he said, "Okay, but just say the word if you do."

Almost at my desk, I pulled up short when my boss called my name.

"Hey, Tate," I replied, turning to him.

"Antonia said you'd gone to see the kindergarten teacher. How'd it go? Is she going to go to bat for us?"

"No, sorry. She's adamant that she thinks she got it all wrong." I shrugged. "She's not changing her mind."

"Shit." He pinched the bridge of his nose. "We've got a good case, but the teacher would've helped."

"The teacher's aide is willing to though." I grinned, feeling pretty pleased with myself, especially when Tate's eyes went wide.

"She will? What did she say?"

I nodded. "That it's her duty." I chose not to tell him that she also said that I was an asshole.

"Fantastic. Well done, Shaw. ."

To be fair it hadn't been difficult to get her to agree, but if Tate wanted to think I'd earned my stripes, then so be it. I liked working for him and wanted to keep working for him, especially when I'd finished law school. A lot of the people I was at college with wanted to go to New York, Boston, Chicago, or any of the big cities for that matter, but I was happy to work for a guy like Tate in a small town like Dayton Valley. It wasn't that I didn't have ambition, I did, but I also didn't want to work from a cubicle with a dozen other lawyers for some big company who had no clue who you were. Helping people to avoid taxes or helping to push through underpriced takeovers was not what I was going to law school for. I loved what Tate was doing. His reputation in Frisco was already big, so the fact he now worked in a small town in Texas hadn't really hurt his business. Only a month before he'd fought a case for a woman in Maine whose boss had fired her because she wouldn't sleep with him. He'd claimed she was bad at her job in advertising sales, but Tate had proved she had the best numbers of all the team, and he got another woman to come forward who'd suffered the same experience. The lady from Maine was now richer to the tune of almost three million dollars.

"You think you could take her statement?" Tate asked. "Maybe prep her in case she's called to the stand. Antonia is pretty busy right now and I trust you to do it."

"You're definitely going to?" I asked. "Call her to the stand, I mean?"

"Might not be necessary if we get enough witness statements to prove most of the parenting was done by mom. I've got some other stuff I can present."

"You going for full custody?"

"Sure am," Tate said, with a grin. "He thought he could push her around. Use his family money to be the big man and show her who's boss. Treat her like shit for asking for a divorce in the first place. Well, he has another thing coming. Mrs. Ranger is a nice lady who just wanted a peaceful, nicer life for her kids."

And that was why I wanted to work for Tate; he cared about people.

"Well, anything I can do you just let me know."

He smiled. "You know I will."

"Okay, I'm going to get back to my list of prospective partners. Catch up with you later."

Tate clamped a hand on my shoulder. "Thanks, Shaw and thanks for doing a great job."

As he walked back to his office, I couldn't help but grin. He was all suited up but had a pair of sneakers on his feet. That was another reason I liked Tate; he didn't conform just for the sake of it.

***

Sitting at my desk, I got the list I was working from up on my screen. For all that Tate was doing was a good thing, I hadn't had much luck in getting anyone to partner with us—it seemed they didn't want to take a chance on a small-town lawyer. Word must have been getting around though, because a couple of women's groups had reached out to us. Problem was they were politically inclined. Tate had his own political viewpoint but didn't want to tie his cause to one, so he'd got me to politely decline. The one group I was hoping would interested was the South-Central Women's Foundation based out of Dallas. They were making big noises in women's rights and advocacy, particularly around equal pay in the workplace and were exactly who we would want to be partnered with. I was about to dial their number from my office phone when my cell started ringing. I looked down and groaned when I saw it was Carter my brother-in-law.

"Carter, I told you no," I said on answering.

"You have no idea what I'm going to ask you," he protested.

"So, you *are* going *ask* me something?" I sighed heavily and sat back in my chair. "If it's about your stupid show then the answer is still no."

"Shaw, man, come on." He groaned.

"I'm right then, that is why you called."

"It's for a good cause, Shaw, you know it is."

Carter was trying to raise money to help pay toward building an animal shelter and had decided that holding a singing contest was the way to do it. Ergo Dayton Valley Idol was going to run over three nights over the weekend.

"Maybe, but I don't know if I can spare the time or the effort," I said. "How about I give you a donation instead?"

Carter ignored me and continued trying to sell the show to me "The first round is on Friday night," he said. "With the judges voting off two of the nine acts each night you're bound to end up in the final. Imagine how great you'd look to everyone."

He was right. It might get me some attraction from the ladies, but I'd still be tied up for three nights over the weekend.

"Tell me again who else has entered."

"Nancy," Carter told me.

"Oh yeah, because she can't say no to you." I felt my top lip curl in disgust at the thought of Nancy. I still got pissed off that my sister had found Nancy in bed with Carter. Okay, so it was innocent because Carter fell on her when he was drugged up on painkillers, but it was still a reason to dislike her.

"The public vote could be down to you and Nancy." His tone was toying, he knew that I'd love to beat Nancy.

"I don't know man," I replied with a heavy sigh.

"C'mon Shaw," Carter pleaded. "Throw me a bone here. I need someone who can actually sing to keep everyone interested because… well, Ellie has entered."

I busted out laughing as Carter remained silent. Ellie, Carter's sister who was married to his best buddy Hunter, had the worst voice I'd ever heard. So horrific, she could barely hold a note. Hunter, her doting husband, just damn well indulged her. According to my sister, he'd even bought her a karaoke machine which no doubt would be brought out every time we had a cookout on the ranch.

"Y'see why I need you? Ellie can't hold a single note, as for Nancy I have no idea. Violet Callahan is… well she's Violet Callahan. Who the fuck knows what she will do."

"Who else you got?" I asked, smiling at the shit show he was facing.

"Pauly Jansen and Bryce Davidson the guy who owns the carwash." He sighed. "It's going to be a disaster; Bryce has to be nearly ninety."

"Stop exaggerating," I replied, scrolling through the website for the Women's Foundation. "He celebrated his seventieth last week. He told me when I took Dad's car in to be detailed."

"Oh, you mean after you took Ruthie Grey out in it and missed your aim on the back seat."

I shifted uncomfortably. "My sister has a big mouth."

"You should know better than to tell Bronte anything. She loves me and we have no secrets."

"Whatever. The answer is still no," I growled.

"Pleeeease." He sounded like Rett, his and Bronte's one and half year old. He was an amazing kid and I adored him but his parents…nah, not so much.

"No and stop begging. It doesn't make you look good."

"I'm not above paying you to do it," he replied. "Name your price."

"What and use up all your profits? It's a charitable gig, what sort of person do you think I am?"

"A big meany, that's the sort of person I think you are," he shot back. "And when I see you again, I'm going to pinch your nipples and make you cry."

I let out another burst of laughter. "You're a dick, you know that right?"

"What happened to respecting your elders and your sister's husband?"

"Like I said, you're a bit of a dick. I mean I like you well enough, you love my sister and you're a great dad to Rett, but other than that…"

"You'll be sorry," Carter said, still sounding a little petulant. "Wait until I tell Rett what a big dimwit his Uncle Shaw is."

The line then went dead.

"You douchebag," I muttered. "Using Rett to bribe me, what the fuck."

Then, muttering to myself about how much I hated Carter, I got on with my work.

***

It'd been a long day only helped by the fact that the Southern Women's Foundation had agreed to a meeting with Tate. Otherwise, I was glad it was almost over. I had no idea what was wrong with her, but Evie had been crying for most of it. When she spilled coffee on my paperwork as she passed it to me, that sent her off the deep end. She ran into the bathroom and wouldn't come out until Tate said he was taking her home. It hadn't been much, but it did mean I had to reprint a whole load of documents again. To top it all off, when I went out to get a bite of lunch, I bumped into Carter who pestered me *again* about the show the whole time I was in the line at the bakery.

"You going straight home?" I asked Tate as he loosened off his necktie. He'd only worn it because he'd been on a Zoom call with a judge.

"I had planned on it. Although," he said, scratching behind his ear and throwing his briefcase into the trunk of his car. "Mom is out of town planning a wedding and Lily is sitting for Jacob, so I did consider going to Delphine's for an early dinner."

"Well, the fried chicken at Stars & Stripes is pretty good if you want to join me for a beer."

Tate considered it for a second and then nodded. "Why not. Thanks, Shaw."

I waited as he locked up his car and then we both made the short walk to Stars & Stripes. It was only half past seven and pretty quiet, but I knew it would fill up later. Wednesday nights were not only fried chicken night, but quiz night too. A couple of the teams that I knew played were already there, by eight the place would be busy.

Tate took a seat at the bar and picked up the menu. "What's good?" he asked. "I know you said fried chicken but the pieces, the wings or the burger?"

"It's all amazing," I replied sitting next to him. "It's Billy the chef's own recipe."

"Okay, I'll try the pieces then." Tate looked over to Penny, whose bar it was, and lifted a hand. She smiled back and held up one finger to indicate she'd be a minute. "You going to join me?" he asked.

I glanced at my watch knowing that Mom would have made a start on dinner. The chicken was amazing though.

"Yeah, why not. I'll take the pieces too." I then pulled my phone from my pocket and shot a text to Mom.

Shaw: *Having a bite to eat with Tate. Don't worry about dinner for me*

I'd only just put it back in my pocket when it beeped with an incoming text.

Mom: *Is he giving you a raise? Make sure you get vegetables. Austen is staying home tonight. Do you think you could talk to him about sex when you get back?*

Groaning I quickly replied.

Shaw: *No. Okay. Not a chance!*

I then put my phone on silent knowing that she wouldn't be able to stop herself from responding.

"Okay?" Tate asked.

"Yeah," I sighed. "Just my mom riding my ass about vegetables and my little brother's sex life."

Tate's brows rose and he huffed out a surprised laugh. "Really?"

"Yeah. She thinks he's sleeping with three different girls and wants me to talk to him about it."

"And say what?" Tate grinned. "I remember my sixteen-year-old self and if I'd been getting action from three different girls, I'd have thought my dick and balls were made of fucking gold and maybe tried for number four."

I laughed and smiled as Penny approached us.

"Hi, boys," she said cheerily. "What can I get you?"

Tate ordered us beers and chicken pieces with French fries—hey, they're potatoes and potatoes are a vegetable. He then turned back to me and finally pulled off his necktie before stuffing it into his pocket.

"Does your mom think you'll dissuade him from sleeping around?"

"I have no idea." I shrugged. "But I'm not going to talk to him about it. Other than checking he's bagging. That's one problem he doesn't need while he's still at high school. I'm pretty sure he is though, I spotted him buying a box only last week and I'd already given him a jumbo box last year."

"Good to know," Tate replied and pushed one of the beers that Penny had placed on the bar toward me. "As the child of an unplanned pregnancy, I can honestly say that is not a road your brother wants to go down."

"Talking of, how is your dad getting on in Jefferson Correctional?"

Tate gave a lobsided grin. "Oh, he's loving it. And boy the fucking irony that he's in a Florida facility called Jefferson."

We both laughed. Jefferson was the name of his mom's man.

"He'll probably be out in another year, but they could throw away the key for all I care."

It was safe to say Tate had a difficult relationship with his dad. I only knew what I'd overheard from mom and dad, but Chet Hallahan, who was a famous rock singer, cheated Kitty, Tate's mom, out of millions in their divorce. He'd also evaded a huge amount of taxes. Tate had been instrumental in getting him caught.

"You like Jefferson?" I asked, taking a sip from my bottle of beer.

He nodded. "Yeah, I do. He's great for Mom. Loves her to distraction, treats her like a damn queen and just as importantly looks after my little sister like she's one of his own. I mean they've only been together a year but the last six months they seem to have taken it to another level."

"He's a good man," I replied. "More like an uncle to me, I guess."

"Yeah, I like him a lot. I'm glad he and mom found each other again."

Kitty and Jefferson had been high school sweethearts until Kitty moved away to Florida. When she moved back to Dayton Valley, she was divorced, and Jefferson widowed. They pretty much got together straight away. I knew my folks loved her and thought she was great for their best friend.

"Anyway." I changed the subject. "What's going on with your love life? No one special?"

Tate's brows arched. He was a good-natured boss so I knew he wouldn't mind me asking.

"Don't really have time," he responded. "And like the saying goes, once bitten and all that."

He'd had a pretty bad divorce; his ex-wife had wiped out their bank account yet still wanted more in the divorce. She hadn't got it, but Tate was still smarting over it.

"A man has his needs though, Tate."

We both glanced over to Penny who was carrying two plates of food toward us.

"True, Shaw, and I get by." He nodded thanks to Penny as she laid down the plates. "So, what about you. Who scratches your itch?"

I almost dropped my bottle of beer as who should stroll into the bar but Nancy. She looked like hell, like she had earlier, but at least she changed out of her coffee-stained tee and was now wearing a red plaid shirt and jeans. Yep, not her best look but my dick still twitched with interest—fucking idiot.

CHAPTER 5

Nancy

Was it not bad enough that I'd run out of tampons and had to go to the store when I felt like shit? Oh, no, apparently not. The gods thought it would be funny to place Shaw in Stars & Stripes just because I'd decided I wanted fried chicken take-out for dinner. And could he try *not* to look so damn sexy all the time. There he was, sitting at the bar, shirt sleeves rolled back, a bottle of beer dangling from between his thumb and forefinger and his hair all mussed up like I'd dragged my fingers through it.

"Shit," I muttered under my breath and recalled how silky his hair felt, giving myself a little quiver down below. "Stupid jerk." Immediately, I shook my head at myself.

Stupid Jerk. Lazy, lazy, lazy, Nancy. You've really got to step up your game girl.

"Hey, honey," Penny called from across the bar. "You here for the usual take-out?"

I nodded and gave a tight smile. Crap, since Minnesota had left me to go travelling, I'd obviously become a creature of habit.

"Take a load off." Penny placed a Topo Chico on the bar, right at the space next to Shaw which was why I pulled it out and shifted it a little to the left before parking my ass on it.

"Hey, Miss. Andrews," Tate leaned forwarded and lifted his beer bottle to me. "Thanks for agreeing to help us out with our case. Shaw said you'd be happy to make a statement."

"No problem." I lifted my glass and smiled. "And please, call me Nancy."

"Well, Nancy, we really appreciate it, don't we Shaw?"

Shaw who was looking down at his food nodded and grunted out what sounded like, 'if we must'.

"Shaw recommended I come here tonight, so I'm guessing you agree on how good the food is?" Tate started to cut into a piece of chicken, his attention taken up by his plate.

"I do. It's amazing. The best thing I've ever tasted."

When Shaw looked up and into the mirror running the length of the bar, he smirked sending my piss straight to boiling point—*again*. I narrowed my eyes at him in my own reflection and pretended to gag. He then infuriated me more by poking at the inside of his cheek with his tongue, moving it backward and forward like he was sucking dick. He evidently hadn't thought that one through. I raised my brow and mouthed silently, 'you like dick?' and then gave him a double thumbs up and a cheesy grin.

He choked on his food and a little light came into my life as I thought he might just keel over and die. But then he took a slug of his beer and stopped. Oh well, I guess you can't win everything.

"You come here often?" Tate asked, dabbing at his mouth with his napkin. He looked over at me and grinned. "That wasn't a pick up line, I swear."

We both laughed but I noticed that Shaw continued to shovel food into his mouth, seemingly disinterested in either of us.

"Well, I love the fried chicken and there isn't really anywhere else in Dayton that you can let loose."

"Yeah," Shaw said, clearing his throat and placing his fork onto his plate, "Nancy likes to let loose."

Before I could even curl my lip in disdain, he smiled and turned to Tate.

"We all do though. We're a real friendly town."

Tate nodded. "Yeah, I get that feeling, even after less than a year here. I understand why my mom and sister love it here." He then leaned forward and spoke to me. "Wait a minute, are you the Nancy who Lily is friendly with?"

I smiled, thinking of my friend. "Yes, that's me."

"I thought the name rang a bell." He clicked his fingers and then pointed at me. "You're the one who helps her out with JJ from time to time."

"I am." It was only with ideas on how to entertain him or useful learning games, but it was Lily who was eager to do those things with him. She was all in on that job and I knew once JJ was too old to need a sitter she'd be lost. Lily had fallen for that little boy hard in the time that she'd been taking care of him.

"She's real helpful, that Nancy," Shaw added, his beer bottle poised at his lips.

If Tate hadn't been sitting at the bar next to him, I was sure I'd have emptied my glass over Shaw. He was being particularly annoying today and I was not in the mood for it.

"Talking of helpful," I replied in a loud voice. "Did Shaw ever tell you how he likes to help his sister, Bronte, with new beauty treatments. Didn't you once tell me about something called Anal Bleaching?"

I tilted my head to one side and furrowed my brow, feigning interest as Shaw almost choked again, this time on fresh air.

"N-No," he finally stuttered. "I'd never let anyone near my ass with bleach, least of all my sister."

Tate laughed loudly and slapped Shaw's back. "Hey, Shaw, whatever floats your boat. Nothing wrong in taking pride in yourself."

"But I didn't!" Shaw turned to me. "Tell him you're joking and that I didn't have my butt hole bleached."

The timing couldn't have been better as Carter's voice boomed, "What the hell?" around the bar which had started to fill up. "When did you get your ass chemically cleaned? Was it when Bronte waxed your balls?"

Damnit, I just knew it!

Shaw made a noise a bit like a strangled chicken and glared first at Carter and then at me.

Before he had chance to speak, Carter drummed out a beat on the bar top. "Anyway, less of your balls and ass, who wants a drink. Hunt is on his way and as usual is late, so it looks like I'm buying."

Sometimes I really wanted to slap Carter. Why'd he change the subject when Shaw was getting more embarrassed by the second? If I tried to start the conversation up again that would make them think I cared about Shaw's butt hole and his testicles and I really didn't. Okay, maybe I had more than a passing interest in his balls, his hole not so much.

Thank God for Tate. "Hang on, back on up there," he said, pushing his plate away and grinning. "You got your ass bleached *and* your balls waxed by your *sister*?"

"No," Shaw snapped. "I did not. What sort of guy do you take me for?"

"A guy with an asshole that needs chemically cleaning," I muttered into my drink.

Without looking I knew Shaw's gaze was on me. I got a poke in the thigh from his finger.

"What did you have to say that for?" he hissed in my ear.

When I looked up, he was turning back to Tate and Carter, who had now moved to stand at that end of the bar. "I did not have my ass bleached, yes I got my balls waxed, but there's no way Bronte went anywhere near my butt."

"Yet you let her near your balls," Carter sighed with a shrug of his shoulders. "Go figure."

"She only supervised," Shaw cried. "Lilah waxed my damn balls."

Once again the good Lord shone down on me.

"You had your fucking balls waxed. What the fuck?" Hunter Delaney bellowed.

Yep, it was ending up being a really good day. Shaw Jackson was practically sobbing into his fried chicken, and I had another insult for him to add to my list.

<u>*Nancy's Bitch List for Shaw*</u>

- Maximus Douchimus
- Captain Shitsmear

CHAPTER 6

Shaw

Not in the best of moods after my dinner at Stars & Stripes, I didn't feel any better when the smell of boy's locker rooms and ass hit me as soon as I walked into the house.

"Damn it, Austen," I called. "Can you please shower after soccer practice?"

Austen's blond head appeared around the door from Dad's office. We'd all used the space for homework and studying over the years.

"Hey. Mom said she and Dad have gone over to the ranch for cards night. They'll be back around eleven."

"So?"

My brother stepped out into the hallway, still in full soccer kit. Dark stains of grass and sweat dotted all over it.

"I think she was kinda warning me," he shrugged, "like, 'we'll be back at eleven, Austen, so don't let me catch any girls in your room.'."

"You've had girls in your room?" I asked, shocked. "I've never had girls in my room."

"That's because you had them on Mom and Dad's couch." His whole body shuddered. "You could have scarred me for life you know. You definitely did Mom."

I thought back to when I'd been caught with Austen's babysitter and grinned. To be fair we hadn't gotten to the sex part, but she had already come all over my fingers.

"Me and Patty didn't actually have sex," I offered, moving past him to go into the kitchen.

"So what?" he asked. "You're telling me you've never had sex with a girl under this roof."

As I reached for a glass and ran the faucet, I felt my little brother behind me – actually, I could smell him. I filled the glass with water and took a long drink before I answered.

"Didn't say that," I replied, breathless from drinking quickly. "Just said I haven't had a girl in my room."

"Well, if you didn't have sex with Patty and you haven't had a girl in your room, then where have you had sex in this house?"

I winked and took another sip of cool water.

"No fucking way," Austen cried. "Please tell me you haven't had your hairy balls rubbing against my sheets?" He gagged, snatched the glass from me and downed what was left. "You've butter milked on my sheets. That's disgusting." He paused and then slammed the empty glass against my chest. "That time when I had crusty sheets and you convinced me I'd had a wet dream, it was you, wasn't it? You dirty bastard."

He began to shake himself out, all the time retching.

"Don't be so dramatic," I sighed as I put the glass into the sink. "It was one time only. All the others were in Bronte's bed."

"Oh. My. Fucking. God." He groaned, his eyes bulging. "That's just weird. Letting her wax your dick is bad enough but having sex in her bed is just… *nasty*."

"She did not wax my *balls,*" I protested. "She supervised and why is everyone so interested in my dick today?"

"Oh, believe me." He grimaced and circled a finger in the area of my junk. "I have no interest in that at all. I'm only repeating what Mom told me."

"Yeah, well I'm gonna kill her for telling you."

"Yeah, well Mom knowing you get your balls waxed is even weirder than you actually *having* your balls waxed."

"Yeah, and that's because Bronte has a big mouth."

I looked him up and down and took in his athletic physique. In the space of a year and a half, he'd changed a lot. No longer the gangly kid who wore mismatched pajamas, over one summer he'd shot up by at least four inches and was still growing. His body had filled out and now instead of Transformer PJ's he wore designer boxer briefs to bed, making sure they rested low enough for us all to see the V he was developing due to soccer and working out in the gym. Mom was right, this kid was having sex and a lot of it.

"Who're you seein' at the moment?" I asked, leaning back against the countertop grateful to be able to change the subject.

He grinned and grabbed an apple from the bowl on the table. "A couple of girls."

"You being careful?"

He bounced the piece of fruit off one forearm onto the other. "Yes. I'm not stupid."

"You're sixteen and you're a guy, Austen, of course you're stupid. We all are at that age, once." He then rolled the apple along his arm, but before it hit his hand, I snatched it up and took a bite. "The book I lent you help?"

He huffed out an empty laugh, the sort we all did when Dad cracked one of his '*funnies*'. "No, not really. All those notes in the margins were stupid."

"They were not," I argued with my mouth full of apple. "Never known me not satisfy a girl."

"Well, I didn't use them. I got expert help elsewhere."

"I thought you said Carter and Hunter were no help at all."

"I didn't get it from them." He frowned and shook his head. "Not quite sure how Hunter managed to bag Ellie and keep her if *his* notes were anything to go by."

Austen's cheeks reddened, clearly he hadn't recovered from his crush on Ellie.

"Who offered their great words of wisdom then?" I asked.

"Minnesota," he replied, smiling big and wide. "He told me about this thing where—"

"Okay, okay, I don't want to know." And I really didn't. Like I gave a shit how Nancy's ex had satisfied her, and more specifically satisfied that magical thing she had in her panties. Instantly the thought of *that* created a shift in my own underwear and I quickly pictured Mrs. Callahan from the gas station in my head to help calm down the beginnings of a boner.

"Honestly, Shaw, it's amazing," Austen said, his eyes bright and excited. "The girls go wild for it. It's like a routine of certain moves. It goes, figure of eight, figure of eig—"

"Austen, no!" I snapped, pinching the bridge of my nose. "I've had no complaints. I don't think I need to change my methods now."

"But there's more to it than that. You do four figure of eights and then it goes stab, stab, stab, repeat. It's awesome. Every freaking time."

My brother looked more than pleased with himself, but I couldn't say it sounded great to me. I mean… figure of eight, stab, stab, stab. What the actual fuck?

"Well, I thought you'd want to know," he continued as he reached for the apple that I no longer found appetizing.

"Why the hell would I want to know that?" I threw my hands in the air in protest.

"Because Minnesota said it made Nancy go wild. Figured you'd want to know as you two are having sex…" He shrugged and then left the kitchen.

A couple of things struck me at that moment, both troublesome.

1. How the fuck did my brother know I'd had sex with Nancy?
2. Why did I want to punch Minnesota in the mouth for disrespecting Nancy by telling a kid what pleased her in the sack?

Damn it. I was in a shit load of trouble either way!

CHAPTER 7

Nancy

After looking at a face full of spots for three days, I decided to treat myself with a facial. Luckily, Bronte had an opening at her salon, so that was where I was walking to when I spotted Shaw kissing Ruthie Grey. It was a little PDA for my taste—it looked kinda like he was using his tongue to mine for diamonds at the back of her throat. All he needed was a helmet with a lamp attached and he'd have been good to go. As I drew level with his car, which they were leaning against, I also heard the amount of fluid involved and it was a lot. There was squelching and lip smacking and it was nothing short of gross. Funny though when he kissed me, it was kinda perfect, which was annoying. I so wanted him to be crap in the sack and less than stellar at kissing, but he wasn't.

Ignoring them, I crossed over the road and almost ran into Evan Redbank, the school janitor, on his bicycle.

"Sorry, Evan," I called, raising my hand in apology as he screeched to a halt.

"You need to watch where you're going, missy." He rolled his eyes, gave his bell a quick ring and then proceeded to maneuver himself around me.

He wasn't the happiest of people at the best of times. I could gear him cussing under his breath as he rode away. Stupidly, I glanced over my shoulder, also stupidly wondering whether Shaw had seen me almost get killed by a seventy-year-old on a rickety bicycle? Unfortunately, he had. He hadn't stopped kissing, oh no, he was still plundering Ruthie's mouth, but his eyes were firmly on me. His hands firmly on Ruthie's ass, but his eyes on me. Ever the adult and annoyed at myself for looking and even having a smidgen of care, I gave him a double flip of the fingers. I couldn't see properly because Ruthie's head was in the way, but I was pretty sure the stupid idiot was grinning. When he lifted a hand from her ass and then flipped me off, I knew he was.

With a huff and a haughty shrug of my shoulder, I continued across the road and made a left onto Calderdale toward Bronte's salon, hoping a nice facial would help me forget about her stupid brother.

***

"What do you mean you're not going to Kitty's birthday party?" Bronte asked, her fingers massaging the lotion around my eyes. "Most of Dayton Valley will be there."

I couldn't say because I didn't wish to see her brother sucking face with Ruthie again. If I did it would sound like I cared and gave a shit that she was getting the orgasms I knew he was so good at giving.

"I don't know," I said with a sigh. "Everyone will be paired off and I know that Alaska and Jennifer still feel bad about Minnesota dumping me like he did."

"As they should." Cool pads were placed over my closed eyelids, and I heard Bronte start to clear everything away. "The boy is an idiot and as his older brother, Alaska should have pointed him right. I mean," she sighed heavily, "if you were dating my brother, I would've."

Jeez, if only she knew!

***

It was only a little while later, when Bronte had just finished waxing my brows for me, that Ellie came bundling into the salon and made my misery complete.

"Thank God you're here, Nancy."

"What's wrong?" Bronte asked, placing a glass of water on the side table next to my chair.

"I just came from the bakery. Hunter likes Jennifer's blueberry muffin cake so I went in to get one, but they were sold out, so I said to Jennifer, "Hunter will be real disappointed and I wanted it to surprise him because he's been so tired recently". She stopped talking and stared at us wide-eyed. "Sorry."

Bronte shook her head. "I can guess why, but why do you need Nancy?"

"I can't bake, if that's what you're thinking." Ask me to cook a meatloaf and I'd be great, but cake… not my thing at all.

"God no." Ellie waved her hand at me and flopped down into a chair the other side of the small table. "I have some news. Jennifer wanted you to hear it first and Trick Denton from the hardware store said you were in here, so she asked me to do it."

That was a small town for you—everyone knew your business and where you could be found at any given time, or so it seemed.

"Okaaay." I nodded indicating for her to lay it on me. Whatever the 'news' was I could guess it was about Minnesota. Why else would Jennifer have news for me? We were friendly but not close enough that she would want me to be the first to know the gender of the baby she was going to be having in a couple of months.

I was right.

"Minnesota called the family last night. He's getting married to a girl from London. They met in Rome a month ago." Ellie blurted it out like it might hurt me a little less if she said it quickly.

"We were only talking about him just a half hour ago," Bronte gasped. "It must have been my sixth sense that made me bring him up."

I didn't have the heart to tell her that it'd been me that had raised the subject of my ex, not her. That aside, I felt hurt.

"Wow," I replied, feeling a little tremble in my bottom lip. "Married?"

Ellie nodded silently and reached for my hand I had resting on the table. "I'm sorry, Nancy. I know he's been gone a few months, but it's still gotta hurt."

I swallowed back the lump in my throat and shrugged. "It's not like I still love him or anything, but we were together a while. He never even suggested we live together, never mind asked me to marry him."

"And he dumped you just before you were supposed to go on a big adventure together," Bronte said glumly.

"Okay," Ellie snapped. "You don't need to remind her."

"You're the one who just told her the love of her life was getting married after a quick romp in the hay with some girl who probably sticks out her pinky while drinking endless cups of tea and eating cucumber sandwiches all day."

"I don't think Brits eat cucumber sandwiches and drink tea *all* day," I said. "And I'm pretty sure he wasn't the love of my life."

"You'd be surprised about Brits," she replied as she picked up a towel and folded it. "I heard they also eat eels straight from that big river that runs through London."

"I think you mean the Thames." Ellie rolled her eyes. "Nancy is right, they do more than eat cucumber sandwiches or eels and drink tea. The point is, Jennifer asked me to tell you because Talia Pitt heard Mr. & Mrs. Michaels discussing flights to London when she was in the travel center picking up a brochure. Apparently, Mrs. Michaels was beside herself and mentioned it was for their son's wedding, and as Alaska and Tallahassee are already married, well even Rett could add two and two together and make four on that one."

"He's not coming home to get married then?" I asked, gently pulling my hand from Ellie's.

She shook her head. "Probably not at all, except for holidays maybe. He's got himself a job at a tech company just outside of London and has moved into her apartment. Actually, he moved in after their second date."

"Could it be just for the Green Card?" Bronte asked, although not sounding convinced.

I shook my head. "No, I don't think he'd do that. If he did then he's not the sort of person I'd want to be with anyway."

We were all silent for a few minutes, until Ellie shifted on her chair and let out a little groan.

"What's wrong?" Bronte asked. "Please don't tell me you've shaved your bush again. What did I tell you about razor burn? It's ugly and as a newly married woman you do not want your hoo-hah looking like the chin of a thirteen-year-old boy who has used his dad's razor after his mom shaved her legs with it."

"No, I haven't," Ellie protested. "You told me you break our life-long friendship if I ever shaved it again."

"So why are you squirming around on that chair?" Bronte's face broke into a grin. "Please tell me Hunter has gone all Christian Grey and slipped some of those balls up there and he's working them from over at the ranch."

"No, the damn opposite if you must know." Ellie pouted. "I feel horny and it's all because he wouldn't have sex with me this morning."

"Oh so the honeymoon period is finally over," Bronte replied and threw her hands into the air. "Thank the Lord. Boy were Carter and I sick of you two disappearing on a night out so you could go have wild sex somewhere."

"You think that's it?" I asked, all innocence.

"What? No way," Ellie blasted back. "His penis is more tired than usual is all. He's tired and his penis is tired."

"Well, I guess all that banging had to take its toll at some point," Bronte retorted with a hint of a gloating smile. "You'd think that hammer would have nailed it by now."

"I may regret this," I sighed. "But why is his penis more tired than usual?"

Ellie screwed her eyes up and placed both hands onto the table. "We agreed we wouldn't say anything, but you know I can't keep a secret. Ugh, why'd you have to ask me that?"

"You don't have to tell us," Bronte replied dismissively. "It's not like we don't all know how often you bang each other's brains out."

I nodded in agreement. Only a month ago I'd caught sight of Hunter's bare ass pumping away behind the gardening and horticulture books at the library. I was shocked. I mean who knew Hunter and Ellie were into gardening and horticulture?

Despite what she'd said, Ellie was evidently desperate to impart her news. She was practically bouncing in her seat, staring between me and Bronte with bright eyes.

"Oh go on," Bronte groaned and dropped down into a chair opposite to us. "Spill it."

"We're trying for a baby and have been for three weeks now."

Bronte gasped. "You never said."

"I'm saying it now," Ellie replied. "So, are you excited for us, and for Rett to have cousin?"

"I guess, but it's kind of spoiled our surprise." Bronte pouted as she looked at Ellie with narrowed eyes.

"No way. Don't you dare tell me you're pregnant." Ellie's eyes widened. "You've already got the eldest grandchild; you could at least let me have the second one."

"I'm not pregnant." Bronte ran a hand down her white tunic and over her stomach. "Do I look pregnant?" She looked pointedly at me.

"No," I replied shaking my head vigorously.

"Phew, thank goodness."

"If you're not pregnant then what's your surprise?" Ellie asked.

Bronte flicked her long braid over her shoulder. "If you must know, Carter and I are trying for another baby too. Have been for two weeks."

"Just great," Ellie sighed. "You're bound to get pregnant first and more than likely have a girl. Just damn well perfect."

Bronte smiled. "I'm sorry but it did only take once for me to get pregnant with Rett, so you're probably right. I'll probably get pregnant before you, and most likely have a girl this time."

"You're crazy," Ellie said, folding her arms tightly over her chest. "Two kids eighteen months and under. You'll never cope. It'll be a nightmare."

Bronte shrugged. "Rett needs to go to preschool soon anyways."

"They have to be potty trained and at least three years old before Ms. Baker will take them," I informed her. "She's pretty strict on her rules."

"No problem. I'll send him somewhere else."

"There is nowhere else," Ellie replied.

Bronte looked at me and grinned. "Why don't you set up your own preschool. You'd be amazing."

"Just so you can have another and make Carter an even bigger douche because he's provided Mom and Dad with their first *two* grandkids?"

"I couldn't set up my own place," I protested. "It takes money and time."

"Didn't your aunt leave you a sizeable sum when she died a few months ago?"

"How did you…" There was only one person who knew—Shaw. That was because I'd taken the call from Aunt Willa's lawyer while arguing with him outside Stars & Stripes one night. Shaw had been in there with some blonde girl and every time he shoved his tongue down her throat, he gave me a thumbs up. I was mad that he'd been looking my way while making out with a girl and told him what a douche he was when he followed me outside. Shaw had then got into it with me about how it was my own fault for staring and how I should just admit I was hot for him. The insults were flying when the call came, and he stayed there I guess ready to carry on our fight when I finished. When my call ended in my shock, I blurted it all out.

I knew Aunt Willa had died a month before in an old person's facility in Chicago, but I wasn't expecting the call to say she'd left me such a huge sum of money. She was my mom's much older half-sister and had no family but a houseful of cats and always said she was leaving her money to a cat charity. Which she had, except for what she'd left to me. I don't think any of us had any clue how rich she was.

"My brother has a big mouth when he's drunk," Bronte explained. "I'd been out with Ellie, so shared an Uber with him that night and that's when he told me."

"Yeah, he really does have a big mouth." I shook my head feeling annoyed at Shaw… again.

"I'm sorry, but it's not like you were his client," Bronte replied, wincing at the fact she'd probably got her brother into hot water. "And I didn't tell anyone, not even Carter."

"I guess it wasn't a secret." I was being honest, it really wasn't. I was just angry that it had been Shaw who'd told her. "You all knew Aunt Willa had died and left me something. I just didn't say what."

"I'm positive Shaw wouldn't have said a word if he'd been sober when he overheard your conversation."

"That's small towns for you," Ellie said with a shrug. "Everyone knows your business."

Yep, everyone did, especially when they had a mouth as huge as Shaw Jackson's.

Nancy's Bitch List for Shaw

- [ ] Maximus Douchimus
- [ ] Captain Shitsmear
- [ ] Shit Talking Cock Womble

CHAPTER 8

Shaw

"What're you doing here?" Hunter asked, looking anxious as he ran a hand through his hair. "Weren't your words 'I'd rather suck Mrs. Callahan's toes than enter'?"

I sighed heavily. "Let's just say the thought of her bunion touching my lips was too horrific. Plus, Carter called last night and threatened to tell Dad it was me who drank his twenty-year old malt last Christmas if I didn't enter."

"Good old bribery and corruption works every time." Hunter looked over his shoulder and then back to me. "You think it'd work on Ellie?"

I looked over to see Ellie arguing with Carter and grinned. I'd finally been 'persuaded' to take part in the Dayton Valley Idol, and it was a first rehearsal. With Ellie there at least there'd be some light relief.

"Why he's making it a singing contest I have no idea," Hunter grumbled. "A talent show would be much better." He grinned. "Not that Ellie could show her talents on stage."

I rolled my eyes. "Really. Do you have to?"

"What?" He shrugged. "I can't help it if my wife is super-hot and fucking awesome in the sack."

"But we don't need to know," I protested about to walk away when something, or rather someone, caught my eye. Nancy was walking in, and she wasn't alone. She was laughing with Tate.

"They a thing?" I asked, nodding in their direction.

Hunter glanced over. "No idea. He's your boss, don't you know?"

"No. He's practically your step-brother, don't you discuss things like dating over game night?"

Hunter raised a brow and then grinned. "Who you interested in, Nancy or Tate?"

"I'm not interested in Nancy. She's a royal pain in the ass, why the hell would I be interested in her?"

Hunter began to laugh softly and with a wink walked away, gathering Ellie in his arms and kissing the top of her head.

"Douche," I growled.

"Who's a douche?"

I jumped. "Carter, do you have to sneak up on me like that?"

"I wasn't sneaking, you were just too busy hating on someone. I repeat who's a douche?"

"Hunter."

Carter nodded. "Yup, I get that. Anyways, just wanted to let you know, you have this in the bag. You're the betting favorite for the win. My sister was just practicing her scales and let's say I've heard nails across a chalkboard sound more musical. As for Pauly, well I do believe I saw every animal in Dayton Valley run for the hills."

"Is Tate entering?" I asked, clearing my throat.

"No. Not sure why he's here. Maybe, he's supporting Nancy."

"They together?" I asked, trying to remember what I'd last eaten. Something had given me a horrible taste in my mouth.

Carter shrugged and looked down at his clipboard. "No idea, but you're up first to rehearse your walk on and I need you to sing the first and last verse."

I felt deflated and beaten, not able to believe he'd managed to trick me into entering. I really didn't want to have to be committed to the contest. My free time was precious. I liked having my evenings free, and I didn't want to spend them singing to a couple of hundred residents who had nothing better to do than listen to their friends and neighbors annihilating popular tunes.

"I'm not sure I can commit, you know."

Carter slapped my back. "No problem."

"Really?" I asked, shocked it had been so easy. "I can leave?"

"Sure." He reached into the pocket of his jeans and pulled out his phone. "I'll just call your dad and tell him about the malt."

"You're a dick, you know that right?"

He turned away, holding up his phone and waving it about, laughing as he did. I found nothing humorous in the situation. I should never have let him know I'd downed the precious malt that Dad had gotten from Mom to celebrate their anniversary. Not only was the booze old, but it was their first anniversary since they'd taken a break from their marriage. They were back together and happy again and Mom had wanted to mark it as a special anniversary.

I'd drunk it one night when I was already tighter than bark on a log. I'd blindly reached for something from Dad's stash after a night clubbing with some old high school buddies. By the time I'd downed almost a full bottle, I realized what it was that I was drinking, but by then it was too late. Stupidly, and drunkenly, I'd called Bronte to ask her what to do. Half an hour later Carter turned up at the house with some cheap whisky and poured it into the bottle.

"This is your one and only time, Carter," I yelled as he continued to walk away.

"Hmm, we'll see."

Feeling pissed and agitated, I swiveled around to walk toward the 'stage' and spotted Tate and Nancy. Their heads were together and they were looking at Tate's phone, huge smiles on their faces. The bad taste returned and I made a mental note to quit having oatmeal for breakfast.

"Need this like I need a hole in the head," I muttered to myself, striding toward the mic.

"Okay," Carter yelled from the back of the ballroom of the Memorial building. "Your entrance could do with some work but that's a minor thing. Right, first and last verse as we agreed."

Rolling my eyes, I looked over to where Dusty Chalmers was about to queue up my music, Dylan Scott's *Nobody*. I gave him a nod and as the opening bars sounded out my phone began to ring in my pocket.

"Sorry." I reached for it, pulled it out and glanced at the screen.

"Did you not see the notice," Carter growled as he stalked back toward the stage. "It states that all phones be turned off." He paused and held up his pointer finger. "And that's off, not silent."

Shit, give a guy a clipboard and he thinks he's God. "Sorry." I held up the phone and clicked on the screen to end the call, it was an unknown number anyways.

"Think you could turn it off?" he asked.

Before I had chance it started to ring again. Unknown number again. I ended it and then shut down my phone. When I looked up Nancy was grinning at me.

"What?" I asked over the mic.

"Nothing," she shrugged, "I just can't believe how unprofessional some people are."

When my music started again, I chose to ignore her and stick to the task at hand. Even though I didn't put my all into it, I knew I still sounded pretty decent. I had a gift, I knew that. Mom had always gone on at me to join Glee club at high school, but I was a teenager who'd wanted to get laid, so I'd left singing to karaoke or in the shower.

When I let out the final note, I looked over to Nancy, expecting to see her full attention. It wasn't on me; she was busy pacing up and down with earbuds in and listening to something on her phone. I guessed it might be her song, seeing as she was drumming a beat against her thigh.

"Thank you," Carter said as he raised a thumb. "Nancy, you're up next."

"That it?" I asked.

Carter tapped Nancy on the back and when she looked at him, he pointed to the stage.

"Oh, right okay." She pulled out her earbuds and walked toward the stage.

"Carter, is that it?" I asked again.

He shrugged. "What else do you want?"

To tell me how amazing I was. To announce to everyone that I was who they had to beat.

"Nothing, I guess."

"What's wrong?" Nancy whispered, nudging me aside from the microphone. "Not enough adulation for you."

"Shove it, Nancy," I replied close to her ear.

"Rather not. Tried it and wasn't that impressed."

"Yes, so you say."

"Shaw," Carter yelled. "Can you get off the damn stage. It's Nancy's turn."

"Okay, I'm going."

I didn't intend on staying and listening to her sing, but as soon as she sang the first words of Lady A's 'Can't Stand the Rain', I knew she was going to be good. She'd slowed down the tempo and with a raspy and haunting voice, made what I thought was a cheesy song sound hella cool. I couldn't stop looking as she lost herself in the music, even if she was only singing a small part of the song.

I watched as her throat bobbed with each note and how her hands gripped the mic' stand and it struck me how damn beautiful she looked up there. Her dark hair was swept over one shoulder and her pouty lips were almost caressing the mic as she leaned in and sang out the words.

"Good, isn't she?" Carter nudged me as he leaned in close to whisper. "And guess what?"

"What?" My gaze was still on Nancy who was being high fived by Dusty.

"You're not the betting favorite any longer, in fact," he said, hitting his hand against his stupid clipboard, "I'd say you're a little overrated."

CHAPTER 9

Nancy

Did you ever have one of those days where you could quite gladly tit punch your co-workers? A day when everything you do gains a scowl or a sharp intake of breath, which is what makes you want to tit punch them. That was the sort of day that I'd had with Mrs. Baker who I worked for as a teacher's aide. She'd even told me I wasn't helping Janey Gualtierra blow her nose correctly—apparently, I was holding the tissue wrong.

I knew what it was all about. She was totally aware that I'd agreed to testify on behalf of Mrs. Ranger in her custody case. Mrs. Baker had refused because according to her she wasn't sure there was a problem between Eddie and his dad. Like hell there wasn't. I saw on many occasions how that little boy withdrew into himself when he knew it wasn't his mom collecting him from school. I'd also seen Mr. Ranger and the kids at Delphine's one night and he'd been on his phone the whole time. Whenever Eddy and Molly spoke to him, or asked a question, he just brushed them off without even looking up.

Anyways, my day had been shitty, and it had got me thinking about what Bronte had said about opening up my own preschool. I would need to hire an actual teacher or more than one, as I wasn't qualified to teach, and that would take a huge chunk of my inheritance until the place started to pay for itself. Without a building I couldn't even start to consider it, and I had no clue whether there was any such building available in or around Dayton Valley. Maybe that should be the first thing that I did, check for a suitable building. If there wasn't anything then it wasn't meant to be. I'd just suck it up and carry on working for crabby Mrs. Baker. The problem was, even if there was a building, I wasn't sure I had the nerve to do it. Mrs. Baker had pre schooled the kids of Dayton Valley for the last ten years and her mom for twenty years before that. Who would even trust me with their kids? I pulled out my phone and dialed a number.

Bronte.

"Hey, Nancy. You, okay?"

"Yeah. No. Yeah."

Bronte giggled. "Well, which is it, honey?"

I sighed heavily. "It's no, but it could be yes, depending on how you answer this next question."

"Okay. Go ahead."

I screwed my eyes closed and tapped a beat on my forehead with my fingertips, beginning to second guess my idea. "It's okay, I've had a bad day and was just thinking…" I trailed off not sure what I was thinking.

"Yes, you were thinking?" Bronte prompted.

"I'm just going to come right out and say it." I inhaled deeply. "If and it's a big if, if I set up a kindergarten were you being serious about sending Rett there? And, and d-d-do you think Ellie meant it too, that she'd send her kid there if she and Hunter had one. I mean *when* they have one because you just know they will with the amount of sex they have."

"As long as they don't have it before us," Bronte grumbled. "I know we had the first grandchild and I know people will say we should let Ellie and Hunter have the second, but I so want to beat them to it."

"Yeah, but whoever has it, would you… I mean if I opened up a preschool would you, would Ellie send your kids to me?"

I held my breath, feeling apprehensive that she might say no. Now I had the idea in my head, I was excited about it. I'd thought I might put the money from Aunt Willa toward a nice house with a yard, but opening a business was just as good an idea.

"Of course we would," Bronte cried. "You're really going to do it? Oh my God, that's amazing news. I can't wait—"

"Hold on. It's just an idea for now. I don't even know if I have enough money. I need to see a financial adviser and find out exactly what the costs would be. I mean it might be over my budget."

"You could add daycare. Do you know how many women in this town would kill for a few baby free hours? Do you know how much they'd *pay* for those few baby free hours?"

"They would?"

"God yes. I was at baby disco with Rett last week and Mimi Dawson actually said those words, 'do you know how much I'd pay for a few baby free hours? If only that old trout Mrs. Baker did daycare.'. Seriously, Nancy, you should do it. I'm sure you could get a loan if the money from your aunt doesn't cover it. What? Hang on a second, Nancy, Carter is yelling something from the bathroom…*good idea, baby…yep, I'll mention it*. Nancy, Carter's made a great point, although how he can hear when I'm in Rett's room and he's having a crap down the hall."

"Okay, too much information, Bronte."

"Sorry, but we like to share in this family. Anyhoo, Carter suggested that you rent a place and he knows just the one."

"He does! W-where?" My hands started to tremble, and I felt a whooshing sensation in my belly. Could a silly idea be about to happen?

"The old bank on Greendale. It's been refurbished with a small kitchen added and there's an apartment on the top floor, sooo," Bronte took in a deep breath, "you could live above and if you negotiated the rent, you might find that it works out less than that fancy apartment that you live in now. And I know how much those apartments cost, Carter lived there don't forget. *We* lived there together when we first had Rett."

She wasn't wrong, the rent on the apartments was pricey, but I'd bought mine outright with the money I received when my folks died. My heart thudded as I thought about them and how they'd died in a fire at their villa while on vacation in Puerto Vallarta. The fire investigator said it was some old wiring and the owner was completely negligent. The insurance payout and the sale of our small family home a few blocks down from where Ellie's family lived was what had paid for my apartment, my car and to put me through a two-year child-development course at San Jacinto.

"I could sell the apartment and probably raise enough money to avoid having to get a loan."

"Oh, God, yes. You bought yours," Bronte said excitedly. "That's even better."

I was pretty sure that she was clapping.

"Who's handling the rental?" I asked, grabbing a pad and pen. "Does Carter know?"

"*Baby you know who's handling the rental on the bank?*"

I held the phone away from my ear and winced and then waited until I could hear Carter shouting. It was mostly indecipherable but think I heard the words 'shit, peace and Belinda.'

"Belinda, Jennifer's sister, just got her realtor's license. She's dealing with it. Would you like me to come with when you go and see her about it tomorrow?"

My brows arched and I placed a hand to fast beating heart. "Slow down, I need to think about it first."

"Ah, quit stalling," Bronte replied. "You need to get in there quick. I'll text Jennifer and get Belinda's number. Then I'll text her and ask her to see us first thing. *Carter, baby can you watch Rett in the morning...thank you I love you.*"

Damn she really needed to learn to move the phone away from her mouth when yelling to her husband.

"Okay, that's sorted," Bronte said a lot more quietly. "I'll text you the details once I've talked to Belinda."

"Bronte, I don't—"

"No don't say don't. It's not a word I like or use."

"But you just said it. You said, don't say don't."

"Semantics."

I heaved a sigh. I knew I wasn't going to win on this one. "Okay, thank you. Let me know what she says."

Bronte squealed with delight and before I knew it, I was jotting down figures on a notepad.

***

I didn't know when I'd felt so excited about anything. Not even Christmas as a child—okay that was probably over exaggerating, but it was safe to say I was ready to pee my pants. The old bank would work perfectly for a preschool. The contractor had turned it into a light and airy building, adding skylights and big picture windows. There were four smaller rooms off the main one and what had been the staff breakroom had been updated with kitchen equipment and cabinets. There was also a whole load of storage, and the main room was large enough to section it off for all the different types of activities; soft play, wet play, storytelling, and nap time could all be covered. Even better there was decent sized yard out back that would be big enough for a sand box and some play equipment.

"You love it, right." Bronte nudged me with her elbow and let out a little squeak.

Chewing on my bottom lip, I gave the room a sweeping gaze and then grinned. "Yeah, I really do. I had a quick look at my finances last night. I mean I'm not a professional or anything, but I'm pretty sure I can afford it if Belinda can sell my apartment. Getting the timing right might be difficult but it's doable."

Bronte clapped her hands together and squeaked again. "Oh, jeez I'm so happy. Rett is going to love it here. Amelia is going to love it here too."

"Is that one of the baby disco kids?" I asked, running my hand over the top of one of the built-in cupboards, thinking about how I could paint it bright colors.

"No, it's mine and Carter's baby."

My head shot around to her. "*You're pregnant*!"

She waved me away. "No, not yet, but it's only a matter of time." There was a noise of a door opening and Bronte grabbed my hand. "Belinda is here. Now don't appear too keen. Make her sweat a little, honey. Who knows, it may get you a rent reduction."

Before I could say anything, Belinda ran toward us, fanning herself with a pamphlet. "Lordy, I'm so sorry. I got caught up with my last client. Who knew that a pink colored toilet could be a deal breaker? I'm here now. What do you think? You like it?"

She grabbed my hand and gave it a squeeze and looked around the room.

"I do. I want it," I blurted out.

"Nancy," Bronte cried. "What did I say about not appearing too keen?"

I shrugged. "But I want it." Turning to Belinda, I said, "I want to sign today. Right now, in fact."

Belinda grimaced. "That's the thing, sugar. I'm sorry but the contractor who owns the building now wants to sell it, and he wants to do it quick. His daughter announced she's getting married and of course daddy must pay—big time. That's what happens when your daughter wants to marry a guy whose dad is Chairman of the country club."

"That's not a problem." Bronte smiled at me expectantly. "Right, Nancy."

I mentally envisaged the piece of paper on my coffee table with numbers scribbled on it. "Yep, it's doable. Definitely."

Belinda groaned. "That's the other thing, we have someone else interested and they already have the finances lined up too."

"You can't have," Bronte yelled, making me jump. "You told Carter it only came into your office two days ago."

Belinda shrugged. "What can I say, it's a desirable property."

"Who wants it anyway? And, what the hell do they want it for?" Bronte asked, putting an arm around my shoulder giving me a sad smile. "Don't worry, Nancy, we've got this."

I looked to Belinda. "Can you tell me who I'm up against?"

She shook her head. "I can't, sugar. It's confidential and it wouldn't really be professional of me to say."

"But Belinda," Bronte said, squeezing me closer to her. "You've known Nancy since kindergarten. And weren't you both in the same high school graduating class?"

Belinda raised a brow. "I can't tell you and don't even try and persuade me otherwise." She cleared her throat. "All I'll say is don't forget who knows everything that goes on in this town."

Bronte and I looked at each other and chimed out at the same time, "Mrs. Callahan."

Belinda smiled. "Okay, Nancy. Let me show you the apartment upstairs while Bronte stays down here and makes a few calls." She winked and then led me away.

A half hour later, I wanted the building even more. The apartment was awesome. It was so much bigger than the one I currently lived in—it had an extra bath and the most amazing open plan living and kitchen area. The best bit was the roof terrace which was huge and had a great view over the town and the valley in the distance.

"You will not believe this." Bronte came rushing towards us as we stepped back into the room. "Mrs. Callahan didn't know at first, but God that woman is good. She said to give her ten minutes, but she called me back in eight. I mean, how does she do that?"

"I have no idea." I shook my head and turned to Belinda. "Does this put you in a difficult position?"

Belinda held up her hands in surrender. "I'm going to step outside and make a call. I'll give you a few minutes."

"So?" I asked as the door closed behind Belinda. "What did Mrs. Callahan find out?"

Bronte rolled her eyes. "She wouldn't say how she got the information, but it's a doozy."

"Go on," I urged.

"It's that damn Ruthie Grey. Her daddy is funding it and it's going to be a karaoke bar with topless male waiters and is going to be called." She took a deep breath. "You won't believe this."

"What? Tell me."

She shook her head. "If I didn't dislike the girl so much, I'd think it was a great idea and a cool name, but I do dislike her."

"*Bronte. Just tell me.*"

"Schlongalong."

Damn it she was right; it was a great name for a topless male waiter karaoke bar.

"I hate her," I groaned. "But I love this building." I hadn't even considered opening my own preschool until a few days ago, but now I couldn't think of anything I wanted more. The old bank was just right for it.

"Okay, we need to get this ball rolling," Bronte said, taking her phone out and stabbing at the screen. "You need to be prepared, get all your ducks lined up if you're going to get this place ahead of that spoiled little princess."

"W-who are you calling?" I asked, the swirl of dread in my stomach telling me I already knew.

"Shaw," she confirmed my fear. "He'll represent you and he'll do it pro bono seeing as he's still in college."

"Bronte, no," I cried, making a grab for her phone. "He can't. He's dating Ruthie." If you could call it that.

"Screwing her brains out is not dating, Nancy. He needs experience, so who better than to represent than his friend."

I was also pretty sure he would not call me his friend. I was also pretty sure he'd say no. Not only because it was me but also because he was screwing Ruthie's brains out.

"Shaw, hey I have a job for you." Bronte winked at me as she spoke into the phone. "You're going to represent Nancy in a real estate deal. No, she hasn't got any contracts… she's just viewed the property…I don't care, Shaw… don't be so mean," she whispered the last part and turned away from me. "Yes, you will… oh my God, I can't believe you just said that." She glanced at me, her eyes wide and gave me a thumbs up, like it was all going to be okay when it evidently wasn't. "Remember what I know… I don't care that Carter used it up already, that's Carter… but I will." She was silent for a few seconds and then grinned. "Thank you, Shaw. I'll let you know when we need you."

She then ended the call and looked at me triumphantly.

"He's happy to do it."

"Hardly happy, Bronte," I sighed.

She shrugged. "In this case the devil is *not* in the detail, honey. Now, let's get Belinda in here and make your offer."

"But I haven't sold my apartment yet," I protested. "I need equipment and an initial layout for staff."

Bronte thrust her hands to her hips. "Do you want this place or not?" I nodded because I couldn't deny it. "You have enough money to get the building, right?" I nodded again. "So, let's just make sure we get it and then think about the rest later."

"Okay. But I'm not positive Shaw representing me is the right thing. He obviously said something about me that you weren't happy with."

She waved me away. "Let's just say he needs to consider the language he uses in front of a lady, and I will be having words with him later." She walked to the door and opened it. "Okay, Belinda, we're ready for you."

Bronte certainly was a force to be reckoned with, but if she could help me to secure the bank then what did I care. It was just a pity it looked like I was going to have to take help from her brother too.

Nancy's Bitch List for Shaw

- [ ] Maximus Douchimus
- [ ] Captain Shitsmear
- [ ] Shit Talking Cock Womble
- [ ] Dildohead

CHAPTER 10

Shaw

When I'd woken up from a great night's sleep, I had no idea what was about to hit me like a Mac truck. I'd yawned, stretched, scratched my balls, contemplated jacking off but decided I'd prefer to eat breakfast and get ready for work. Then just as I was getting into my car, my phone rang out, blowing my mind.

Distracted by Mom yelling at me to make sure I picked up her dry cleaning from town on my lunchbreak, I answered it without looking to see who the caller was.

"Yup."

"Shaw? Shaw Jackson?"

"This is he. Who am I speaking with?"

The person on the other end let out a shaky breath. "My name is Aurelia Devonshire, Monique Devonshire's mother."

I sat back against the seat with a bump and stared out through the windshield. Wow, I hadn't heard from or about Monique since she'd run off with our history professor after he'd got her pregnant over a year and a half ago. It had obviously been pretty big gossip for a while, but mainly because he was married to the Dean who was just about to star in her own reality TV show about running an Ivy League college.

"Okay," I replied. "And?"

Thinking about Monique and Professor Ritter didn't boil my piss any longer. I knew it was good riddance; I mean could I really see myself settling down with a woman who didn't eat grilled cheese sandwiches and hated Elvis Presley? No way!

"There's no easy way to say this, but Monique has passed away."

I may not have had feelings for her any longer, but I felt my heart drop to my stomach and my mouth went dry.

Dead.

How the fuck could she be dead? She was my age. People in their early twenties didn't die.

"H-how?" I managed to stutter out.

"Aggressive bone cancer." Monique's mom drew in a breath and was silent for a beat. Then she rushed out. "You need to take custody of your daughter."

"Wait, what?" I bolted forward, my chest colliding with the steering wheel. "I don't know what she told you, but her baby was not mine."

"I know she claimed it was Jonathan Ritter's but I'm afraid a DNA test says differently. Besides which he's never wanted anything to do with Tia. All he was interested in was getting my daughter into bed and then enticing her from her future with promises of marriage. He wasn't even divorced."

Suddenly feeling hot, I loosened my tie and undid the top button of my shirt. "I can promise you, Mrs. Devonshire, that kid isn't mine. We always used protection, besides which I had mid-terms so was real busy studying and had no time to…" I paused trying to choose a suitable way to tell a mother I hadn't been having sex with her now dead daughter. "Spend time with Monique around then."

"Condoms break young man, and Monique said Tia was a month early. She's a petite child so we didn't question it. That, young man," she said sharply, "means, the *quality* time you spent with my daughter before you became busy studying has resulted in Tia being yours."

It was at that point not only did my heart drop to my stomach, again, but the ass fell out of my world too.

***

Walking into the office, I ignored Evie's morning greeting and headed straight for Tate's office. I wasn't sure I could speak without breaking into a scream.

I didn't want or need a kid at this point in my life. In fact, I would have rather gotten a dick piercing and I hated needles. Coming off the phone from Monique's mom, my mouth was as dry as a bone and my heart was beating so loud, I was sure my mom would hear it inside the house. Speaking of, I hadn't even considered going back inside and talking to my folks about the call. I knew my mom and after giving me a lecture about safe sex she'd be ordering a crib online. As for my dad, well I wasn't sure I could stand to see his disappointment. They'd been great about the whole *Bronte getting knocked up before she was married* thing, but I wasn't sure they'd be so cool with me. Dad had always drilled it into me to be sure I was covered, *literally*, where birth control was concerned.

'Son, respect yourself and the woman by ensuring you're both protected,', he'd said and then slapped me on the back and handed me a packet of condoms. 'And if you can't then be sure to abstain.'

No, I didn't need his discourse, what I needed was good solid advice, so who better than Tate.

"Hey, Tate," I said, wrapping on the door jamb with my knuckles. "You got a minute please?"

Tate looked up from a document he was reading through and smiled. "Sure. Come on in."

Closing the door behind me, I went over to the visitor's chair at his desk and dropped down into it.

"What wrong?" Tate asked, frowning. "You don't look so good. You're a little pale."

"I had some news this morning and I'm not sure what to do with it."

"Okay." He pushed his chair back and stood up, made his way to my side of the desk, and sat on the edge of it. "I'm guessing it's bad news." He placed a firm hand on my shoulder and gave it a squeeze.

Blowing out my cheeks, I stared up at him wishing that it was just a fucking nightmare and I'd wake up soon. The noise of the street outside, along with my blood pounding in my ears, told me it most definitely wasn't.

"I got a call from the mom of an ex-girlfriend about a half hour ago." Tate crossed his arms over his chest and nodded. "And well, shit…"

Tate's desk phone trilled out and he turned to pick it up. "Sorry not now, Evie. Hold all my calls please." He replaced the handset to the cradle and gave me a smile. "Sorry, Shaw. Carry on."

"According to the woman—Monique's, mom. Well, according to her I have a baby and she wants me to take custody of it."

Tate's eyes widened. "*What*?"

"Yeah. So, well, shit." I scrubbed a hand down my face. "Apparently Monique died and the baby who I thought she was having with our history professor wasn't his. They've done a DNA test, so the only other person it could be is me." I stabbed at my chest with my thumb. "It's my baby, Tate and Mrs. Devonshire wants me to take her because she's getting married again and doesn't want to bring up another kid."

"Wow, way to go Grandma," Tate remarked, shaking his head. "Do you think the child is yours?"

I shrugged. "I have no clue. I mean the dates would work, but I always, always used a condom."

"She cheated on you with the professor?" I nodded. "Any chance she could have been seeing someone else, as well as him?"

I shrugged. "I have no idea. I never thought she'd cheat on me with one person, never mind two."

Tate sighed and scratched his ear. "Yeah, well, people we trust can often surprise us."

"I certainly never thought it of Monique." I sighed.

"Okay," Tate said. "Let's consider the facts. You say you always used protection and she said the baby was the professor's?"

"Yep, to both. She told me that she was pregnant, and it was Professor Ritter's. I didn't question it because I always used a condom. I mean, we would have known if one had ever broken, right." I sighed. "I don't get it, she told me Ritter didn't use protection. We weren't exactly sexually active around that time, so it added up."

"But he's done a DNA test and it's not his?"

I nodded. "Mrs. Devonshire is sending me the results. She also said that Monique must've lied that the baby was a month early, which kinda puts me back in the frame."

Pushing to his feet, Tate moved over to his chair to sit down and immediately started to type on his keyboard. "First things first. You get your own DNA test done. Where does the grandmother live?"

"Wichita."

"Okay, we'll get you a flight out there as soon as we can. Call me mistrusting, but you should take the baby's DNA in person." He paused and jotted something onto a legal pad. "Who's less likely to be emotional about all this, your mom, or your dad? Whichever one it is, take them with you."

I groaned and Tate looked up.

"You have to tell them sometime. Plus, we want to be sure you don't get coerced into signing something while you're in a sensitive state. In fact…" Tate clicked on something on his Mac screen and then picked up the office phone. "Hey Evie, could you organize two flights out to Wichita for Thursday? Also reschedule the pretrial meeting with Anna Duke for Friday or the following Monday instead… yeah, it's a video conference call… that'll be me and Shaw… great. Thank you." He replaced the receiver and looked up at me. "Okay. You have the grandmother's number?"

I nodded and flashed my mobile at Tate. "Yes, I do."

"Call her and tell her that she and the baby need to be available Thursday. Don't take any shit from her. Tell her you're going there to get a DNA sample and you'll have your lawyer with you."

"What if she can't make it?" I asked, glancing out of the glass office to see Evie on the phone, probably booking flights.

"Well, it'll be a good opportunity to practice your skills as a lawyer. Pick her weakness and play on it." He grinned.

"Basically, tell her to be there if she wants me to even consider taking the baby."

"You got it." Tate sat back in his chair and crossed his arms over his chest. "Now, in the meantime, take the rest of the day. Go and tell your folks and then get over to the Houston Testing Center on Maple and pick up a test—actually get two just in case."

Swallowing hard, I nodded.

"It's going to cost you a couple of hundred bucks. Do you have enough money?"

"I do." I'd barely spent any of the small salary that Tate paid me, what with working and studying, it wasn't a problem.

"As your lawyer, I'll cover the air fare."

"Tate, I can't ask you to do that," I protested.

"Shaw it's fine." He smiled and pushed his chair away from the desk. "It can go toward my pro bono hours and the flights will go down as expenses. Now, go. Go see your folks and then get yourself to Houston. I'll get Evie to text you the details about the flights. Okay?"

"Thank you, Tate. I can't tell you how much I appreciate this. All I wanted was your advice, so this is above and beyond."

Tate grinned and then picked up his pen. "Like I said it'll go against my pro bono hours."

Leaving his office, it felt like it was now only a hundred-pound weight on my shoulders rather than a thousand. Tate Hallahan was a good man. I knew he'd more than likely already used up his pro bono hours. He was doing this as my boss and friend, and I was lucky to have him as both.

"Oh, and Shaw," he called as I reached the door. "Your sister called and asked if it was okay for you to take on Nancy Andrews as a pro bono for her realty deal."

Fuck, I cursed in a whisper and turned back to face him with a smile. "Yeah, she did mention it."

"I'm more than happy with you doing that." He started to shuffle some papers on his desk. “It’ll be great experience for you and she’s doing us a solid by testifying so I’m happy to throw her a bone right back.”

Smiling tightly, I left the office. As I left the building, vowed that representing her would most definitely be the last bone that I’d ever throw Nancy Andrews way ever again.

CHAPTER 11

Nancy

It had been three days since I'd looked at the bank, and I'd almost bitten my nails to the quick waiting to hear back from Belinda as to whether I was the only person who'd offered on it. I just hoped that Ruthie had changed her mind and decided Dayton Valley wasn't the place for a topless waiter karaoke bar.

Apparently, the contractor who'd upgraded the building was away visiting family and didn't want to talk business until he got home—which was going to be in another two days. I mean, did he want to make himself some money or not?

Apart from that stress, I was about to go on stage for my turn in the first round of Dayton Valley Idol and feelings were running high. Young Dulcie Rogers had just got through, even though Mr. Callahan had voted no. That hadn't gone down too well with the audience crowded into the hall. The barrage of abuse he'd got had resulted in Dulcie's dad being banned from the gas station by Mrs. Callahan.

"You set?" Carter asked, as Garner McGillicuddy, our emcee finished introducing me.

"Yes but remind me again why I agreed to this."

He grinned and slapped my back. "'Cause it's for a good cause and you're a sucker for my baby blues."

He fluttered his eyelashes at me and grinned. Yes, he was definitely pretty with nice eyes, but they weren't quite the right sort of blue.

Damn it. Why the hell was I thinking about Shaw?

Talking of which, my attention moved to the steps leading up to the backstage. There was the man himself, looking like he'd lost a dollar and found a dime. He'd been like that the night previous too, at our final rehearsal. So much so that Carter had sent him home because he was dragging down the mood. No one had got so much as two words out of him, even his singing had been lackluster normally he sounded like an angel.

"Go, go, go," Carter yelled down my ear and pushed me toward the stage. Taking one last quick glance at Shaw, I ran to where the microphone was waiting for me.

"Hello," Jim Wickerson, our head judge called up to me. "And who are you and what are you going to sing for us tonight?"

The audience, who it had to be said was probably well over half of Dayton, all groaned. He asked everyone who they were, even though we were all locals and most of us had known him all our lives.

"She hasn't changed her name since she went to school with your grandson, Jim." It was Henry, Ellie and Carter's dad. I knew it was him even though the stage lights blinded me. He'd said pretty much the same thing every time Jim had repeated the question.

"Henry, pipe down," Jefferson called. "Don't you know that Jim has an important job." There was laughter in his tone, and I got the distinct impression that the whole thing was a joke to everyone, except for Carter.

"Sush, baby," that was Kitty. "Just let Nancy do her thing."

"I'm Nancy Andrews and tonight I'm going to sing Lady A's *Can't Stand the Rain."*

Jim nodded, Mr. Callahan rolled his eyes and Delphine clapped her hands together like a performing seal.

Once more second guessing how I'd let myself be talked into taking part, I swallowed and opened my mouth to sing. As soon as I let out the first note, I was lost in the music and nothing else existed. The words, the tune, the melody were the only important things. The bank, my weird relationship thingy with Shaw, the fact that I was pretty much alone in the world, floated away into the ether. It was just me and the song.

I'd always loved singing, even as a small child, any opportunity I got to give my family a song I would. It wasn't like I wanted to be a singer or anything, but I could hold a tune and I enjoyed the feeling it gave to me.

When I finished, the audience applause was deafening, and I couldn't help but break out a huge grin and do a little bow.

"Way to go, Nancy."

"Woah, Nancy. Amazing tubes, honey."

"Go Nancy."

When the applause died down, all I could hear was my heart thudding. All I could *feel* was my heart thudding. I glanced to the side and almost peed myself when I spotted Shaw clapping and smiling like *now,* he'd lost a dime and found a dollar. He looked handsome and happy, as though I'd just given him the world. I wasn't expecting to feel my heart swell as much as it did—it felt like it was glowing inside my chest. A little ball of sun underneath my silver sequined vest top.

As the judges all gave their opinion, I didn't really listen to them. I was too busy trying to figure out what the heat in my chest meant. I glanced back at Shaw, but he'd stopped clapping, he was no longer smiling and was now back to glowering. The thrill I'd been feeling slowly ebbed to a whisper until it finally died, and my own mood turned grey.

"Thank you, Nancy," Jim said. "Let's hope the audience vote for you to get through to tomorrow's semi-final."

"For Pete's sake, Jim," Jefferson hollered. "Of course she's going to get through."

People started to chime out their agreement and when I heard Bronte calling for a new head judge, I slunk off the stage.

"Well done." Carter ruffled my hair and grinned. "Let's see what Shaw can come back with. Hopefully, it's better than his rehearsal."

"I am here, you know."

We both turned to face a scowling Shaw. He was scuffing his toe along the wooden boards of the stage and there was deep crease between his eyes.

"You sure you're up for this?" Carter asked.

Shaw glanced at me and then pulled his shoulders back. "You betcha." He then stormed out onto the main stage, even though Garner hadn't finished introducing him, and in the next three minutes he absolutely killed it. He sang the first notes of *Nobody* and instantly the audience looked up at him in rapt attention. His voice was beautiful, deep and melodic and the way he gripped the microphone stand had me thinking all sorts of things. Leaning into it, his eyes closed, Shaw looked every inch a rockstar. He was good.

He was so damn good in fact that I almost threw my panties on stage.

Expecting him to milk the applause, I was surprised when he simply asked, "Sorry to rush, but am I through?"

All three judges gave him a yes, but while Mr. Callahan was over doing his role and going on and on about melody and timing, Shaw walked off the stage.

"I know he's pissed at something, but that's just rude," Carter muttered, turning his gaze from Shaw back to his clipboard. He groaned. "Jesus, help us. Ellie, you're up."

Ellie squealed and clapped her hands and jumped up and down on the spot. "I'm so going to kill this."

"No fucking kidding." Carter frowned and pushed his sister toward the stage.

As she did a little bow, I heard Hunter yelling. "Go baby. You can do it."

"I beg to differ," Carter said, shoving some yellow foam into his ears. He then held out his palm, where another pair of earplugs balanced. "Seriously, take them. You'll thank me for it."

The first note that came out of Ellie's mouth wasn't too bad, but the second, third, fourth and so on were hideous. Fingers down a chalk board sounded better. She was supposed to be singing Whitney Houston's *Greatest Love of All,* but there was nothing about it that resembled the original song. When the three judges shouted 'no' simultaneously, I heaved a sigh of relief. Carter slapped his thigh with his clipboard. "Hell, yeah." It took a couple of seconds for it to register with Ellie, who continued warbling.

"Garner," Carter yelled across the stage. "Get her off."

"But I haven't had my feedback," Ellie protested. "I think I've been judged unfairly." She pouted and looked from the judges to Carter.

Carter took a step onto the stage. "I'll give you your feedback, sis. You're shit, now get off."

Ellie stamped her foot. "Why are you so mean to me?"

"I'm not, I'm truthful. Now move, we have two more people to sing and very little time."

"Well, thank you and commiserations, Ellie," Garner said, moving to center stage and putting a hand on Ellie's back. "Let's hear it for nurse Ellie, everyone."

With that she finally moved off, throwing a death stare at the judges as she did. It was so mean it even scared me, not as much as her singing had, but it scared me all the same.

***

Stars & Stripes was almost full to busting when I finally got there to meet 'the gang' for drinks. They didn't have to invite me along, as I wasn't with Minnesota any longer, but they still included me in any plans. Yes, I felt awkward from time to time, especially when they all insisted on PDA-ing the hell out of each other. Generally, though, it was great to have people other than four-year-old kids and a crotchety old teacher to spend time with.

I knew that Alaska felt guilty about how his brother dumped me, but he had no need. If I was being truthful and dug up my feelings from deep within my heart, he and I had been having problems for a while. They were little things. He stopped staying over both nights on the weekends. He'd started to complain about the mess in my bathroom, which he'd never done before. The main thing was when he'd called me Annalise one time, at least I'm pretty sure he did. I tried to pretend to myself I'd misheard, after all he didn't look guilty, hadn't flinched, or colored up. I pushed it from my mind and decided it hadn't happened, but deep down I knew it had. Then when I collected his stuff from around my apartment to give back to him, a piece of paper fell out of the pocket of his jeans. It had the name Annalise and a number on it with the words, '*next time maybe you can stay longer'*. It kind of proved I wasn't hard of hearing.

Anyway, safe to say, when Minnesota left, I wasn't totally heartbroken. Maybe a little heart sore would be a better description. I felt stupid and foolish for believing that he wanted to travel the world with me before we decided to settle down together. It had all been a bunch of lies on his part—the stupid, handsome idiot. Truth be told, if I thought about settling down with Minnesota it didn't make me feel all warm and fuzzy, he'd probably done me a favor.

"Hey, Nancy," Hunter called from the high-top table everyone was standing at. "Got you a beer."

I nodded my thanks and made my way over to the three couples. There was no Shaw, or Lily, who sometimes tagged along and then spent the night complaining about the fact that she had to drink Coke.

"Hey guys." I gave them all a wave and then took the beer being offered to me by Carter. "Thanks, I need this."

"You were amazing," Bronte gushed, pulling me into a hug. "I mean I know he's my brother, but you were even better than Shaw."

"What about me?" Ellie asked in all seriousness. "Did you not think I was robbed?"

Everyone stopped and stared at her, and I felt a little uncomfortable as she watched us all with wide-eyed anticipation.

"Sure, baby," Hunter finally replied. "They just weren't ready for your brilliance."

Through a cough, Carter spluttered, "Fucking pussy."

Slapping him against the chest with the back of her hand, Bronte smiled sweetly at Ellie. "There's always next year, honey."

"Shaw was pretty good though," Hunter quickly added, steering the conversation. "He's got the old, tortured rockstar thing going on."

"Yeah, what's that all about?" Carter asked. "He hardly waited long enough to hear if he'd got through, he was in such a foul mood."

Bronte shrugged. "No idea. I know he went to Wichita with Tate the other day. Maybe it's a tough case they're working on."

"Where is he anyway?" I took a swig of my beer, being careful not to give anyone eye contact.

"Said he had stuff to do," Carter responded. "Speaking of."

He raised a brow at Bronte and held up five fingers making Bronte giggle. Ellie's head swung around and she gasped before grabbing ahold of Hunter's arm and tugging on it. I smiled, fully expectant of some sort of madness to follow.

"Babe, what the hell." He grimaced and pulled away from her. "That hurts."

"That didn't hurt," she protested. "But what will hurt is your blue balls if you don't get me pregnant before *them. They* are leaving in five minutes to have baby making sex and we cannot let them get ahead of *our* schedule."

I was right the madness was about to begin. Not for the first time though I was glad I had them and their crazy in my life. They'd certainly distracted me when Minnesota dumped my ass.

Carter burst out laughing and I swung my gaze to him as he said, "You ever think his swimmers might be, kinda like, drowning rather than front crawling toward the finishing line known as your eggs."

"For fuck's sake Carter." Hunter slapped him around his head. "Do not talk about my swimmers not being viable and certainly do not talk about your sister's, *my wife's,* lady parts."

"Well, you haven't got her pregnant yet. How long you been trying?"

It wasn't enough that Bronte and Ellie were in competition, Carter and Hunter were going to join in too. Turning to Hunter, it occurred to me that it was like watching a mixed-doubles tennis match.

"Not long." Hunter pouted in response to Carter. "A few weeks."

Carter tapped his bottle against Hunter's. "You do remember that I put a baby in Bronte's belly just the one time of skinny dipping in the pool of pleasure."

Bronte groaned. "Really?"

"Lollipop, come on, you know it's true."

"I know you're a dipshit," Hunter replied. "Talking about my spunk like that."

"There's nothing wrong with his swimmers anyway," Ellie added, poking Carter in the shoulder. "I know for sure that he has a lot and they're very strong. I've seen them under the microscope. Dr. Peterson let me look."

"When the fuck did you do that?" Hunter asked, as he reared back to look at her.

We all turned to look at Ellie who was sporting a wary smile.

"Did you—?"

Surely she hadn't! Had she? By the look on her face, I knew she had, and I cringed second guessing my joy at being part of this mad inner circle.

"Oh shit," I muttered.

"Yes, baby I did. I needed to know if we were up against any problems."

I started to laugh as Hunter's face morphed into a picture of horror. His eyes were wide, and his mouth dropped into a perfect O as he gasped loudly.

"So when you ran out of the bedroom with your mouth full, it wasn't like you said, because it tasted of beef jerky?"

"Hunt' you asshole," Carter cried. "I don't want to know about my sister and what she does with your jizz."

"Oh my God, Ellie." I grabbed a hold of the table to steady myself as I was laughing so hard. "You didn't."

She put her hands to her hips and glared at Hunter. "You wouldn't beat off into a cup, what was I supposed to do?"

"You were supposed to give me longer than a week to knock you up, Ellie. That's what."

"Doesn't mean they're any good just because the doctor said they are," Carter said. "I mean having them in your mouth must have contaminated them."

"I brush not only my teeth but my tongue too, you douche. Unlike you who Mom used to have to force into the bathroom."

"Well, if you ask me," Bronte said, taking a sip of her wine. "I think it's a total waste of spunk. But I'm glad you're good to go, Hunt'. That does mean though Carter that we need to get busy if we are to provide grandchild number two. Make those five minutes three and we are out of here." She knocked back the rest of her wine and then tapped Carter's watch. "The clock is ticking baby."

"Hunter, let's go." Ellie snagged his beer bottle and slammed it down onto the table. "Sorry, Nancy, hate to run but we kinda need to get home quick."

I shook my head. "No problem, it's fine."

"Yeah sorry, Nancy," Bronte said as she started to move away from the table. "Maybe my brother can keep you company." She nodded toward the bar and there was Shaw being handed a bottle by Penny. He turned and when he saw us looking in his direction, rolled his eyes.

Hunter and Carter finished their drinks, while both of their wives waited impatiently. While it was amusing to watch, I was also disappointed. I'd been looking forward to a few beers and letting loose after the stress of the contest and worrying about the bank.

"I guess I'll go too," I sighed.

"No," Bronte protested. "Have a drink with Shaw and see if you can find out who pissed on his grits."

At that exact moment, Shaw arrived at the table not looking any happier than he had earlier.

"What's going on?" he asked. "Where's everyone going?"

"Home for sex," Bronte replied with a smile.

"To get pregnant," Ellie added.

As they all practically ran out of the bar, Shaw turned to me and frowned. "Seriously?"

"Yep, seriously. They're all in competition to see who gets pregnant first."

"No," he snapped. "I didn't mean that. I meant seriously I'm left here with you."

You ever feel like you want to dick punch someone, just for being a dipshit? Yeah, exactly!

<u>*Nancy's Bitch List for Shaw*</u>

- [ ] *Maximus Douchimus*
- [ ] *Captain Shitsmear*
- [ ] *Shit Talking Cock Womble*
- [ ] *Dildohead*
- [ ] *Dipshit Cockhead*

CHAPTER 12

Shaw

"You want a drink?" I asked Nancy. "Or you could go, either is good with me."

She narrowed her eyes at me and then grinned. "I'll get a vodka tonic please."

I looked pointedly at the beer in her hand. "You sure you want to mix?" I leaned closer. "You know what tends to happen if you get too drunk."

"And what's that?" Nancy swallowed hard and I knew she knew. It was good to see the hint of pink on her cheeks, knowing she felt uncomfortable.

"That," I whispered closer to her ear, "would be me fucking you until you scream."

Clearing her throat, Nancy moved back a step and while it was almost imperceptible, I saw her pull her thighs together and squirm.

I filled the space she'd created. "You do remember how I stripped you naked? And how I then licked every inch of your skin, your pussy and then those amazing tits."

Damn it, my dick was getting hard just talking about it. Nancy bent over in the Delaney's barn was pretty good too but, in a bed, she was a whole other ball game. Nancy in bed was amazing, she was unabandoned and free and knew exactly how to please a man.

"You still wanna get drunk on vodka then Nancy?" I whispered in her ear. "Maybe repeat that night."

"I think," she said, tucking her hair behind her ear and moving her mouth close to my ear. "That maybe I should stick to beer because it's not like I'd ever let that happen. Twice was enough."

I raised a brow and shrugged. "Think it was more than twice on one of those occasions, but I'm not one to split hairs."

Nancy's eyelashes fluttered like she was remembering everything. In fact, I was pretty sure she was close to asking me to just bring the whole bottle of vodka. I didn't blame her though because we were more than compatible in the sack—like I said, I was in lust with her pussy.

"Just get me a drink, Shaw." She moved a step away again. "I've had a shit week and need something strong."

"Okay," I said, holding up my hands in surrender. "Vodka and tonic coming right up."

God knew how much later and we were both well on our way to being drunk. Problem was, neither of us were happy drunks. We looked like we'd been sent for and couldn't go as my Grammy used to say about people who looked morose.

"Oh my God," Nancy sighed. "What the hell is wrong with us? We're in the prime of our lives and yet we're both standing here staring into our drinks and looking miserable." She pointed at herself. "*I* should be out with friends, dancing and having a great time. Instead." She looked me up and down. "I'm here, with you."

"Hey," I protested. "Don't think I like it any more than you do. I could be at a kegger tonight, playing beer pong or strip poker."

"So, why aren't you?"

I looked up at the ceiling, thinking about it. "I fucking hate frat parties and I have something going on that's kinda making me shit company."

"Oh, has that something been going on for the last twenty-two years or so? Because got to say, Shaw, you've always been shit company."

I couldn't help but laugh. She always had a cute but snarky remark for me, which often made me smile, even if it was only when she'd turned her back.

"Glad I can cheer you up." Nancy winked and took a slug of her vodka. "Okay spill it. Tell me what the current something is."

She then grabbed a spare stool and plonked herself down onto it, settling in. Normally, I'd have told her to fuck off and mind her own business, but whether it was the alcohol or the fact that my head felt about to burst with it, I opened my mouth and let it all spill.

The whole shazam; Monique, Professor Ritter, the baby that may or may not be mine and the fact that Tate had done me a solid by flying to Wichita with me to tell Monique's mom she was crazy if she thought that sweet blonde-haired cutie was mine.

"Holy fuck," Nancy gasped her eyes going wide as she gripped the tabletop. "And you're sure she's not yours?"

I thought back to the little girl running around and babbling about dollies and Legos as I watched her, desperately trying to see any resemblance to Professor Ritter. Of course there wasn't one; Mrs. Devonshire was right, Tia did not belong to our history professor. She was fair not dark and did not have a chin with perfect right angles at the bottom corners.

"No, I'm not sure. I *am* sure she isn't the professor's kid though. I've seen the kids he has with the Dean and let me tell you, they are *not* pretty girls."

"Shaw! You can't say that," Nancy gasped.

"But they're not. Honestly, all three of those girls look like Ritter in a dress. They don't have one feminine feature amongst them. You know the eldest one has a huge Adam's apple, bigger than mine."

Nancy blinked slowly. "I'll pretend you didn't say that. And you do know there are laws against saying things like that…" She sighed. "Yes, of course you do, you're a trainee lawyer."

I shrugged. "Just saying what I saw. I won't tell if you don't."

"So, what you're saying is, the fact that the baby is pretty means she could be yours."

"Nooo, no way." I shook my head vigorously. "What I'm saying is, she's definitely not Ritter's kid. However, the fact she isn't his means that there's a ninety-five percent chance that she's mine."

"What's the other five percent?" she asked taking a drink.

"That Monique sat on a dirty toilet seat."

Before I had time to blink, Nancy's vodka came out of her mouth and hit me smack bang in the middle of my chest, dripping down my shirt.

"Please tell me you actually know the facts of life," she gasped, wiping at the alcohol on her chin.

"Yes, I do, you idiot. It was a joke."

"What gives with the five percent then?" she asked.

As the liquid slowly ran down her neck toward her cleavage, I shifted feeling a little tight in the crotch department and shrugged. "I don't know, I didn't want to appear too cocky, I know how these things turn out. You're confident about something and it generally turns to shit. Plus, there is a five percent chance she may have banged someone else."

A hand was held up in front of me. "You know for an educated man you sure talk like Jeremy Brenton at times."

"No way, how the fuck dare you?" I glanced around the bar, worried someone may have heard her.

Thankfully, everyone was too busy taking advantage of Penny's happy hour. I was relieved because no one wanted to be likened to Jeremy Brenton. He was in our class in high school and was the biggest douche on the planet. The guy carried the panties of whichever girl he was dating in his jeans pocket and regularly used them to mop his brow in gym class.

"You know he's working at a strip joint in Middleton Ridge?" I asked, totally pissed at her.

"No way." Nancy sat back on her stool. "Who the hell would pay to watch *him* strip?"

"No one," I replied, picking up my beer and rolling my eyes. "He's the janitor."

"Oh, that makes sense." She eyed me warily. "You think you'll be okay? You think Tate will help you get it fixed?"

"I hope so." I swigged back the last of my beer, *hoping* that my *hope* wasn't misplaced. "Anyway, less of my crap, what's made your piss so sour?"

"Ugh, Mrs. Baker." She screwed up her face and pretended to gag. "She's being a total bitch to me. Ever since I agreed to testify for Mrs. Ranger, she's just taken every opportunity to pull me up on my work, and be basically, well… a bitch."

I'd never liked Annie Baker. She'd always been a crotchety old buzzard who wasn't so hot on little kids having fun. Which was pretty shitty because she owned the only preschool in Dayton Valley.

"You know she made Carter sit facing the wall once?" I offered.

"What did he do? Pull some girls pigtails or something?" Nancy laughed and her face went from pretty to just plain beautiful.

"Nope." I shook my head. "He spoke during quiz night."

Nancy screwed up her brow and she still looked cute. "What at preschool? "

"No, you idiot." Now it was my turn to laugh. "In here, the summer before he knocked up Bronte. We were in here having a drink and the quiz was going on, and Carter asked what we were all drinking. I mean everyone knows you don't talk during quiz night."

"What like fight club?"

I rolled my eyes and tried not laugh. I couldn't have her thinking she was fucking funny. "Yeah, just like fight club."

"Why come in here then? If you can't talk on quiz night what a shit idea to come in here for a drink. Why would you do that?"

"Duh." I shrugged. "You get free grilled cheese sandwiches at the end of the night."

She thought about it for a few seconds and then nodded. "Yeah, I get that. When is the next quiz night, because I'll be right here!" She stabbed a finger on the table and when she wobbled a little, I knew it was probably time for us to quit drinking. "And you know what," she continued. "I will be talking."

Laughing, I reached for my bottle. "Imagine how fucking pissed she'll be when you open your pre-school."

"Well I won't if Ruthie gets the old bank." Narrowing her eyes on me, Nancy made a small growling noise. "You know, your girlfriend, Ruthie."

"She's not my girlfriend, Nancy."

"Oh yeah, sorry. I forgot you're just 'banging her'." She did air quotes and giggled.

"Ruthie likes people to think we're dating. She's always grabbing me when people are watching or if we happen to see each other in public. For me it's more a mutual gratification thing and it hasn't happened for a while." Not since I'd last 'banged' Nancy seemingly, but I didn't mention that. "Anyway, Tate says I have to help you get the building, so it's practically yours. I'm that good.

"Yeah, about that," she replied, picking at the table with her thumbnail. "I'm not sure it's in my best interest to have Ruthie's...whatever you are... working on my behalf."

"Why the hell not?" I asked. "And let me be clear, I am not Ruthie's anything. No way. No how, not ever."

"It's a conflict of interest though. Like I said you're having sex with her. What if you let slip something and she uses it to get the building?"

I shifted in my seat to fully face her. "It won't happen because I'm a professional. I promise you; we barely talk."

Nancy snorted. "Will that be because she's a grade A bimbo?"

"No," I snorted back. "Because usually her mouth is full of my dick."

Nancy rolled her eyes. "You're so gross."

"That's what she said."

"Shaw, are you ever serious about anything?"

"I can be," I replied with a shrug. "And I will be when I'm winning the old bank for you."

"I told you, I'm not sure it's a good idea." She sighed and took a swig of her drink and a tiny droplet escaped. It slowly dripped down her chin and I held my breath waiting for it to drop onto her boobs. She caught it with the back of her hand and wiped it away.

"Fucker," I muttered under my breath.

"Which means," Nancy continued, clearly not having noticed that I'd been waiting for some soft porn boob action. "That I think I should ask someone else to represent me."

I wasn't sure why the words came out of my mouth. Maybe it was the boob thing, or maybe it was my pride because I wanted to prove to Nancy that I could win the bank for her, who knew, but I said it.

"I'll make you a promise," I said, taking hold of her hand. "That I will cut all ties with Ruthie until you have the keys for the bank in your hand."

Nancy sat back on her stool and raised her eyebrows. "Let me get this straight. You'll forgo sexy time just so that I'll use you to broker my real estate deal."

"I can't believe I'm saying this, but yep. I'll forgo sexy times so that you'll use me to broker your real estate deal." The words were ground out and kind of made the back of my throat itch, but if that was what it took, then so be it.

Nancy looked surprised. Shocked. Gob smacked as an English college friend of mine would say.

"You're joking, right?"

I shook my head. "Serious as a heart attack, baby."

She blinked three times, downed the rest of her vodka, slammed her glass on the table and held out her hand.

"Well, I guess we should shake on it then."

We shook and I fleetingly thought about how soft her hands were.

"We have a deal then?"

Nancy nodded. "We have a deal." She stood up. "I'll get the next round and then we'll discuss what you're going to do about the kid which may be ninety-five percent yours."

I have to admit I watched her ass as she walked away, but I still hated her.

CHAPTER 13

Nancy

The crowd cheered and I took a bow. My rendition of Mae Muller's *'Dependent'* had gone down well. Maybe not quite as well as Shaw's version of Elvis' *'A Little Less Conversation'*. The douche had a standing ovation from the whole audience. I even saw some of the high school girls fanning themselves and jumping up and down on the spot squealing when he did a little Elvis leg shake.

"Well done, Nancy. That was amazing," Garner said as he waved me off. "Now, can we please welcome Mrs. Callahan to the stage."

As I walked into the wings, Mrs. Callahan breezed past me the feathers from her headdress wafting up my nose and causing me to sneeze.

"Pretty good out there," Carter said giving me a huge grin. "I think my brother-in-law may have some competition."

"I don't know," I said with a shrug. "I think he may have the high school girls' vote." The town had the final vote. There would be a ballot box in the library and then on Monday evening the winner would be announced on the stage.

"Did you not see the high school soccer team and how they were all gaping at you?" Carter winked. "I think it's going to be a tight result."

We both then swung around as Mrs. Callahan started to sing, '*I Am What I Am'* as she pranced around the stage cracking a whip.

"I never agreed to that," Carter gasped. "This is a family show."

"Well, Mr. Callahan seems to be enjoying it." I pointed to where Mr. Callahan was up on his feet waving his arms in the air and shouting, 'Way to go Snookums' as he slapped his own ass. I shuddered and looked at Carter. He was drawing his finger across his throat at Skeeter Mackenzie who was in charge of playing the music. Definitely my time to leave.

As I left the Memorial Hall, I saw Shaw leaning against the wall and wondered what had bitten his ass because he was kicking at the ground with the toe of his boot.

"Evening," I mumbled as I walked past with my head down. "Nice performance again."

"Yep, I know."

Conceited idiot. He didn't even seem embarrassed by his declaration. I carried on walking half expecting some lame ass insult but there was nothing. When I reached the edge of the sidewalk, I twisted to look over my shoulder. Shaw was still looking down at the ground and ignoring me. Shrugging I continued walking and made my way across the high street and close by to Jacob's print shop. The light was on, and I could see that he was in there. He was bending over the counter and had his head in his hands. Since his wife left him and his son JJ just over a couple of years back, he'd been doing okay. Better than okay in fact. He was running his business, bringing up JJ, with the help of Lily, and had even started to coach the Junior Valliant's, Dayton Valley's under ten's soccer team. The last couple of weeks though he'd started to look like he had the weight of the world on his shoulders. I contemplated knocking on the window to check if he was okay, but when he picked up his phone and started to talk into it, I decided to continue home.

The night was warm, with a soft breeze, so I took the long route home. I kind of wished I hadn't when I walked past the parking lot of the feed store and saw Hunter's truck parked up. For an instant I wondered why the hell it was there at ten at night, but when I saw the windows were steamed up and it was rocking from side to side I knew why. My thoughts were compounded when I heard Ellie yell, "*Oh my God, that's it, impregnate me, baby.*" It struck me that they had their own house so why on earth were they in a corner of a parking lot in town? Then I realized it was Hunter and Ellie so there would be no logical reason.

Giggling to myself I carried on home relishing in the fact that I actually loved the little town that I lived in. The residents were a weird bunch of people, but they were my people and I loved them too.

"You took your time."

I looked over to where the voice was coming from and almost screamed. Leaning against the wall of my apartment building was the last person that I expected to see…

"Minnesota! What the hell are you doing here?"

He pushed away from the wall, stretching out his long limbs to stride toward me. His dark blond hair was a little longer than it had been before he left, but I guess he had been travelling the world.

"I missed you, darlin'," he said, running a hand through said hair and giving me his trademark 'I'm going give you the night of your life' smirk.

"I repeat, what the hell are you doing here?"

"Came to see you."

I looked up to the dark sky and mentally counted to ten. If I didn't, I'd be likely to slap him across his damn face. Also, looking away from him meant that I didn't need to look into his gorgeous brown eyes. I'd lost count the things he'd made me do just by looking at me. Bracing myself for the fall out, I lowered my gaze to Minnesota's.

"Does your fiancée know that you're here?" I asked, crossing my arms over my chest.

At least he had the decency to look away with embarrassment. "Can we at least go inside."

He had to be joking. If we went inside, then I was damn sure he'd end up inside me and I did not want to be that woman.

"No. Just tell me what you want?"

"I want to talk to you."

He reached out to touch me, but I took a step back. "We have nothing to talk about. You dumped me before *we* were supposed to go traveling. And you then went and got yourself engaged to some girl who eats cucumber sandwiches and drinks tea with her pinkie in the air."

He frowned. "She eats what now?"

"What she eats isn't important." I waved him away. "What is important is the fact that you're engaged, Minnesota. You're engaged yet are standing here telling me that you missed me and want to talk, when I know exactly what that means."

"And what does it mean?" Now I was getting the 'damn you're cute and I wanna fuck you', grin.

Huffing out a breath I scrubbed my hands down my face. "God you are so frustrating. You think you can just strut back here and pick up where you left off before you left me. Left me to go alone on the trip that I should point out, I organized the itinerary for. Then on that that trip you set up a new life in London and get engaged to someone. Someone who you've known for a *month*." I blinked rapidly. "We were together for almost two years, and not once did you suggest that we get engaged. Not once, Minnesota."

"I know," he sighed. "And I'm sorry that I took you for granted. If you want to be engaged, then—"

"No!" I held up my hand urging him to shut up. "I do not want to be engaged and certainly not to you."

He had the damn nerve to look affronted. Like *I'd* hurt *his* feelings.

"But why?" he asked in his whiny, teenage boy who just got his PlayStation confiscated voice.

"Because," I replied, equally as teenager-y.

"At least think about giving me a second chance." He actually pouted. "Please."

Then before I had a chance to knee him in the balls, he pulled me into him and planted his lips on mine. I can't say it wasn't nice because it was.

They were soft and familiar, and I might have sighed a little and thrust my hips towards his penis.

"Well, well, well."

I pulled out of Minnesota's arms and twirled on the spot. Shaw was standing there looking like he might snap someone's neck. The way he was staring at the man holding my hand I guessed it was Minnesota's neck that was in danger.

"This is nothing at all like you think," I said, pointing between me and Minnesota.

"None of my business," he replied. "Nice to see you back, Minnesota."

"Shaw."

"Seriously," I cried taking a step away. "You honestly think that I'd go back to him?"

Shaw shrugged. "Like I said, none of my business. Y'all have a good night."

He then turned and left, and I felt like I wanted to run after him and pull him back and beg him to believe me. But then the total moron turned around and shouted.

"Oh, and Minnesota, she's kinda taken a fancy to ass play since you've been gone."

Nancy's Bitch List for Shaw

- [ ] Maximus Douchimus
- [ ] Captain Shitsmear
- [ ] Shit Talking Cock Womble
- [ ] Dildohead
- [ ] Dipshit Cockhead
- [ ] Scrote Noggin

CHAPTER 14

Shaw

Last night had been the final of Dayton Valley Idol and both Nancy and I had smashed it again. The person eliminated had been Mrs. Callahan. She'd been singing *'It's Raining Men'* while wearing a purple leotard and pink tights. She sounded pretty good to be fair to her but Mr. Callahan taking his life in his hands buzzed her. The whole of the room fell silent except for Mrs. Callahan who stomped around the stage yelling that he wouldn't have buzzed had she let him wear the strap-on. At least that was what we all thought she said, but Carter just about managed to get his hand slapped over her mouth by that point.

That meant that tonight was the big vote, and I was desperate to beat Nancy. Why? Because I was a competitive tool, but also because I was pissed at her. Something deep inside my stupid head had got me following her home on the semi-final night. When I'd watched her make her way home, I felt bad for her. She'd done an amazing performance but had no one to celebrate with and was going home alone. I knew our circle of friends supported her, but they hadn't shown. Jennifer and Alaska were getting close to the birth of their baby so had stayed home and Ellie and Hunter were taking advantage of Carter directing the show and getting a head start on him and Bronte making a baby. My mom and dad were there cheering me on, as were our extended family of Jefferson, Kitty, Henry, Melinda, Jim and Darcy, but Nancy had no one. That was the main reason why I'd followed her, because I wanted her to have someone to get excited with. Then I'd found her with him, the dickweed who had dumped her and gone and got engaged to someone else while on his travels. That was why last night I'd barely even looked her in the eye, never mind spoken to her. I was simply pissed.

"Big night tonight, Shaw." Tate slapped me on the back as he joined me at my desk. "Feeling confident?"

I shrugged. I was, but I didn't want to come across as too big a dick. "Nancy is pretty good and the boys' soccer team seem to quite like her."

Tate let out a loud, deep laugh which reverberated around the office. "Well, my mom told me that there were a few high school girls who loved your Bruno Mars last night."

I'd sung *'When I Was Your Man'* and had to admit I had given the group of seventeen and eighteen-year-old girls who were sitting on the front row, all my eye contact.

"What's the prize anyway?" Tate asked.

"Apart from bragging rights, a two-hundred-dollar voucher that can be spent in any of the stores in town. However, I for one will be spending all of my winnings at Stars & Stripes."

"I like your confidence." Tate sighed. "On other news, I've heard from the DNA center."

My heart started to thump wildly. Whatever Tate told me now could shape my life in a way that I hadn't expected. I wanted to be a dad at some point, but not sure now was the right time. I was a softie for kids though and seeing that helpless little girl had got me thinking. It had me considering how I could fit my life around her and make plans for both of us. Then it struck me that she might not be mine and I had to push all those thoughts and feelings away. I had to harden my heart until I knew the truth. It was still a scary place to be though.

He placed a hand on my shoulder. "No, don't panic. They contacted me because of the delay."

"Okay. What about it?" They'd told us it would only take seventy-two hours at most and that had been four days ago.

"They've had to evacuate their building for the last three days because of some problem with the A/C. They called me as they couldn't reach you and I was listed on your contact sheet."

"Okay." I swallowed back the fear and excitement that had been bubbling up. "Did they say how long they'd be delayed."

"They hope to be back in by Wednesday and then it'll be seventy-two hours from then. Which means by Sunday at the latest you should know if you're a dad or not."

"Okay," I blinked slowly. "And then I might have to break the news to my mom and dad."

"You haven't told your folks yet?"

I grimaced. "I chickened out. I have told Nancy though."

"Not the same Shaw. You *need* to tell your mom and dad. Anyways, I got the feeling that you and Nancy don't exactly get along."

I looked down at my empty desk and smirked. We did and we didn't, but that wasn't a story for my boss.

"We get along fine some of the time. She's easy to talk to." And fuck.

"That may well be true but that still doesn't alter the fact that you need to tell your folks about the baby."

I glanced around the office.

"It's okay." Tate laughed, squeezed my shoulder and started to walk away. "There's no one around to hear your news. Go home and tell your momma she might be a grandma."

He was right, I needed to tell Mom and Dad.

When I pulled up to the house Dad's car was in the drive and I smiled. Since he'd moved back home after him and Mom had their blip a couple of years back, Dad made sure that he got home at a decent hour. Before then he'd worked way into the evening. I glanced at the clock on my dash—six-thirty, he really had turned over a new leaf. Taking a deep breath, I decided it was time that I spilled the beans.

"Mom, Dad, I'm home."

It wasn't typical for me to announce that I was home, but more than Dad's working hours had changed over the last year, my parents had suddenly turned into horny teenagers, along with my brother. It wasn't unusual to find them in a compromising position when they weren't expecting anyone to come home.

Mom came rushing out of the living room waving her arms and shushing me. It appeared that she was minding Rett, and he was sleeping.

"Sorry," I whispered. "I didn't mean to wake him."

Mom stood in front of me with her hands on her hips. "Oh, you haven't woken *him*."

She looked about ready to bust one of those blow-up boobs of hers.

"Who pissed on your grits?" I asked, taking off my jacket and hanging it up.

"What the hell have you been doing?" she hissed.

"What?" I veered back. I was pretty sure that she might be about to breath fire in my general direction.

Dad then appeared, gently closing the living room door behind him. "You have some explaining to do."

"What the hell is going on?" I no longer cared whether I woke Rett. He was their problem. "Why are you two so damn angry with me. I loaded the dishwasher this morning, I brought down my dirty laundry hamper and I got rid of the ring I left around the bathtub, so what the hell am I supposed to have done?" My heart began to thud almost out of my chest. If Carter had told them about the booze incident, I would nail his balls to one of the Delaney ranch's fence posts with a rusty nail. I was a lawyer though and I could argue my way out of this. "You better have some proof of whatever you're accusing me of."

"Proof! Proof, is that what you want?" Dad asked.

"Yes sir." I stood up straight and put on my best lawyer face.

Dad moved to the door, opened it and then waved for me to go inside the living room. "Go on."

I rolled my eyes and dragging my feet, to give me time to come up with a good argument, walked into the living room. When I got inside the first thing, and only thing that I saw a kid fast asleep on Mom and Dad's couch. That kid was not Rett though. That kid was petite, had a pink pacifier between cupid bow lips and was wearing pink dress and white tights with pink rosebuds on them. That kid was definitely not rambunctious and loud Rett.

"What the hell?"

"Yes," Mom said moving next to me. "And don't shout we just got her to sleep."

"W-what the he—"

"Yep, you already said that son. I think you need to think of something else to say, like why the hell has a sweet little girl been dumped on our doorstep with her favorite doll, her birth certificate and a note that said she's yours and you need to take care of her."

My mouth dropped open as I looked at Tia, the blonde-haired cutie who I'd only met a few days ago. As my heartbeat thudded in my ears, I couldn't take my eyes off her, I couldn't hear what my mom was saying, except that I knew that she was talking because she was holding my hand and pulling on it, like she always did when she was giving me a lecture which she thought would benefit me.

I took a step toward the couch and held my breath as Tia moved, rubbing a hand against her nose so that it dislodged her pacifier.

"Shit," Dad hissed. "Please don't make her cry. She has your damn loudmouth son, let me tell you."

I turned to him and with a surprise feeling of sadness, I sighed. "She might not be mine."

"What?" Mom cried and then slapped a hand over her mouth before saying in a much softer voice, "What?"

I ushered them out of the room and into the den across the hallway.

"The note said she was yours," Mom said, once we'd all held our breaths for a few beats in case our moving rooms had woken Tia.

"Yeah well Mrs. Devonshire will say anything to avoid having to take care of her."

"You already knew about her?" Dad asked, running a hand over his already messed up hair. "And have you been having an affair with a married woman?"

"No, I haven't."

"What then?"

"Well if you let me explain." I raised my brows. "Can I continue?"

"Yes, honey," Mom said giving Dad a withering look. "Carry on."

I took a deep breath. "I went to Wichita to give my DNA. *She*, who is the kid's grandma, was supposed to wait until we got the results back."

"When the hell did you go to Wichita?" Dad looked at Mom. "Did you know he'd gone to Wichita?"

"Of course I did," she replied, her eyes on me. "I made him a ham and pickle sandwich to eat on the plane. What I didn't know was that it was to go and find out whether he was a father. I thought he went on business, seeing as he went with Tate."

"So Tate knows but you didn't think to tell us?"

"Dad, stop shouting, you'll wake the baby." I pushed the door so that it was slightly ajar. "Tate was there as my lawyer and if you must know he told me to tell you."

"And why didn't you?" he asked. "Because I've got to be honest son, a little heads up would've been good."

"I was waiting to see what the test results came back with, and they've been delayed." I pressed my fingers against my temples where a dull ache was building. "I didn't think she'd dump Tia on the doorstep."

"Her name is Tia." Mom got a dreamy look in her eyes and placed a hand against her chest. "What a beautiful name."

"Don't get all starry eyed, Mom," I warned. "She might not be mine."

"What about her mother?" Dad asked.

I sighed. "Remember my girlfriend from college who ran away with the professor." They both nodded. "Well Tia is hers, but Monique died."

"Oh my goodness." Mom flopped down onto the sectional and grabbed my hand. "Honey that's awful."

"Aggressive bone cancer. She told me that Professor Ritter was the

Tia's dad, but he's done a DNA test and he isn't."

"She's yours then?"

"I don't know Dad. She could be but the dates don't work out, or at least they wouldn't, but Monique told her mom that Tia was a month early. Her mom thinks she was lying. You can see Tia is small and petite so it would be easy to get away with it."

Mom looked toward the door, undoubtedly thinking about the cute little girl across the hallway. I saw the shine in her eyes, and this was exactly why I hadn't told her.

"Don't fall in love with her, mom."

Her gaze swung to mine. "She is so blonde. Just like you as a baby."

"Mom." My tone was warning but I could see it was too late. Cuteness coupled with a sad story meant that my mother was already in love and would protect Tia with her life.

"What did the note say?" I asked.

Dad pulled a piece of paper from his pocket and handed it to me. "Your mom heard the doorbell and when she opened the door she was there, sitting on the welcome mat."

I scanned the note, and it was short and sweet.

Shaw, she is your child. Time for you to take care of her.

I folded it up and stuffed into my own pocket. "What time was that?"

"About five. Your dad was coming home early so I was in the bedroom…" She trailed off.

"I get the picture." I shook my head really not wanting to get the picture. I pulled out my phone. "I should call Tate. He is my lawyer."

"Yes, honey, maybe you should." Mom stood and rubbed a hand down my arm. "I'll go check on her."

She was about to leave the room when Dad let out a strangled moan. Mom rushed to his side.

"Jim, honey, what's wrong?"

"This is terrible."

"I know it's not ideal, Dad, but—"

"Not that," he hissed, gripping his hair. "According to her birth certificate she's two weeks older than Rett which means you made the first grandchild and the first granddaughter and that means Bronte is going to be way beyond pissed."

CHAPTER 15

Nancy

The vote for the winner of the contest was in and most of the town were gathered in the Memorial Hall for the result. The only person who wasn't was Shaw, neither were his mom and dad. Bronte was with Rett who every time Carter appeared from the side of the stage whooped a cheer and waved her and Rett's arms in the air.

There was one other person who was also a no show, and that was Minnesota. I was grateful that he wasn't. I didn't want to have to deal with him after the other night. I'd sent him off home, but only after I promised to let him explain. Honestly, I didn't want his explanations. Too many things added up to the fact that he'd actually been a shitty boyfriend. Regardless of whether he regretted leaving me or not, I didn't want him back. I still had no clue what had happened to his British fiancée but had the feeling I wouldn't like what I found out.

"Where's Shaw?" I asked Garner as he paced in front of me looking at his script and distracting me from my thoughts.

"Hmm, no idea. Carter just got a text to say to start without him, something had come up." He glanced at me. "Sorry but I'm trying to memorize this."

I rolled my eyes. One because Shaw couldn't be bothered to turn up and two because Garner's 'script' was just announcing our names.

"What happens if he's not here to collect his award?" I asked.

Garner shrugged with a little too much attitude for my liking. "I don't know, Nancy. Ask Carter."

"Ask me what?"

Carter gave us a grin and smacked Garner's ass with his clipboard. Garner screeched like a teenage girl and jumped about a foot in the air.

"What happens if Shaw doesn't turn up to collect his award?"

He laughed. "You don't get it by default, Nancy. I'll give it to him. Besides you might win."

I snorted. "Doubtful. Have you seen that sign that the girls from the high school have made? It's huge."

It almost covered the whole first two rows that they'd managed to get seats in since they'd been queuing at the door since they'd got out of school that afternoon. It was pink and sparkly and had Shaw We Luv U in bubble letters. Even the sticks that they held the banner up with had been covered in pink tape and feathers.

"The soccer team's one for you is pretty cool." Carter smirked and pointed out to the audience.

"It's embarrassing. It makes me seem like some sort of… well, a whole manner of things."

The three of us leaned to one side to look out into the crowd and there in neon orange and green was my sign.

"Nancy we want you to ride our feces?" Garner turned to me and shuddered. "What is wrong with these kids?"

"It's not feces Garner," Carter said with a sigh. "Put your glasses on."

Garner took his glasses from the top of his head, put them on and read the sign. He turned back and gasped.

"Don't worry about it, Garner," I said, patting his arm. "I'm not going to do it."

Garner was the high school guidance counsellor and was looking at me like I needed to be kept in a locked cage well away from eighteen-year-old boys.

As Garner walked away, Carter and I burst out laughing. It was kind of funny even though it was highly inappropriate.

"I reckon that could be a thing though," Carter said, nodding toward the audience.

"What? Me riding the faces of the soccer team?"

"God no." He grimaced. "That would be disgusting. No, I mean riding someone's feces. I think that could be a thing."

"Carter!"

"Not for me," he cried. "What do you take me for. No, I reckon that it could be a thing for some people, just not me."

God, sometimes I had to wonder about him.

A half hour later and there was still no sign of Shaw, but Garner and I were on stage as he was ready to announce the winner. When he told everyone that Shaw couldn't make it the high school girls practically yelled the place down. Carter even had to get security to throw them out and seeing as security was Hunter and Billy Daniels, the high school's former QB1 and now college football star who was home visiting, they weren't too concerned.

"Ladies and gentlemen, we have our result," Garner said to a chorus of oohs and aahs. "Are you ready for it?"

Everyone yelled they were and then Garner made a huge show of opening the envelope, accompanied by a drum roll from Trudy Johnson of the school marching band.

"Garner hurry up," someone called from the back of the room. "I have my woman waiting for me back home."

Everyone turned to see who it was they all burst out laughing when they saw that it was Kingsley Riley from the livestock auction who everyone knew was gay. It was the worst kept secret in town,

Anyways, Garner shook his head and continued to milk the crowd.

"And the winner is…"

Another drum roll.

"It's—"

"I'm here. I'm here." It was Shaw rushing onto the stage, looking flustered but a whole lot of sexy with his hair messed up and his tee tucked into the waistband on his jeans on one side and untucked on the other.

"What the hell?" I muttered. I turned to the wings to Carter. "He can't just rock up here like he's the star."

Carter shrugged and then turned away to talk to Mrs. Callahan who was still complaining about being eliminated. The woman never gave up. I'd heard that she was making Mr. Callahan sleep on the couch even though they had two spare bedrooms.

"What's wrong," Shaw asked as he sidled up beside me. "Afraid that you may cry in front of me when they hand over the trophy?"

I frowned. "Whatever, Shaw. I don't really care whether you win or not. Let's face it you're only going to spend the vouchers in Stars & Stripes."

He shrugged and I moved away from him to the other side of Garner.

"Get on with it," Henry Maples shouted from the audience.

Garner pouted and gave a dramatic roll of his eyes. "The winner is…" He nodded at Trudy to do her stuff and when someone took a breath in the audience, he held up a palm to shut them up. "And the winner is… it's a tie."

"What the hell?" Someone cried.

"No way," a high school girl yelled.

"All that damn drumming for nothing," Henry cried. "No offence, Trudy."

Trudy smiled, glancing over at Austen, Shaw's brother who looked less than happy to be there, and blushed. It appeared that both the Jackson brothers had game.

"What happens now?" Shaw asked, frowning at me like I'd fixed the result.

Garner looked panic stricken as he leaned back to look to the wings for advice from Carter. "I… well, I… *Carter*!"

Carter came shuffling onto the stage, and I say shuffling because Mrs. Callahan was clinging to him. Her arms were wrapped around his and her feet were firmly planted on the floor as Carter dragged her in like they were doing a paso doble routine on Dancing with the Stars.

"Mrs. Callahan," he gritted out, "get the hell off of me."

"No, not until you agree to let me into the sing off."

"No. You were voted off!"

"By my own husband, surely there's a rule against that."

"Carter," Garner yelled, almost busting my ear drum. "What do we do now!"

"Okay," Carter said looking down at the limpet on his arm. "I warned you."

Carter shook Mrs. Callahan off like a dog shaking a rag. She went flying across the stage on her ass and landed on the judges table, on her back with her legs and arms flapping in the air like a break dancer. Mr. Callahan stood up and as he did, he caught her leg sending her in a spin.

"Oh crap on a crapstick," Garner muttered as Mrs. Callahan screamed loud enough to be heard in Florida.

Crap on a crapstick indeed because she spun clean right off the table and onto judge Delphine's lap. Amid all the chaos the audience were howling with laughter and seemed not to care any longer that proceedings were taking an age.

Carter gave Mrs. Callahan a perfunctory check and then took the microphone from Garner.

"Okay folks in the result of a tie it did mean a sing-off."

"God damnit," Henry yelled. "Is this night ever going to end."

"Thank you, Father," Carter growled in his dad's direction. "Appreciate it." He then shook his head. "Anyways, it *did* mean a tie." He looked at his dad. "But in light of the fact that we all have stuff to do tomorrow, I declare a tie."

"We know that," Shaw said. "You already told us."

"What that means," Carter continued. "Is they split the winnings, and each have a trophy. Well, they will do once I ask Jacob Crowne to order another."

"Just a minute there," Mr. Callahan said, banging on the table and totally ignoring the fact that his wife was scrambling off Delphine's knee with her ass in the air. "The rules say that there is one winner and one trophy and one set of vouchers."

"Well, I'm in charge this year," Carter said, pinching the bridge of his nose. "And I'm saying that they share. Next year if you're in charge then you can decide what happens if there's a tie."

"Shit we haven't got to sit through this again next year, do we?" Henry cried.

"Dad, please." Carter pointed a finger in Henry's direction. "I do not want to have to evict you."

Henry stood and held his wrists out in front of him. "Sheriff, quick take me away now. I give myself up." Melinda, Carter's mom, then reached up and dragged him back into his seat.

"Thank you, Mom." Carter turned to the wings and snapped his fingers.

A girl I think was named Peggy ran on with the trophy and a gold envelope and handed them to Carter. Before she left, she turned to Austen, winked and blew a kiss.

"Shaw," I whispered. "What the hell has your brother been doing to the girls in this town?"

He looked at Austen who was running his tongue along his top lip and looking Peggy up and down.

"I have no fucking clue. It's like the kid has a golden penis all of a sudden."

I chuckled because Shaw sounded a little more affronted than he should. I was still giggling when a gold, two-handled cup was thrust into my arms.

"You get this one and I'll order another for Shaw, unless you want six months each."

"Nope, want my own," Shaw said, crossing his arms over his chest.

"Fine." Carter sighed and then ripped open the envelope and pulled out some of the vouchers. "These are yours, and these are yours." He then pushed the open envelope against Shaw's chest and then turned to the audience. "And that folks, is it. Thank you and good night."

Carter then dropped the mic' and practically ran from the stage leaving the mayhem behind him.

I looked at Shaw and he looked at me and we both shrugged.

"Fancy spending a couple of those vouchers at Stars & Stripes?" I asked, feeling magnanimous. Plus, he looked kinda hot and I was pretty sure that a night of drinking alcohol might end in sex. Okay, so I'd said never again, but Minnesota coming home had thrown me for a loop. I wanted to prove to myself that I wasn't still attracted to him, and you know what people said about getting over someone.

"Sorry Nancy, I have to go home."

I blinked rapidly. First an apology and then he used my proper name without any hint of an insult. And he was turning down my awesome sex skills, because he knew as well as I did that was what was on the cards. I could see it in his eyes.

"Okay, no worries." I smiled at him and then noticed that as well as ideas of sex in those eyes of his there was some sadness. "You okay?"

"Yeah, sure." He frowned and started to walk away.

As I watched him leave something cracked in my chest. I'd never seen him take such slow steps or his shoulders so sloped. It wasn't Shaw at all. As he reached the wings, he paused, and I took a step closer. I was going to give him a hug. He looked like he needed it. Then he turned around and tilted his head on one side.

"Hey, Nancy."

"What?" I asked, a small smile on my face. Clearly my offer had been too good to resist.

"You should know that your ass looks kinda big in that skirt."

He turned and left, and you know what, I couldn't help but watch his ass and think that his was not big. At. All.

Nancy's Bitch List for Shaw

- [ ] *Maximus Douchimus*
- [ ] *Captain Shitsmear*
- [ ] *Shit Talking Cock Womble*
- [ ] *Dildohead*

- ☐ Dipshit Cockhead
- ☐ Scrote Noggin
- ☐ Assilicious

CHAPTER 16

Shaw

When I walked into the house, I was shocked by the sound of a toddler crying. I mean I knew that there was a child in the house, how could I forget? It was more that I didn't think about the fact that they cried or needed feeding or diaper changes.

When Rett came over, Bronte and Carter, or Mom and Dad took care of him. Normally I'd make sure that I disappeared as soon as bodily fluids got involved. Now though, jeez, if Tia *was* my kid, then I'd have to learn pretty quick what to do. There was no question that I'd get my folks to do it, or that I'd give her up for adoption. Family was important in our… well, family. They'd never forgive me if I'd declined the honor of being her dad. In fact, I was pretty sure my mom would keep Tia and put me up for adoption.

"Shaw, honey," Mom called from the kitchen. "How did it go?"

"I won."

She screeched and ran out to launch herself at me. There was a child's sippy mug in one hand, so it was a one-armed hug that she pulled me into. "I'm so proud of you, baby."

"So did Nancy," I told her.

Mom pulled back to look at me. "She did?"

"Yep. It was a tie. We shared the vouchers, and she got the trophy until Jacob Crowne orders another one."

I thought back to Nancy and how hot she'd looked tonight. The crack I'd made about her ass was not true at all. Her ass looked amazing in the tight skirt she'd worn. I'd just needed to do something that made me feel normal and not like a guy who'd had a baby left on his doorstep.

"How's Tia been?" I asked. "Although I'm guessing the crying means not so good."

"Oh no," Mom replied. "She's been great. It's all just a little strange for her. I'm just doing her some warm milk."

"Did we even have formula in the house?" I was shocked. Rett didn't drink it, so I had no idea where my mom conjured these things up from.

"She drinks real milk now, honey." She patted my chest. "I can honestly say that Mrs. Devonshire might not have wanted that gorgeous little girl, but she took good care of her, that's for sure. Her bag is full of some beautiful clothes."

"Good for Mrs. Devonshire," I said sarcastically before blowing out a breath. "Okay, what do I need to do?"

It was at that moment that the front door burst open, and my sister barged in, throwing her hands in the air.

"Tell me, is it true?"

"What?" I asked. "That I only tied with Nancy at the talent show. I know it's embarrassing, and I apologize to the whole family."

"No, you idiot." She slapped my arm and then cupped her hand behind her ear. "I'm guessing that noise of a crying child answers my question."

"Speaking of," Mom said. "I really need to go and get her milk before she bursts your dad's eardrums. I'm hoping it'll settle her." Mom rushed back to the kitchen leaving me with my annoyed looking sister.

"Yeah, it's true. I'll tell you all about it sometime, but basically my girlfriend who got pregnant by her history professor didn't, apparently."

"She lied to you and slept with someone else?"

"Seems that way."

"Bitch." Her brow furrowed and her nose crinkled, and I knew she was building up to something. "You do know that I wanted the first granddaughter, right?"

Damn, here was the meltdown that Dad had been worried about.

"I know, but she may not be mine. And you can still beat Ellie to the title in the Maples' family." I chose not to tell her that Rett might not even be the first grandchild. You had to choose your battles with my sister.

After she'd thought about it for a second, she nodded, meltdown averted. "Yeah, you're right." She cupped my face with a cool palm. "What are you going to do?"

"He's going to take care of her," Mom said as she passed us. "Until we find out. However, I'm confident that little girl in there is a Jackson. She's loud, she sleeps like the dead and she fills her diaper to a nuclear level."

We watched her disappear into the living room and I felt Bronte's hand curl into mine.

"She's amazing, isn't she?" Bronte sighed.

"She sure is."

"I hope I'm half as good a mom."

I turned to see unshed tears in her eyes and pulled her in for a hug.

"Don't get emotional. I told you, you can still beat Ellie to it if you try hard."

A little while later after Bronte had left and Mom had shown me how to change a dirty diaper, my maybe daughter was lying contented in the toddler bed that Mom and Dad had in Bronte's old room which was now set up for Rett.

"What do you think, son?" Dad asked as he turned up the baby monitor. "You think she might be yours?"

"I have no idea, Dad. I mean she could be. If Monique was lying about her due date, then yep in all probability, she's mine."

I scrubbed a hand down my face and groaned. Being a dad *now* was not in my life plan but weirdly I felt equal levels of trepidation and excitement, which in and of itself was scary. Maybe it was the fact that having a kid would be a test. I was competitive by nature and having to prove myself was something that I thrived on. College was a prime example. I needed to be better than the best and prove that a guy from a small town with a population of less than ten thousand people could be a great lawyer. One better than all those kids with 'the third' as part of their names and whose families vacationed in the Hamptons and owned big city law firms. Theodore Templeton the 3rd being a prime example. The kid was a dick who barely scraped through his classes, yet even before law school he had a junior partner job lined up at his dad's firm once we graduated.

"Okay." Dad nodded. "It sounds like Tate already has you covered regarding what you need to do next from a legal standpoint. So, me and your mom will help with the practical stuff. Right Darcy?"

Mom smiled. "You know we will. It's going to be hard for you, honey, what with work and law school."

"No Mom, you've almost raised your kids, although Austen might take longer than Bronte or I." She blinked at me and shook her head in disapproval. "Seriously though, I thank you, but you don't have to help out. If she's mine, then she is my responsibility. I'll organize some day care for while I'm back home."

"What happens when you're back at school though?" Dad asked. "Texas Tech is closer to home, but you still have to work hard and there'll be nights where you have to study late. You don't want this to affect your future, so Tia will stay with us and me and Mom will help take care of her when you're not home."

Damn it. I never cried but now I felt like contesting Tia for biggest baby in the house. Bronte had been right about Mom being amazing and Dad was too. They should have been enjoying the freedom that having three practically grown kids brought. They should have been organizing vacations and road trips and slowing down at work, yet here they both were offering to start again with my child.

"You have no idea how much I appreciate both of you right now." I drew in a breath and looked between my parents.

Mom gave me her sweet, loving smile, the one everyone got when she wanted you to know that she was right.

"Don't sweat it, son," Dad said. "You'll pay us back when we're old and infirm and you have to wipe our asses."

He pushed up out of his chair and ran a hand down Mom's hair. "I think we all need a drink." He walked to the door. "Oh, except for you, Shaw, you're on night duty so you need to be sober. Me and Mom? Well, we're going to get wasted."

CHAPTER 17

Nancy

I looked at the trophy that had been on my shelf for twenty-four hours and sighed. I thought I'd feel amazing at winning the contest, but I felt deflated. I had no idea whether that was because I'd have to share the victory with Shaw or because it was over. It being over meant that I wouldn't be seeing people every night. I'd be going back to lonely nights in my apartment.

Okay, I knew that deep down the person that I'd miss the most would be Shaw. That was purely because I loved sparring with him—honestly. I also was fully aware that being lonely may well push me toward Minnesota who'd been blowing my phone up with messages. There were begging ones, apology ones and even some dirty ones and I was on the brink of cracking.

There was no disputing the fact that Minnesota Michaels was hot. Even with his crooked bottom teeth he had model good looks and a swagger to go with it and all that made him dangerous. He was dangerous to my heart because I knew if I let him back in, he'd let me down again. I knew deep down he wasn't the one for me which was why it hadn't taken long for me to get over him, but he was also good for me too. He made me laugh, he made me feel sexy and good about myself. He told me all the right things; he certainly didn't tell me my ass looked big in a skirt that I knew for a fact it looked amazing in. Pauly Hansen, Dusty Chalmers and Beatrix Benedict, who was ninety and who in her youth had been a successful pageant queen, had told me how great it looked. Beatrix had even offered to put me in touch with her old pageant trainer, obviously I'd politely declined. The point being, Minnesota certainly didn't tell me things that might hurt my feelings. He told me that I was beautiful, had perfect lips and gorgeous hair. Shaw on the other hand said I wasn't so ugly he needed a bag on my head when we had sex, that I had cock sucking lips and my hair was great for wrapping around his fist while he, in his words, 'fucked me into oblivion'. It was also very clear what he and I were to each other, or rather had been to each other, and that was Fuck Buddies. He didn't owe me any sweet talking, whereas Minnesota had been my boyfriend. He was supposed to say those things. He wasn't supposed to dump me just before we went on the trip of a lifetime. He was not supposed to cheat on me with a girl called Annalise, or at the very least *think* about cheating on me with a girl called Annalise. Oh, and let's not forget that he got engaged to someone else while on *our* trip of a lifetime.

No, I would not be answering any calls from Minnesota Michaels. I said what I had to say in the parking lot the other night and that was it.

"Nancy, darlin', open up."

What the…

The man himself was knocking at my door. Text messages were one thing to ignore but his physical presence with only a door dividing us was another thing exactly.

"Nancy, I know you're in the there. I still have your phone linked to my phone on that app you insisted we both had."

"Because we were travelling around the world and I didn't want either of us to lose the other in a foreign country," I yelled as I stomped toward the door. "But when you told me I wasn't welcome on said trip, I kind of thought that you'd remove it."

I yanked the door open and glared at him as he leaned nonchalantly against the doorjamb and grinned at me.

"Maybe me not removing it was a sign," he said, looking me up and down.

"Yeah, it was," I snapped. "That you're a dick who can't be trusted."

"Ah c'mon baby. I told you that I was sorry. I should never have—"

"No, Minnesota, I should never have got involved with you in the first place." I took a deep breath. "We sat in this apartment, lay in my bed for hours planning that trip. I was the one who researched everywhere that we wanted to go. I was the one who created the itinerary, the one who lost thousands of dollars on plane tickets that I couldn't get a refund on. I was the one left behind feeling like there was something wrong with me because you had to wait until the cab was here to take us to the airport before you told me you'd rather travel alone halfway around the world than take me with you, on the fucking trip that was my fucking idea." I took another breath. "Minnesota."

To his credit he slumped a little, but such was his ego it wasn't long before he lazily stretched his toned body and smiled his all-American boy smile. The fucking smile that he always, always gave when he knew he was about to entice me into bed. Well not tonight, Romeo.

"Go home, Minnesota." I tried to push the door closed but he placed his foot against it to stop me. "Move your foot."

"Please Nance, let me come in and explain.

"No, I neither need nor want an explanation from you. Go away and leave me alone." Suddenly I felt weary and everything about the man in front of me just made me feel worse.

"Is there anything that I can say to put this right?" he asked.

His voice said he was contrite, the puppy dog look on his face said he was contrite, but the glint in his eye and the way he stood tall and straight told me he was not sorry at all.

"Why did you come back?"

He paused for a beat and then grinned. "For you of course."

"No, Minnesota. The real reason. You didn't come back for me."

"You don't know that," he replied. "You can't say that."

"I can because it's true. If you truly wanted me then you'd have come back before now, and you certainly wouldn't have got engaged to someone else." I pushed him back away from my door. "She dumped you, didn't she?"

It was quick and I almost missed it, but he winced.

"Thought so." I nodded and sighed. "Goodnight, Minnesota."

He took a step back of his own accord allowing me to slam the door. Once it was closed, I rested my forehead against it and listened as Minnesota's footsteps retreated along the hall to the elevator.

"Thank God," I whispered and pushed away from the door.

I wanted the damn day to end. Everything with Minnesota, the arguing with Shaw, the crap going on at work with Mrs. Baker, all of it had made me feel drained. All I wanted was to take a bath and then go to bed and sleep.

That was why when my phone rang, my heart sank. Maybe Minnesota hadn't got the message. However, when I picked it up, I almost lost my breath when I saw that it was Belinda. She must have news about the old bank.

"Belinda," I said hurriedly. "What have you got for me?"

"Hi sugar, I'm so sorry to bother you this late at night."

"It's fine. I'm anxious to get this done so I really don't mind." I crossed my fingers and silently prayed. "Did I get it?"

"I've been trying to get in touch with Shaw for the last two hours but he's not picking up and now it's getting critical."

Damn Shaw and damn Belinda for not calling me sooner.

"Okay, what's the problem?" I asked, already plotting Shaw Jackson's murder.

"The owner got back to me. He wants a quick sale and has said it has to go to sealed bids."

"Sealed bids?" My heart sank. "Honestly?"

"I'm sorry, Nancy but yes. I also know that the other party has put theirs in already." She lowered her voice. "I got that info on the quiet so don't tell anyone that you know. That's why I was so desperate to get a hold of Shaw, so he can get yours in."

"Can't I do that?" I asked, mentally working out how much. "What do I do, just write it down on a piece of paper?"

"Normally sugar, but he's being awkward. He wants it to come from your lawyer along with your business proposal. It's not usual I admit, but he's the one with the building and therefore the power, so can I guess he can ask for whatever he likes." She sighed heavily. "Like I said he's being awkward. You have no idea where Shaw is do you? I mean you could do it yourself, but it'll look much better coming from your lawyer."

Damn Shaw Jackson.

"How long do I have?" I asked.

"You have… two hours and counting. He said any bids not in by then lose out and seeing as there's only you and Ru…I mean another party you'd be handing it over to them."

"I know it's Ruthie, Belinda. Mrs. Callahan worked her magic."

Belinda chuckled. "Okay, well we all know how Ruthie is when she's determined and she's real determined about this, so we need to get in touch with Shaw asap."

"Okay." I closed my eyes and mourned the hot bath that I wouldn't be taking. "I'll go over to his folks house and see if they know where he is."

"Good plan, sugar and in the meantime, I'll try and get you an extension. I'll tell the owner that you've been out of town or something. Oh, and he did say you can email it as it's such short notice."

"How nice of him," I groaned, not feeling like it helped me at all.

"Good luck, sugar."

As soon as Belinda rang off, I snatched up my keys and headed out of the door determined to find Shaw, even if it I died trying.

Nancy's Bitch List for Shaw

- ☐ *Maximus Douchimus*
- ☐ *Captain Shitsmear*
- ☐ *Shit Talking Cock Womble*
- ☐ *Dildohead*

- [ ] Dipshit Cockhead
- [ ] Scrote Noggin
- [ ] ~~Assilicious~~ Fat Ass
- [ ] Fucknuckle

CHAPTER 18

Shaw

Tia was grouchy and no matter what I did, she wouldn't stop crying. I'd tried to do silly voices with her doll and an old teddy bear of mine, but apparently, I was no children's entertainer.

I'd sent Mom and Dad off to their card night with Henry, Melinda, Jefferson and Kitty and told them that I'd call Bronte if I needed any help. When they left, she was fast asleep, so I was convinced it would be a breeze. A half hour after my folks had gone and Hurricane Tia started.

"Come on, sweetheart," I whispered against her cheek, desperately trying to soothe her. "What's wrong, hey?"

Her diaper was clean, I tried calming her with some warm milk like Mom had, and I'd even given her a soother despite some mom's website I found which recommended not to at her age. It was in the bag that Mrs. Devonshire left, so I guessed she usually had one.

"Tia, sweetheart, come on. Please don't make me call my mom."

"Momma," she said in between sobs, and it broke my heart. She didn't have a clue why her Momma wasn't here so no wonder she was so upset.

"Do you want me to call my mom?" I asked but got no response, just more crying.

For some reason I didn't want to say the word 'Grandma', just in case it she wasn't. I didn't know why but something in my heart told me that maybe this baby could be mine. I'd found myself searching her face for features that resembled me or someone else in the family. Like Mom said she was pretty loud like me and my brother, and sister. Sometimes she screwed her nose up and I could swear it was Bronte looking up at me. Maybe I was seeing things that weren't there and I had no idea why. Why the hell did I want this screaming bundle of blonde hair and rosy cheeks to be mine? It wasn't the best time for this to be happening, but now she was under our roof, and I'd spent time with her the feeling wouldn't go away.

Then she screamed loud enough to burst my eardrum and for a moment I had second thoughts. Groaning, I lifted her higher over my shoulder and rubbed her back like Mom had said would comfort her. It wasn't helping so when there was a knock on the front door, I silently thanked whoever had been listening to my prayers.

"Okay, let's see who has come to see us." With Tia still screaming in my ear, I walked down the hallway to the front door. Pressing a hand on her back to make sure I didn't drop her, I swung the door open.

"Nancy." Well, that was a surprise.

"Hey." She frowned and pointed at Tia. "Did Bronte and Carter have a baby already? Because it's a big one if they did."

As Tia screamed again, I shook my head. "Nope. Long story." I stood to one side. "You'd better come in."

"Are you sure?" she asked. "I could come back another time."

She looked disappointed, so I shook my head. "No, it's fine and to be honest I could probably do with your expertise."

Nancy looked back down the driveway to where her car was parked behind mine. She then turned back to me and nodded before stepping through the doorway.

"So, what's the story?" she asked as I led her into the living room where an array of toys and Legos was scattered around. "Unless you don't want to tell me of course."

I jiggled Tia up and down and felt the sweat prick my brow. "I will but please Nance, tell me what to do first. She's had some warm milk, she's dry, she even burped as loud as my dad after Mom's fried chicken, so I don't think she has a stomachache."

She held her arms out. "Give her to me."

Handing her over, I sighed with relief, but only because I had some back up. The screaming didn't stop. Nancy cradled Tia against her and took her over to the couch. She laid her down and immediately started to undress her. She took off the little pink knitted cardigan I'd put on her because I thought she might be cold and then pulled open the buttons on the white all in one sleep suit thing that mom had dressed her in after she'd shown me how to give her a bath. Underneath that was an all-in-one vest and Nancy removed that too. Once Tia was down to her diaper Nancy started to blow on her stomach and as if by magic the screaming toddler stopped crying. When Nancy started to draw shapes on her little pudgy belly with her finger, Tia started to giggle. They were light and free, and her little chuckles filled my heart.

"Amazing," I gasped. "How the hell did you do that?"

Nancy glanced up at me. "She was hot is all. It is pretty warm in here."

I grimaced. "I cranked up the heating because I read that babies need to be warm. I also put that pink cardigan on her."

"Yes, they do," Nancy replied her gaze going back to Tia. "But it's like eighty degrees out there, Shaw. She'll be plenty warm, just don't put her under the A/C."

I blew out a sigh of relief. "Thank you so much. I don't know what I would have done without you. I didn't really want to call Mom and Dad back from cards night."

"You seemed to be doing okay, and she's happy enough now." We both looked at Tia whose eyes were drooping. "I'll put her onesie back on. Where is she sleeping?"

"She's taken over Rett's room as well as in here, but you can put her on the couch for now so I can keep an eye on her."

Nancy rolled her eyes and smiled as she gently started to redress Tia, minus the cardigan, while I went to turn down the heating. By the time she'd finished, she was fast asleep. She then gently lifted her and went to place her on the couch stacking a couple of cushions down the side of her. Tia immediately turned on her side, rubbed her nose with her tiny fist, wiggled her little ass and then fell into a deep sleep.

"You're a miracle worker," I said, looking down on the sleeping child.

"Like I said, you were doing okay, it's just experience. I work with little kids, and I also did a child development course."

"I know but I just wish I could have settled her." I scrubbed a hand down my face. "It's a lot to remember."

"You going to tell me what's going on?" Nancy asked, gently stroking Tia's stomach.

I laughed. "I may or may not have a kid," I replied, inviting her to sit down so that I could continue to tell her the whole story.

"This is the child who may only be ninety-five percent yours?" she asked.

"Yep, that's the one."

"That's why you were late last night for the talent show?"

"Yep, pretty much. Mom took care of her while I was there, but I wasn't sure whether to leave her or not."

"What happens if she's not yours?" She glanced over at the couch where Tia was still sleeping. "If it's the five percent that wins out?"

I shrugged. "Mrs. Devonshire doesn't want her, and I have no idea if Monique was seeing anyone else other than me and the prof." I blew out a breath. "I can't let her go into the system though Nance. I couldn't forgive myself. I'd always be wondering."

"If she's not yours though." She leaned forward and grabbed my forearm. "It's a big responsibility, Shaw, and you're just getting started in your career."

Her hand felt warm and comforting and when she gently rubbed my skin, something shifted in my chest. I couldn't think about that though.

"Shaw, it's a huge sacrifice too," Nancy said bringing my attention back to the matter in hand.

"But if she is mine then I'll be in the same position." I lifted one side of my mouth into a resigned smile. "You know the day that I found out about her I was sure that she was not what I wanted or needed in my life. I think I even silently offered to have my dick pierced instead." I grimaced and she laughed.

"Hmm that would be interesting."

"Not that you'd see it," I replied with a smirk. Who the hell was I kidding? She'd have been the first person I'd want to experience it. Like I said, magical pussy.

"So, junk hardware aside, you're saying you'll keep her even if she isn't yours?"

"That's about the size of it I guess."

Nancy blew out her cheeks and shook her head. "I'm just… shocked."

"Shocked that I have a kid or shocked that I want to take care of her?"

She didn't answer immediately but stared at me. "A little of both?" she said it like it was a question.

"Well, me too because apart from getting used to the idea of being a dad, I'm also seriously considering the piercing." I laughed and rubbed my hands up and down my face. "Okay, so tell me what you're doing here? I don't think you came here to have sex under my mom and dad's roof."

She smiled and she looked so damn pretty. Her dark hair was falling around her shoulders and her lips were all pink and pouty, and if she wasn't such a pain in my ass, I could seriously consider… nope I wasn't going there.

"I don't want to bring my crap to you now, Shaw. It'll wait." She waved me away and moved to stand up.

"No don't," I said nodding for her to sit down. "You obviously wanted to speak to me about something so spill it."

Tia shifted on the couch and we both froze. When she settled again, Nancy shook her head.

"Honestly, Shaw it's fine. I'll give Tate a call."

"Is it about the bank?" She worried her bottom lip. "Come on, Andrews, spill it."

She sighed. "I need a written bid for the purchase and the owner is being a little dick about it, otherwise I'd do it myself."

"What do you mean?"

"He's doing sealed bids and wants them professionally written along with my business proposal. Like I said I'd do it myself, but Belinda says he wants it from my lawyer." She reached into the huge purse I hadn't noticed her bring in and pulled out a buff-colored folder. "It's all in here and I was kind of hoping that you'd help me with it."

I took it from her and opened it up. She certainly had all the information in detail, it would probably only mean that I'd need to type it up on Hallahan & Associate Lawyers headed paper. The problem was I didn't have any at home, it was all in the office.

"There is another problem though," Nancy said tentatively.

"Yeah, what's that?"

She looked at her phone which was on the couch next to her. "I only have one hour and twenty-two minutes to get it to him. Seeing as he lives near Dallas, he's said that I can email it."

"That solves one problem," I said, getting up. "I thought I'd have to go to the office for some notepaper. Let me get my MacBook and I'll be right back. Or," I glanced over at Tia who I was pretty sure was going to wake up screaming soon, "at the risk of sounding like a misogynistic asshole, could you take care of Tia while I do this in dad's office? Otherwise, if she wakes, I know I'm just going to want to take care of her."

My gaze went back to the couch and something in my chest kind of pinged. I had no idea what it was, but it was warm and comforting. Nancy's hand on my knee startled me.

"I don't think that's you being a misogynistic asshole at all. I think it's you being a good friend and a good father."

I laughed emptily. "She might not be mine don't forget."

"Hmm, she is kinda too pretty to belong to you." Nancy laughed and scuffed my shoulder. "This doesn't mean that we're going to be friends by the way. You're helping me, so I'm helping you."

"God," I replied, grimacing like I could smell the worst shit ever. "As if. I'd rather kiss Mrs. Callahan than be friends with you."

Forty minutes later after she'd settled my 'daughter', and got her back to sleep, I was seriously reconsidering having Nancy Andrews as a friend because, and don't ever repeat this, she was pretty awesome.

CHAPTER 19

Nancy

Shaw Jackson was possibly a father, and I wasn't sure how to deal with that. I mean it wasn't unusual for guys our age to have kids, but Shaw? Shaw, the man who drove me crazy at any given opportunity?

I had to admit he was pretty good at fatherhood, from what I'd seen. Okay, so there were things that he still needed to learn, but he clearly wanted to try and be the best dad possible, if that was how things turned out. Although, to be honest, I was pretty sure he was going to want to keep her even if she wasn't his.

On top of all that, he'd done a great job on my proposal and my bid. I defied Ruthie to have produced anything more professional than what Shaw created. He'd printed me a copy and when Belinda called around to my apartment earlier, she'd been beyond impressed. After having a time limit put on sending it, the owner had said he'd decide in the next couple of days, asshole. But, as Belinda said, he had all the power so what could I do except hope that I'd finally beaten Ruthie at something.

Our feud wasn't just a recent thing. It all stemmed back to high school where she'd been a little bitch to anyone who wasn't in her inner circle. You guessed it, I was not in her inner circle of cheer leaders and pageant queens. She also hung around Shaw and his buddies like a bad smell. That was what I thought anyways. I'm not sure Shaw did, considering he was often seen under the bleachers with his tongue touching her tonsils. She wanted him from the moment she transferred to our school in the sixth grade from Tuscaloosa. Before then I had a feeling that Shaw was kind of sweet on me. He asked me to dance at our little sweetheart's party that was held in the school hall. Then the next semester Ruthie joined the school and like a shiny new toy everyone wanted to be her friend. The more people she gathered around her, the more she saw herself as the Class Queen who got whatever it was that she wanted. Shaw Jackson never looked my way again, until prom and we know how that ended.

"Damn it," I muttered to myself. Now I was mad at him again. "Stupid asshole."

"What are you talking about?" Lily asked as she thumbed through the magazine she'd been pretending to read ever since she'd arrived at my apartment.

"Nothing." I was at one end of the couch, she was the other. I poked her thigh with my toe. "What are you doing here anyway? Shouldn't you be helping with the preparations for your mom's party?"

She looked over the top of the magazine and rolled her eyes. "My mom plans weddings, do you think she'd let anyone plan her 'Big Birthday Party that isn't a 50th'?" I shook my head. "No exactly."

"Did you have the talk with them about all moving in together?" I asked.

Lily's candy pink braids bobbed as she nodded. "Yep, unfortunately. I was enjoying being treated like a princess while they tried to pluck up the courage, but they told all of us a few nights ago when we like went to dinner in Middleton Ridge. It was so funny, we all had to pretend that we had no idea. Tate and Hunter made this big show of gasping, like they'd just been told the weirdest piece of news and then Hunter asked Mom what her intentions were to his dad and whether she planned on having any more kids. I mean he was joking around but Mom was like really embarrassed." She started to laugh, throwing her head back and I envied her new, big family.

"You seem happier than you have in a while," I said as she gave a happy sigh.

Her cheeks pinked and not for the first time I wondered whether there was a boy involved in making her more cheerful.

"I'm always happy."

"Hmm okay." I raised a brow having seen her in some less than stellar moods over her dad and how he'd hurt her mom. "Anyway, how's work going?" I asked.

"Erm, yeah, good. JJ is doing well. He's enjoying first grade."

I frowned because she looked kind of sad about it. "What's wrong, is the job not going so well?"

"What?" She stared at me and then plastered on a smile. "No. No it's good. I guess as JJ gets older, he'll need me less and less. I should think about asking Jennifer if I can do more hours at Cake Heaven."

"He's still not quite eight yet, Lily. I think you've got some time yet. Anyway," I said, poking her with my toe again. "Tell me about the party. I bet it's going to be amazing." I didn't mention that I might not go, even though Bronte had threatened to drag me there.

"God yes. You should see the decorations she's putting up. She even managed to get some with 49 on them." She grinned. "I don't know why she's so bothered about celebrating being fifty next year."

"Maybe Jefferson will whisk her away somewhere next year." I gasped. "Maybe he'll propose when she's fifty."

Lily's eyes went wide, and she wore an expression which said she had news.

"What?" I asked. "What do you know?"

She got herself comfy and threw the magazine to one side. "Okay, so you can't breathe a word of this, but he took Tate and me to one side after dinner and asked for our permission to marry Mom."

I jumped up and down in my seat with excitement. I loved Kitty and Jefferson and they totally deserved to be happy. "Oh my god, no way. That's amazing."

Lily nodded enthusiastically. "I know right. He showed us the ring because he wanted to check he'd got one she'd like."

"And?"

Lily swooned back and held her hands to her chest. "Nancy, it's amazing. Beautiful in fact. He loves her so much."

"What's it like? I need to know."

"It's this gorgeous oblong shape emerald with diamonds around it and there's diamonds all around the band. It's like a thousand times more gorgeous than the ugly thing that my dad got her when he started to make money." Lily rolled her eyes at the thought of her dad who was currently in prison for fraud. "Jefferson said the emerald is just the color of Mom's eyes and it's a princess cut because she is his princess."

We both sighed dreamily and for one bizarre, ridiculous moment images of Shaw entered my head. What the hell was I thinking.

"It's going to be a beautiful occasion," I said and then thought back to Lily's happy mood recently. "You taking anyone?"

If I wasn't mistaken, she blushed as she shook her head. "God, no. Men are off my list of things to do at the moment. What about you?"

I burst out laughing. "That'll be a no."

"Minnesota is going." She winked at me.

"No, not happening. I found out that he got dumped and that's the reason he came home. Not for me or because he missed me, but because he was smarting and needed his ego rubbed. And I don't want to be the one to do it."

"What about Shaw?" she asked with a smirk.

"Please tell me you haven't told anyone about him and me."

"No, but you do like him." I shook my head because I knew if I said the words, 'no I do not', they wouldn't sound genuine. "Liar," she said and threw the magazine down on the floor.

"I'm not."

Lily rolled her eyes. "Deny it all you like, Nancy, but it's a big fat lie and you know it."

She might well have been right, but there was no way that I was admitting it. No, Shaw Jackson was not good for me or my vagina and other than professionally, I needed to stay away from him.

***

It had been two days since I'd put in my bid for the bank. I still hadn't heard anything. I also had seen anything of Shaw. With having the baby to take care of I didn't really want to pester him about it, but I was getting kinda anxious that Ruthie already had the keys and was measuring guys up for G-strings and dickie bows. That was why I decided to stop by Tate's office and see if he had any news.

"Hi Evie," I said as I got to the reception desk.

She looked up at me with wary brown eyes and gave me a tentative smile. I had no idea what was going on with her but recently every time I'd seen her, she looked scared or as though she was about to cry.

"Oh hey, Nancy. What can I help you with?"

"Is there any chance Tate could spare me a few minutes? Shaw has been helping me with a real estate deal and I haven't heard from him."

She blinked. "Shaw is here. Don't you want to see him?"

"He is?" I asked surprised, having fully expected him to be at home taking care of the baby, or at least trying to sort things out.

"Yes sure. I think he's free too, let me check." She pressed a button on her desk phone and after a few seconds spoke into it. "Hi, Shaw. Nancy is here and was wondering if you could spare her a couple of minutes… sure, will do." She put the receiver down and gave her attention back to me. "He said go on down to his office. It's the second on the left."

"Thanks, Evie." I took a step away and then turned back. "Are you okay, because if you ever need a friend, I'm a good listener."

She chewed on her bottom lip and then gave me a half smile. "I'm okay thanks, Nancy. It's just one of those months you know."

"Okay, but please don't feel you can't come to me."

"I know, and I really appreciate it." The office phone rang startling her and she stared down at the phone for a few seconds before picking it up and mouthing sorry to me.

I took that as my cue to leave and go and see what Shaw could tell me. When I reached his office, the door was ajar, and he had his head down reading something on his desk. I pushed the door open wider and poked my head through the gap.

"You okay to see me?" I asked.

Shaw looked up and relaxed back in his chair. "If I must."

"Listen I'd rather eat dirt than have to deal with you, but you gotta do what you gotta do, so here we are."

"Yeah," he sighed hooking his hands behind his head, "I get that. Have you heard from Don Jennings about the bank?"

I shook my head. "No, I was kind of hoping you had."

He beckoned me in and then clicked on his keyboard. As he hummed while he typed, he didn't seem like a guy whose life might be about to change forever.

"How's Tia," I whispered, glancing over my shoulder at the door.

"Mom has her today and don't worry, everyone knows about her. I figured living in Dayton Valley it was pretty pointless trying to keep her a secret."

Yet again he surprised me. I'd have guessed he would he kept it quiet for as long as possible.

"You haven't heard about the DNA test yet?" I asked.

"Nope." He carried on looking at his computer screen. "Maybe today. Right," he said swinging his chair back in my direction. "I've emailed him and asked if we can have an answer by the end of today. I think that's pretty fair seeing as he put a time limit on you. Although, I have to be honest, Nance, I did a damn good job with that business proposal and purchase bid."

He smiled and I'll swear that the room got brighter. I gave myself a little shake for even having good thoughts about him.

"You're feeling confident then that we'll win?"

"When am I not confident."

Yeah, not often.

"That's great, I really appreciate it." I stood and thought about shaking his hand, but enough of my skin had touched his for one decade. "Let me know and good luck with Tia."

He shrugged. "What will be will be." He saluted me. "Be careful out there, Nance. You never know the danger on the streets of Dayton."

With a disdainful shake of my head, I left him humming and typing away. When I got to reception Evie wasn't there, but I could hear her soft voice talking to Tate whose deep baritone was assuring her that everything would be okay. I was right, there was definitely something going on with her. I'd offered to be a friend and that was all I could do. Evie wasn't from Dayton Valley originally, only moving here about four years ago. I didn't know her well, but we'd mixed in the same social circle a couple of times as she was friendly with Jennifer, Alaska's wife. Apparently, her mom died when she was young, and her dad was a little strict so she'd decided to move somewhere where she could be free to do what she wanted and live her own life. She put a pin in a map, and it landed on Dayton Valley. As luck would have it the day that she came into town, Bobby Patrick's assistant walked out on him, and he was late to show Evie the apartment that she was thinking of renting above Cake Heaven, which was how she got to know Jennifer. In the space of a half hour Evie bagged herself an apartment and a job, which for me kind of proved that pin was meant to land on Dayton.

Hoping that she was okay, I wandered out into the bright sunshine and decided that I was going to treat myself to coffee and cake at Delphine's. There was no work because the kindergarten plumbing was being upgraded, at last. I'd done all my chores and there wasn't anything that I could do about the bank until Don Jennings got back to us, so coffee and cake it was.

The bell above the door tinkled as I walked in, and Delphine immediately looked over and waved. She was filling sugar dispensers a job I guessed she had to do a few times a week seeing as we Dayton folk generally liked our coffee sweet and hot.

"Hi Nancy, sweetheart. Grab yourself a table and I'll be right over."

"I'm in no rush, Delphine."

I looked around and it was fairly quiet as it was in between lunch and dinner. There was a table free by the huge plate window that had a gold-colored steaming mug of coffee etched on the glass. I sat down and settled in, taking my kindle from my purse and feeling a sense of contentment for once. Hopefully by the end of the day I'd be on my way to owning the bank and starting the next phase in my life.

As I sat back and waited for the coffee and brownie cake that I'd ordered from Delphine, I took a second to look up from the romance that I was reading. When I looked out onto Main Street the couple across the road took my attention.

"What the hell?" I moved my seat closer to the window and peered through between the etched streams of steam. Shaw was standing in the alleyway between the food market and Stars & Stripes and damn Ruthie Grey was hanging of him with her arms around his neck.

Something happened to my stomach. It not only turned upside down, but it went inside out and twisted too. Suddenly the idea of cake didn't seem so appetizing. He was supposed to be working for me. He'd sworn that he would steer clear of her while this was all going on. He was going to stay away until I had the keys in my hands, they were his words.

"Here you go, sweetheart." Delphine placed the no longer needed cake in front of me along with a mug of coffee.

"Thanks, Delphine." The words were forced out of my dry as a dessert mouth.

"That boy." Delphine sighed and then laughed as she pointed to where Shaw and Ruthie were standing. She leaned closer to me. "I have no idea what he's doing with that girl. Between us, sweetheart, she's trouble."

I should have felt glad that I had an ally in Delphine, but nausea still swirled around my stomach and besides which we were kind of related. Garth her husband was my mom's second cousin, so she had to be in my corner.

"Anyways, you enjoy your cake, sweetheart, and I have some casserole for you to take home."

She gave me a wink and walked away leaving me looking between the cake and the couple across the road.

Nancy's Bitch List for Shaw

- [ ] Maximus Douchimus
- [ ] Captain Shitsmear
- [ ] Shit Talking Cock Womble
- [ ] Dildohead
- [ ] Dipshit Cockhead
- [ ] Scrote Noggin
- [ ] ~~Assilicious~~ Fat Ass
- [ ] Fucknuckle
- [ ] Bronocchio

CHAPTER 20

Shaw

I felt like I'd been defiled. I smelled like a cheap brothel and was pretty sure I was pregnant with the amount of testosterone that Ruthie Grey has running around her body. I had to wonder how I'd ever got myself involved with her. Right, her tits and ass had something to do with it. They weren't in Nancy's league, but then the time I first hooked up with Ruthie I had no idea how spectacular Nancy's tits and ass were. Ruthie was mildly less annoying than Nancy, but that made for things to be a little boring. In truth the only thing we had in common was sex. She was pretty good at it, yet weirdly once again she was second place to Nancy. Anyways, the point was that Ruthie had basically humped me in the alleyway between the food market and Stars & Stripes. She caught me unawares and dragged me off the street and begged me to tell her what Nancy had bid for the old bank. Obviously, I denied the opportunity to help her. Aside from being a professional, I didn't want Ruthie opening some bar that would have the women of Dayton going crazy over half-dressed men. It wouldn't even entice shiny new women into town; we were hardly a party destination. Now if she'd decided to open it in Middleton Ridge I could understand it, but Dayton was not going to make her a millionaire.

She was insistent and I was lucky to come out alive. Alive and with my manhood still intact. Once I told her that I wouldn't be giving up the amount of Nancy's bid she grabbed ahold of my dick and gave it a squeeze, well it was more a vise like clamping which when I get chance I will inspect for bruising.

"Hey, honey," Mom said as I closed the front door behind me. "I just put Tia down she was dead on her feet even though I know you wanted to see her before bed."

I felt a thread of disappointment run through me. "Oh, okay."

Mom cleared her throat. "There's a letter on the kitchen table for you."

"What?" I could tell by the look on her face what it was.

"It's here." She rubbed my arm. "How do you feel, honey?"

"I don't know." I shrugged.

"Go and open it and then we'll see what we're dealing with."

I nodded. "Yep. Open it and then decide what we need to do."

"Dad will be home soon. He'll know what to do

I nodded again, bent to kiss Mom's cheek and then went to find out my destiny.

Walking into the kitchen the only thing that I could see was the white envelope propped up against the ugly salt and pepper shakers that my mom had on the table. They were given to her by my grandma just as she started with Alzheimer's and as they were the last gift she gave to Mom before she went into the nursing home, we had to use them. Have you ever seasoned your dinner with a naked Santa and Mrs. Claus?

"Here goes," I whispered as I picked up the envelope and stared down at it.

My feelings were such a one-eighty from when I first heard about Tia that it was making me wonder if someone had slipped me something in my food. Maybe it was Mrs. Devonshire to be sure she didn't have to keep Tia.

"Shaw, honey just open it."

I turned to see Mom standing in the doorway and she was clutching Tia's blanky. Her eyes were wide, and she was chewing on her bottom lip. If this said Tia wasn't mine, I was pretty sure she was going to be devastated.

I took a deep breath and ripped open the envelope and pulled out the letter, skimming to the important part. Shit. My breath was ragged, and my hands shook as I tried to get my emotions under control. The whooshing sound in my ears was probably loud enough for Mom to hear.

"Well?"

I swung around to face her and let my hand drop to my side as I took a deep breath.

"Oh Shaw, I knew that you'd fallen in love with her, but I didn't want to say anything." She made a move towards me, but I held up my hand.

"No, Mom." For the first time in forever, I felt tears forming. Mom gasped, I looked down at the paper and then back up. "She's mine, Mom. Tia is mine."

My five feet three mom ran and tackled me, almost knocking me over as she squealed with joy.

"Ssh," I said around a laugh as she clung to me. "You'll wake Tia."

"Oh, who cares. She's yours, Shaw, and she's so damn beautiful. I didn't want to say it and tempt fate, but I think she looks just like Austen when he was little, except she doesn't have that lazy eye thing going on. Good thing we used Grandpa's eye patch because that worked a treat on him—"

"Mom. Mom, calm down." I wrapped her in my arms and hugged her tightly. "Shit, my life is going to totally change."

She pulled back and looked up at me. "I know, honey, but we'll be here to help you. Dad already said that we'll go shopping at the weekend for anything she needs. And Bronte will get over the fact that she hasn't had the first grandchild and first granddaughter in the family."

"You know what, Mom," I grinned. "I hope she doesn't. I love the fact that I managed to piss her off for the next fifty years or more without even trying."

Mom blinked. "Well, I certainly hope that you put some effort in while making that baby."

"*Mom*."

"Just saying. Reproduction is one thing but at least make the girl feel good while you do it." She slapped at me with the muslin square. "She is going to push a head out of her tiny little nunnie for you."

"Oh God, please help me."

Right at that moment the doorbell rang saving me from having to listen to further rhetoric from my mother about women's vaginas and pushing things out of them.

"I'll go."

"We will continue this conversation, Shaw," Mom called after me as I left to answer the door.

"No, we won't, Mother." I called as I pulled open the door. "Nancy."

"You piece of shit." She poked her finger into my chest. "How could you. You knew how much I wanted that building, but you had to do it didn't you? You had to tell her what my bid was."

"What the hell." I held the door open wider and invited her in with the sweep of my arm. "Want to come in and start again?"

She walked in but didn't stop talking. "I saw you, Shaw. I saw you with Ruthie, making out where you thought that no one would see you. Well I saw you, *Shaw*."

"Hang on a minute." I held up my hands in surrender. "You think because you saw me with Ruthie that I told her what your bid was?"

"I know you did, Shaw because only a half hour ago I got a call from Belinda telling me that Ruthie got the bank. She outbid me, Shaw."

"What? You're joking, right?" I shoved my hands into my pockets and leaned my top half closer to her. "Seriously, she told you that?"

"Half an hour ago. She got a call from Don Jennings saying that he was selling to Ruthie. Apparently," she said with a head wobble. "Her revised bid was higher, and apparently her business proposal was better."

"Son of a bitch. That was a great bid, and that proposal was some of my best work. I even added fifty cents on the end in case she bid the same amount."

"No Shaw," she said, pacing away from me. "It's clear that your best work was in the alleyway earlier today."

"I didn't tell her anything. I swear."

"So how the hell did she know? And why the hell is she allowed to do a revised bid? That wasn't part of his deal. He gave me a deadline and he can't just change that for one person."

"Yeah, well, Nance," I said with a heavy sigh. "He has."

Nancy's lashes were brimming with tears, and she had her arms wrapped tight around her waist. I knew she wanted the bank, but I wasn't sure I realized how much. I moved closer to her and held my hand out.

"Nance, I swear to you, I didn't tell Ruthie anything. She tried to get me to tell her, but I didn't, and she practically left her scent on me. In fact, I felt defiled."

"How the hell did she find out then?"

"Hey, Nancy." My mom appeared from the kitchen. "Are you two okay out here? It sounds like you might have a problem."

"Oh hey, Darcy." Nancy ran a hand through her hair. "I'm so sorry for disturbing you. I'll leave you to it, you must be having dinner soon."

"We're having lasagna honey and it's cooking away. How about you stay, I've made plenty

"No, thank you, but," she said. "I couldn't possibly. I—"

"I won't take no for an answer." Mom approached Nancy with her arms open wide. Just as she did everyone. "Now, let's got get a glass of wine and see if we can't sort out whatever it is that has you two raising hell in my hallway and threatening to wake my granddaughter."

Nancy gasped. "You got the results?" Her mouth dropped open. "Why didn't you say."

I grinned. "Well, you kind of didn't give me a chance."

"That's amazing."

"It's a shock is what it is," I replied. "But I'm going to do the best I can."

"I'm just going to go into the kitchen and let you two sort out whatever the problem is," Mom said, reminding me that she was there. "And you're staying for dinner Nancy, no argument."

As Mom disappeared something soft happened to Nancy's face and I was struck by how beautiful she was when she wasn't screaming at me or throwing insults my way. The point was though, she was here to chew me a new one not to congratulate me on becoming a father.

"Listen Nance, he can't do that just allow Ruthie to put in another bid and not you."

"Is it illegal?"

"No, not necessarily. What is illegal though is bidder collusion."

"Which is what?" Nancy asked.

She looked so despondent I felt a deep need to hug her but that would indicate I cared, so I folded my arms instead.

"I can't be sure that's what's happened, but it's basically you scratch my back and I'll scratch yours. That must be what happened, because I sure as hell didn't tell her what your bid was. She told me her original one though, and I promise you it was almost eight grand under."

"How much?" Nancy's eyes went wide. "And she told you?"

"Yes, she did." I ran a hand through my hair. "Well, you couldn't say let slip it was much more a brag."

She blinked. "Did you then let slip what my bid was?"

"No! I'm a professional and a damn great poker player, so no way did I even give a hint that your bid was higher.

"So why not just sell to me?" she asked, shrugging. "Instead of getting her to bid more."

"I don't think that she has put a revised bid in."

Nancy's eyes flashed. "What?"

"I think that either Don Jennings has number blindness, or he's accepted her bid for a reason."

"Being?"

"He's a contractor, Ruthie needs a contractor so I'm guessing that she offered a little sweetener just in case and the tale of a revised bid is to put us off the scent."

Nancy collapsed back against the hall wall. "Do you think so?"

I shrugged. "I intend to find out."

"How do you intend to do that?" she asked.

"Go and see Ruthie."

"She won't admit to that," Nancy scoffed.

"Oh wow, you of such little faith, Miss. Andrews."

She groaned and hit her head back twice. "Damnit, you're going to sex it out of her, aren't you?"

"What? God no."

"How then?"

I grinned. "Leave it to me."

"You have no idea, do you?"

I took the fifth on that one.

CHAPTER 21

Nancy

I wasn't sure what to think about the bid situation. Shaw seemed pretty clear on the fact he hadn't told Ruthie anything, but how the hell had she found out otherwise?

"Seriously, Nance," Shaw said, putting a hand on my elbow. "I'll sort it."

I looked up at him and his eyes had to have that stupid glint in them. The one that made them bluer than usual. The one that made my heart add an extra thud to its beat. I swallowed and pushed off the wall… and then Tia started to scream.

Shaw let out a breath and took a step back just as Darcy appeared in the doorway.

"I'll go, Mom. I know it's early days but she's not settling here too well," he explained as he walked off down the hallway to one of the bedrooms.

"He's so good with her already," Darcy said as I heard Shaw greet Tia.

I followed her back into the kitchen where she took a seat at the island. "Sit down, honey."

"Thanks, Darcy." I took the stool next to her and leaned on the white granite. "So, a new grandchild. How does it feel?"

She blinked and shrugged at the same time. "Can't say I'm not shocked. I thought Bronte would be providing us with grandbaby one and two but clearly not."

"Probably not as shocked as Shaw," I replied. "When he told me about her, he was sure she wasn't his. Well, I think he said he was ninety-five percent."

Darcy shook her head. "Don't get me wrong, I'm mad at him. He's got a huge future in front of him and as much as I love that little girl already, she's going to make things difficult for him. Jim and I are forever telling all the kids to be careful and then we end up with two grandchildren before expected. I mean we all know the drama around Bronte and Carter, I know they're fine now, but jeez there was a time when I wasn't sure that would happen."

I laughed because I'd been a part of that shitshow for a brief misunderstood moment. "I think we all got front row seats."

Darcy rolled her eyes. "Oh, don't remind me. And now as well as this I have Austen to deal with. Going around acting like he's Dayton's answer to Hugh Hefner."

"He'll be fine." I wasn't totally convinced on that, after all he shared DNA with Shaw. "You're okay about Tia though?" I asked.

"Oh yes, she's a beautiful little thing and I know Shaw will do good."

At that moment the door pushed open and the man himself walked in. He was holding his arms out and there was something stinky and yellow down the front of his shirt.

"Mom," he groaned. "She puked on me."

Darcy and I looked at each other and burst out laughing as Shaw stood in the doorway looking like he might be about to cry.

***

After Tia and Shaw were cleaned up, and Tia finally fell back to sleep, we were all, including Shaw's dad, Jim, sitting down to dinner. I had to admit it felt a little weird. Austen wasn't there for me to chat and have a laugh with as he'd gone to soccer practice and then for burgers at Delphine's. Darcy and Jim were lovely and asking me questions but were treating me like I was Shaw's girlfriend, or at the very least a friend. I was neither. I felt like I wanted to say, 'you are lovely, but I'm here because your son was supposed to be working on my behalf but is actually doing a crap job'. Clearly, I couldn't and didn't say that. It still felt like I was in an alternate universe though.

"Do you have a financial advisor, Nancy?" Jim asked, after I explained all about my plans.

I shook my head as I had a mouthful of lasagna. I finally swallowed and wiped my mouth.

"No, I do know that I need one though."

Darcy's eyes gave off an excited glow and she grabbed Jim's arm. "Oh, Jim," she cried.

"Darce let's just get this straight. This will be Nancy's decision."

I looked between them wondering what on earth the secret conversation was that they were having.

"You remember what Dad does for a living, right?" Shaw asked as he poured himself some water.

I shook my head. "No, I'm not sure that I do."

"He's a financial advisor, honey," Darcy cried, jumping up and down in her seat.

If anything proved her boobs weren't real, that did because they barely moved, and she was bouncing like crazy.

"Darcy," Jim growled. "What did I say?"

"It's Nancy's decision, Jim, yes, I know. So, what do you think, Nancy?"

"You don't need to say tonight, sweetheart," Jim replied, giving Darcy a nudge with his elbow. "Don't let Darcy push you into saying yes, but I'd love to take care of your finances for you."

"You would?" I was shocked. This was a such a nice gesture. "Are you sure?"

"I work for a lot of people in this town, so while I'm saying it's no big deal, I'd also like to reduce my fee for you."

"Oh God, no Jim I—"

"No, Nancy, no argument. What you're wanting to do for this town is something good. If only for the fact that it sticks one on Annie Baker, the old buzzard." Jim took a long swig of his water and then slammed the glass on the table. "You know she told Bronte that Rett needed more discipline."

I had heard on the grapevine that after Rett had spent one day at the kindergarten Mrs. Baker was saying he was wild. He wasn't. He was a cute little boy who had a personality. Knowing that Bronte and I were friends she'd kept me well out of that loop.

"The point is," Darcy added. "Is that Jim will check out your finances cheaper than the does for the rest of the town. You'd be silly to say no."

"Mom," Shaw groaned. "What did Dad say?"

"I know, but it would be great for Nancy to have your dad help her out. Dad doing her finances and you doing her legal stuff." Darcy started to giggle. "And anything else."

"No Mom!"

"Oh my God, no. We are nothing like that," I cried.

"What the hell, Mom!"

"Well, I just thought." Darcy shrugged but had a little smirk twitching at her lips.

It was time for me to go. I shouldn't have even stayed for dinner in the first place. I couldn't have Darcy thinking those kind of things about me and Shaw.

"Well you thought wrong, Mom," Shaw said, pushing a piece of bread into his mouth and giving me the side-eye.

"I just thought that you seemed to spend a lot of time together and Shaw is doing the real estate thing for you for nothing, so I just—"

"Mom, it's my pro bono hours. I have to do so many, you know that." Shaw glared at her. "Nancy and I would never… no just no."

I narrowed my eyes on him and scowled. "You don't have to sound so vehemently against it." I hissed. "You do know what that word means, right?"

Shaw's brow furrowed. "I'm not sure, do you think you could explain it to me."

"Oh gosh," Darcy cried. "I was right about you two. Why didn't you just say?"

"Darc, what did they say?" Jim rolled his eyes. "Were you even listening?"

Darcy tutted and blinked before turning her attention back to me. "You both are just so hot together. Can you imagine the babies that you two would have?"

"Fuck, Mom!" Shaw threw his napkin down on the table. "Will you give it a rest. I've only just become a father, don't even think about me having any more kids for a long time yet."

What the hell was Darcy saying, how the hell could she even think about me and Shaw having babies? The thought was… well, it was awful. This was like a nightmare, and I really needed to wake up.

"Shaw watch your mouth, son," Jim said and then turned to Darcy. "But he has a point sweetheart."

"Oh, come on, Jim, don't tell me you don't see it. They're hot for each other." Darcy clapped a hand over her heart and gazed between me and Shaw.

Shaw pushed his plate away and turned to me. "I'm sorry about my mother, Nancy. She tends to get a little excitable about stuff that isn't anything to do with her. Because," he turned to Darcy, "she's too damn nosey."

"It's fine," I replied, shifting uncomfortably in my seat. "I need to get going soon. I have an early start in the morning."

"Please don't let Darcy scare you away," Jim said, giving his wife a nudge in the ribs. "Stay for dessert."

"Please do, honey," Darcy said with a sigh. "I'm sorry."

I looked at Shaw who was looking down at the table and decided that it might just torment him if I stayed. Who wouldn't want to torment Shaw

Jackson if they had a chance.

"I'd love to stay for dessert, thank you."

Jim patted my hand and then he and Darcy got up and started to clear the table. I sat back in my chair and picked up my glass of water and turned to Shaw.

"Your mom is kind of excitable, isn't she?"

He looked up and gave his head a small shake. "She's a nightmare but I guess I'm used to it."

"She means well."

He grinned. "Imagine us having kids together though."

"I know, right." I gave him a cross between a smile and a grimace.

"Fucking hideous," he replied.

My heart thudded hard, and I felt like he'd punched me in the gut. I knew we didn't get along, but that was just mean.

"Can't think of anything worse," I responded, crossing my arms over my chest. "In fact, I think I'd rather kiss Jim Wickerson than you ever again."

He smiled. "Same here and he's really not my type."

"Here we go," Darcy said gleefully placing a plate down on the table. "Strawberry pie, kids and you know what they say about strawberry pie."

Shaw sighed. "What would that be, Mom?"

"It's an aphrodisiac." She gave us a huge wink.

"Wow," I replied. "Is that so."

"It is," Darcy answered, cutting into the pie as Jim sat down. "So, I'll give you two a big piece each."

Shaw groaned and I cleared my throat.

"You got plans for after dinner, Nancy?" Darcy asked.

"Yes," I said, making sure to kick Shaw under the table as I crossed my legs. "I'm going to visit with Jim Wickerson later."

I wasn't sure whether it was the size of his piece of pie which made Shaw choke or the fact by association he may end up kissing the local pig farmer.

Nancy's Bitch List for Shaw

- [ ] Maximus Douchimus
- [ ] Captain Shitsmear
- [ ] Shit Talking Cock Womble
- [ ] Dildohead
- [ ] Dipshit Cockhead
- [ ] Scrote Noggin
- [ ] ~~Assilicious~~ Fat Ass
- [ ] Fucknuckle
- [ ] Bronocchio
- [ ] Asshobbit

CHAPTER 22

Shaw

I'd had a terrible night. Barely any sleep because Tia had cried pretty much all night. Mom had offered to have her in her and dad's room, in bed with them, but that wasn't how it was going to be in the future. Mom wouldn't always be there to help me out. One day it may be just me and Tia in the house, on our own, and I had to learn to deal.

"You look like shit," Tate said as I opened the door to him.

"Thanks, boss." I yawned and scrubbed a hand through my hair. "It was a bad night."

He came into the house, and I led him to the kitchen where Mom had already put on a pot of coffee before she went off to see my grandma in the nursing home.

"Where's Tia?" Tate asked, pulling out a chair at the table.

"She's sleeping. I put her down about ten minutes ago for a nap.

Thanks for the few days off by the way." I took two mugs and filled them both with strong, black coffee. "She's just not sleeping at night. I think it's all too strange for her."

"You should be sleeping while she does," Tate said, taking the mug from me. "According to my mom anyway. I have no clue."

"Yeah, mine said the same, but I'm too nervous about sleeping through and her needing me." I sat opposite Tate and sipped at my second cup of the morning. "I'm scared she'll get out of bed and somehow let herself out of the house."

"I'm sure she won't. And she'll get used to you all soon."

"I hope so because she keeps asking for her mama."

Tate shook his head and looked genuinely sad. "She's only been gone a couple of months. It's sad but Tia will soon forget her, and you'll become her world instead."

"Her tired world," I said through another yawn.

"Once I've gone lay down for a while." Tate sat back in his chair and picked up his coffee. "So, the reason I called was to check that you know what you need to do next."

I nodded. "I do. Social Services are going to call around sometime this week. Mrs. Devonshire has already been in touch and done what she needs to do to ensure that I have custody of Tia. I have to get her birth certificate changed as I'm not named on it but as it says unknown it shouldn't be too much hassle."

"I bet the grandmother couldn't wait to sign the poor kid over." Tate shook his head and curled his lip. "I can't say I took to that woman when we visited her and the fact that she's just abandoned Tia makes me realize how right I was about her."

Tate's relationship with his dad wasn't great because he felt abandoned by him, so I wasn't surprised at his dislike for Tia's grandmother.

"You shouldn't have any problems at least," he continued. "So, I hope you're ready for fatherhood, Shaw."

Was I? I hoped so, but at almost twenty-three who would be? It was a scary thought that this was now my life—teething, sleepless nights and toilet training, but I'd do my very best to be a good dad. It was a challenge and I'd never been one to turn one of those down.

"I've got to be," I answered.

"I have good vibes about it, Shaw," Tate said, leaning forward and slapping my shoulder.

"I just hope I don't let her down."

"Believe me, as the son of a father who constantly let me down, I don't see that from you." He took a drink of his coffee and when he'd finished pushed his chair back. "Anyway, I'd better get going. I just wanted to stop by and check that you were okay."

We both stood and I held my hand out to Tate.

"Thanks again, for everything, Tate. I don't think I could have done it on my own."

He shook my hand in both of his and smiled. "Don't doubt yourself Shaw. You've got this covered. Now, will I see you at Mom's birthday party at the weekend?"

I shrugged. "I hope so, but with the baby, I don't know."

"Lily has arranged for a couple of the high school girls to come and take care of JJ and Rett, and any other kids who are there, so I'm sure Tia would be okay with them. It's not like she's a tiny baby and you'd be on hand if they needed you. Mixing with other kids might be good for her."

"Bronte and Carter are coming over tomorrow with Rett, so she'll at least know him by then I guess."

I did want to go to the party seeing as it was going to be the biggest event Dayton had seen since Ellie and Hunter's wedding. Memories of that night brought a smile to my face, not that anything like that would ever happen again of course. Nancy and I were strictly business from now on.

"It does sound doable," I replied. "So hopefully I'll see you there."

"Great," Tate said. "And get some rest. Oh and what's happening with the old bank deal for Nancy? Is there anything that I need to do while you're away from the office?"

Shit, I'd totally forgotten that I'd told Nancy that I'd go and see Ruthie for her. With the long, sleepless night it had gone right out of my head.

"He's gone with Ruthie."

"What?" Tate eyebrows almost disappeared into his hairline. "I saw what you sent him and that was a great bid and business proposal. Ruthie must have offered some serious money to beat that."

"That's the thing." I sighed. "She was eight grand under."

Tate's eyebrows came back down and furrowed together. "How did you find that out? Or do I not want to know?"

"Believe it or not Ruthie told me." I shuddered as I recalled how she pinned me against the wall down the alleyway. "I didn't give her any information about Nancy's bid, so I was shocked when she called around to tell me that she'd lost out."

Tate crossed his arms over his chest and nodded slowly. I'd already learned this was what he did when he was mulling something over, so I gave him a little time.

"Are we thinking bidder collusion?" he finally asked.

"I think so."

"We have to prove it though and I guess we can't do that until the sale goes through and Don starts doing the work. He is a contractor, am I right?"

"Yes, he is and I'm pretty sure that's how Ruthie got it. She told me she'd got a contractor ready to go but I didn't think for one minute it was Don. Not until Nancy told me that she'd lost the bid."

"Damn it. Do you want me to deal with it?"

I shook my head. "No, it's okay. I'll go and see Ruthie later."

"I'm not sure that's a good idea, Shaw," Tate replied, sticking me with a concerned look. "She could accuse you of bullying tactics."

I hadn't thought of that. Knowing Ruthie's dad if he found out we'd had a conversation even hinting that she pulled out, he'd have me in court faster than a prairie fire with a tail wind.

"Let me think on it," I replied. "I'll see if I can come up with something that doesn't land us with a coercion charge."

"Okay, but call me if you need help."

"Will do," I replied and waited for him to leave before I cursed loudly. I had no clue what to do.

***

"You sure she's yours?" Carter asked as we all sat around watching Rett and Tia toddle around the yard, chasing each other. "She's far too pretty."

"According to the DNA result she is," I replied. "And I think you'll find she looks just like me. Isn't that right Mom?"

"I think she's more like Austen to be fair, honey," Mom replied as she gazed lovingly at her grandchildren.

"She's a lucky girl then," Austen said, looking up from his phone which he been pretty much stuck to since dinner had ended an hour ago. "Because I am pure perfection according to the girls of Dayton Valley High."

"Oh my goodness," Bronte sighed. "I far preferred it when he was a gangly kid who wore mismatching pajamas and idolized us. Didn't you, Shaw?"

"I never idolized you."

"Yes, you did," I argued. "You followed us both everywhere because you were desperate to be with us and be like us."

"He even cried when you went away to college," Dad added.

"I did not." Austen's lips pouted just like he was six again and Mom was right, Tia looked just like him.

"Yes, you did." Mom reached over and ruffled his hair. "You sat at on the driveway every night waiting for him to come back. Crying and asking, 'when's Shaw coming home, I miss him'."

"Pathetic behavior from an eleven-year-old," I said with a grin, earning myself a double flip off from my baby brother.

"She is cute though," Bronte said our attention going back to the two toddlers. "And it's good they seem to like each other."

I watched as my daughter, which still sounded weird, ran around with her cousin squealing in delight as Mani, Bronte and Carter's dog now lumbered around with them.

"He's okay with them?" I asked.

"Mani?" Carter looked at me like I was stupid. "He's the gentlest most caring dog you could ever meet. You know that."

I must admit the big black and tan dog of unidentified breed was pretty soft and had always been great with Rett. I guessed that things changed when you had your own kid. You clearly became more paranoid.

"How's she been today?" Mom asked, her eyes still on the kids.

"A bit grizzly." I exhaled a heavy breath of disappointment. "This is the happiest she's been all day."

Right on cue Tia let out another belly chuckle.

"She'll get there, honey," Mom replied. "She just needs to get used to her new normal."

"I guess so."

I wondered if I was doing what was right for Tia by keeping her? Maybe I should have insisted that Mrs. Devonshire keep her until I got to know her a little better. Then we could have had visits and sleepovers, to introduce Tia to us all gradually. Then again, Mrs. Devonshire had made it clear that option was not on the table. There was nothing like getting married and leaving the country to show you didn't want to care for your granddaughter any longer.

"Do you keep calling yourself Daddy to her?" Bronte asked. "Because you should. She needs to know that you are."

"It felt a bit strange saying it. Like it got stuck on my tongue or something." I swallowed remembering how weird it had felt.

Dad slapped my back. "You'll get used to it son. You haven't had time to adjust. I mean look at Carter he passed out when he found out he was going to be a dad."

We all looked at my brother-in-law who had gone a deep shade of red. Being ginger it wasn't a good look on him, even if he was a handsome bastard.

"I'm still paying for that you know," Carter said.

"And you will be, honey, until Rett leaves for college at the very least." Bronte winked at him, and I knew that she wasn't lying.

"How do we know who our parents are?" Austen asked. "I mean how do we know who our mom and dad are and who are grandparents are, and our aunts and uncles."

"Because we told you," Dad said.

"Yes, but how did I know that you and Mom were the ones who loved me the most?" Austen's hair fell into his eyes and for one moment, with his mouth gaping open, he looked like a little kid again. Certainly not the boy who'd suddenly discovered his penis was for something more than windmilling.

"Mom and Dad don't love you the most." I nudged Bronte's foot with mine, getting her to join in. "In fact, they're not your mom and dad."

"That's true," Bronte added looking serious. "They adopted you because you were left at the orphanage because you were ugly. No one wanted to take you."

"Don't be so horrible to my baby," Mom protested. "He's gorgeous and he was very much wanted."

"Yeah," Austen said, flipping both me and Bronte this time. "I was wanted because after you two they thought that they couldn't be that unlucky a third time."

Dad leaned closer to me and muttered, "I do believe there was wine involved."

I burst out laughing and Mom threw him one of her hard stares that she used when she wanted us to shut up.

"Was I a drunken conception?" Austen cried. "Oh my god! Really? Please tell me Mom at least knew what was happening."

"Don't be so ridiculous, Austen." Dad's deep voice boomed around the yard. "Of course, she knew."

"We were not drunk either," Mom said trying to placate him. "You were very much planned. I may have had one glass of wine, but there were oysters and candles involved too. In fact—"

"God, Mom, no. I don't want to know," Austen cried, screwing his face up in disgust.

"All you need to know is that we love you and you were wanted. Do not listen to your brother and sister, well they were once we signed your adoption papers from the ugly kid orphanage."

That was it, we all burst out laughing at Mom's joke, even Austen cracked a smile. Then suddenly Mom cried out as Rett, and Tia toddled past us as fast as their little legs would allow.

"Stop! Be careful of the—"

It was too late, Tia tripped over the kid's bucket that had been abandoned in the middle of the lawn and went flying flat on her face.

"Shit!" I cried and before she'd even let go of the huge scream that she was building up to, I picked her up and cradled her against my chest. "It's okay, sweetheart," I soothed as I walked back to my seat. "Daddy's got you."

"Oh my," Mom said, her voice cracking. "I think I'm going to cry."

As Tia threw her little arms around my neck, clung on for dear life and sobbed the word daddy, I was pretty sure I was going to cry too.

CHAPTER 23

Nancy

It was official, I hated Mrs. Baker. My boss was a total bitch. Somehow, she knew that I didn't get the old bank and she actually laughed in my face. Actually, laughed in my face and said, 'tough cookie sweetheart'.

Like I said total bitch.

"Nancy."

Talking of the total bitch. "Yes, Mrs. Baker."

"I need you to take the trash out," she snapped.

"Is Davey not working today?" Davey Jacobs was our janitor and a nicer man you couldn't wish to meet. He was almost sixty-five and probably should retire seeing as he had arthritic knees, but he came into work every day with a smile and a whistle. "He's not ill, is he?"

"He's around." She crossed her arms over her chest and blinked twice, daring me to question her.

I was just about sick of her behavior since she'd found out I'd offered to be a witness in the Ranger custody trial. She'd been hateful before that but was even worse now.

"I'll go and find Davey," I said and gave her a smile.

"The time it takes you to find him you could have taken it out yourself."

I nodded. "I could, but with respect Mrs. Baker I'm not paid to take out the trash." Just looking at her made my blood heat up. She was a totally odious woman, and I had no idea why I'd ever agreed to work for her. The pay wasn't great, but it was close to home without any travel expenses. God, I was so disappointed that I hadn't got the bank because I'd been so excited for it. It felt pretty desolate that it was no longer an option.

"Don't forget, young lady, I'm the one who pays you. That means if I ask you to take the trash out then you take the trash out." Her thin lips, with her usual coral lip color, twitched but the smile didn't appear. I wasn't even sure her mouth muscles knew what a smile was.

"But why do you want me to take it out?" This worm was turning. "We have a janitor. I'm not paid to do it."

"I just do."

At that moment Melody Simpkin a little four-year-old who loved to dress in soccer kit every day, came running over squealing.

"Miss. Andwews, Miss. Andwews, Bobby fell and hurt his knee. He's cwying." The way she couldn't say her r's was adorable.

"Oh goodness, Melody. Where is he?"

"I'll go," Mrs. Baker said. "You take the trash out."

Goddamn this woman was an evil bitch. She knew I wouldn't argue in front of one of the kids. The only comfort I had was that Melody looked disappointed that it wasn't me going with her.

As Mrs. Baker left with Melody, I stormed off toward the three huge black bags that the trash had been emptied into. When I picked the first one up, I almost told the old crone to shove her job and her trash up her ass. It was heavy and I had to pretty much drag it to the dumpster outside.

When I finally got it there, I looked up and sagged. There was no way I was going to be able to heave the bag into the dumpster. The bag was too heavy, and it was too high. I did consider leaving it and then going to find

Davey but knew that Mrs. Baker would pitch a fit if I did.

"Okay, Nancy," I muttered. "You can do this."

I bent at the knees lifted the bag in my arms and then straightened. I tried to heave it up so that I could throw it in, but my arms just weren't strong enough.

"Need some help, Miss. Andrews?"

I let the bag drop to the floor and turned to see Shaw. My heart skipped a thousand beats because he was standing there in jeans and a black t-shirt looking sexy as hell, and he was pushing Tia in her stroller. What the hell was it about men with babies? Damn it, he looked good. His hair was a little disheveled, he had a little stubble and the way he was gripping the handle of the stroller his biceps were bulging pretty nicely.

"Hey, what are you doing here?" I blew out a breath and dropped the bag to the floor.

"I came to see you, and it seems like it was good timing."

I glanced back at the bags, but my attention was on the little cutie dressed in a lemon dress with white rosebuds.

"Hey, Tia." I stooped down in front of her and tickled her chin. "Do you remember me?"

Tia giggled and reached her chubby little arms out to me.

"Can I pick her up out of the stroller?" I looked up at Shaw who was looking down at us. He was rubbing one of his beautiful biceps and the look on his face wasn't one I'd seen before. He kind of looked serene even though he'd just found out he was now a father and would be responsible for someone else for the next eighteen years or so.

"Shaw," I prompted. "Is it okay?"

"What?" He blinked. "Yes sure, of course you can. So, what's with the trash, is Davey sick or something?"

I picked Tia out of the stroller and held her in front of me and pulled a silly face which made her giggle. Shifting her to my hip, my attention went back to her dad.

"Mrs. Baker made me put the trash out even though Davey is around." I cradled Tia's head against my chest and put one hand over her ear. "But she's a b.i.t.c.h."

Shaw laughed. "She can't spell and doesn't know what that word means, Nance."

"No, but she's learning new words every day. Imagine if that was the next one."

"Today's is toast," Shaw said with a laugh. "Well, it was more like Oast."

"You said toast?" I asked Tia giving her wide eyes. "What a clever girl."

Tia's hands reached out and slapped at my face as she grinned at me. I snuggled her close and breathed in the smell of her baby shampoo.

"She's doing so well, Shaw." I grinned at him over his daughter's shoulder. "She's so happy."

He shrugged and I thought I saw a little color to his cheeks. God he was cute. "She seems to be getting happier each day." He cleared his throat and pushed the stroller back and forth a couple of times. "She called me daddy yesterday."

"Shaw." I held my breath for a few seconds and then let it out and grinned. "That's amazing."

He shrugged. "Got to admit I wasn't expecting it so soon."

"Like I said she's learning new words every day." I reached out for his hand and pulled on it. "You're truly doing a great job with her."

As my fingers linked with his, it felt like my heart had been jumpstarted. Immediately I pulled my hand back and went back to cooing over Tia as Shaw coughed.

"Thanks. Anyways, you want me to dump the trash for you."

"Please. Oww…" Tia pulled at my hair and before she could put it into her mouth, I disentangled her tiny fingers from it. "That would be great."

As Shaw walked over to the trash, Tia's gaze followed him and when he glanced over and waved, she went all shy and nuzzled her face against my chest. God, even his daughter had a silly crush on him. Not that I did of course. Not in a million years!

When she didn't lift her head, I knew she was falling asleep, so I put her back into her stroller and dropped the back so that she was lying down. As I checked her, Shaw came up by my side.

"She fallen asleep?"

"Yes almost, is that okay?"

He nodded. "The trash is done. It was fucking heavy. You shouldn't be lifting that."

"Tell old bitch Baker that."

"Well you can when you resign."

"Hah." I laughed humorlessly. "That won't be happening."

He tilted his head and grinned. "What? Are you're going to run your own pre-school *and* work here?"

My heart started to thud. "W-what?"

"I've got proof that Ruthie and Jennings colluded over the bid. Well," he said giving a one shouldered shrug. "It looks that way."

I closed the distance between us. "How? Why?" I covered my mouth with my hands. The hope that maybe I was going to fulfil the dream that just a month ago I didn't know that I had.

"I told you about bidder collusion, right?" I nodded, unable to speak. "I made a few calls to suppliers and bingo, four suppliers confirmed that Jennings had deliveries due in six weeks. All to be delivered to the bank."

I gasped. "They really just gave up that information. For real?"

He grinned. "I was honest that I was the lawyer working on behalf of the purchaser, I just didn't mention which purchaser."

"So what happens now?"

Tia moved in her stroller and both Shaw and I looked down at her, but when she let out a little contented sigh we straightened.

"What were we saying?" Shaw asked.

"You were going to tell me what happens next."

"Oh yep. Okay, so I'm going to speak to Ruthie's lawyer about it."

"Not Ruthie?" I asked, feeling a tinge of something odd in my chest.

Shaw shook his head. "No. I don't want anything to come back and bite our asses on this." His jaw was tight, and I got what I thought was probably his court game face.

"Will he question how you got that information?"

"He might but the point is, Nance, I have the information. How I got it doesn't matter. I'm going to suggest that he speak to his client about changing her contractor at the very least and if she does that, I'm guessing Jennings might revisit the bids."

I dropped my head back and looked up at the sky, with a groan.

"Hey," Shaw said, putting a hand on my shoulder. "There's a real good chance Jennings will kick back on her bid if he doesn't get the contract. If I were you, I'd secure a contractor. You don't want to get the place and then can't find anyone to do the work for the next six months." He grinned. "Just don't use Jennings."

He reached to the back pocket of his jeans and pulled out a card. "Here's the card of the guy who did Hunter and Ellie's place. He did an amazing job."

I looked down at the card. "What if he won't commit because I can't?"

"He might ask you for a non-returnable deposit. If that doesn't swing it for him then we'll look for someone else."

The card felt like it was burning my fingers as I thought about the prospect of soon having ownership of the bank. The possibility of that was mostly down to Shaw and the work that he'd put in over the last couple of days, all while dealing with becoming a dad.

"I can't thank you enough for this, Shaw," I whispered.

As I looked up at him, something shifted inside of me. There was no doubt that I'd been attracted to him, specifically his penis, but now I was beginning to like him as a person too. It felt like I could ask for his support if I needed it and I'd not had that from a man since my dad had died.

He shoved his hands into his pockets and shrugged. "Just doing my job."

"Well, I appreciate it." And I truly did. I knew it was his job, but he truly seemed invested in this on my behalf.

Tia let out a little grizzle and Shaw bent to check on her. "I should get her home. It's almost time for her lunch."

I bent next to him, kissed my fingers, and then placed them against the chubby red cheek of the sleeping baby.

"If you need any help with Tia let me know."

He nodded once and turned the stroller and started to walk away. He almost got to the gate when he turned around. "Hey Nance, you done a lifting course?"

I shook my head.

"Then unless Mrs. Baker wants you to sue her don't ever lift those trash bags again."

Wow, he really was making it difficult for me to hate him lately.

"Also, when you bend over to pick it up, it isn't a great look for your ass."

Yep, that was the Shaw I hated.

Nancy's Bitch List for Shaw

☐ Maximus Douchimus
☐ Captain Shitsmear
☐ Shit Talking Cock Womble
☐ Dildohead
☐ Dipshit Cockhead
☐ Scrote Noggin
☐ ~~Assilicious~~ Fat Ass
☐ Fucknuckle
☐ Bronocchio
☐ Asshobbit
☐ Jerkass

CHAPTER 24

Shaw

Tia had the shits. Her cheeks were bright red, and she was grizzly. Mom told she was teething and to call Bronte to see if she had a teether that I could have. It was the one thing that wasn't in the huge bag that Mrs. Devonshire had left with Tia.

Bronte was on her way around, but so was Ellie.

Okay, so my mom had twenty-six years, or something experience as a mom, but I wanted a professional opinion. Ellie was a pediatric nurse so who better than to come over and ease my new father nerves.

"I'm telling you, honey, it's her teeth coming through." Mom crooked her pinky finger and put the knuckle into Tia's mouth. "Yep, she's biting down and sucking on it."

"It's not like I don't believe you, Mom, but I just want her checked out." I ran a hand through my hair and watched as Mom pulled her finger from Tia's mouth.

"I hear you. You're being cautious, I get that." She ran a hand down Tia's face and gave a soft smile. "She's quiet now let's leave her and see if she'll take a nap."

I nodded and checked that her baby monitor was on before following Mom out of the room.

"I guess we need to paint that room," Mom said as we walked down the hallway.

"It's Rett's room though."

"But now it's Tia's too." When we walked into the living room Dad was there, in his chair reading some papers. "Hey, Jim, I was just saying to Shaw we should paint the baby's room. Now that it's Tia's room."

Dad put his papers down on the floor and looked up at Mom. "When you say we, I guess you mean me."

"Dad, I'll paint it, if necessary, but we don't have to."

"You live here, honey," Mom said. "Rett doesn't so the room should be more suitable for Tia than Rett."

"We could do it half and half," I suggested. "Put two toddler beds in there. I mean I'll buy one for Tia."

"It should be pink though," Mom pouted. "All little girls want a pink room."

"We might not be here for long though, Mom." I'd been thinking that maybe we needed to leave and get our own place. It was just a scary thought. Mom obviously thought so too.

"No. You can't leave." She pulled me into a tight hug. "I don't want you to go yet. We only just got her."

I laughed and pulled away from my mom's arms. "It's not me you want to stay then. It's Tia. Thanks for that, Mom."

"Shaw, son, you should know by now that your mom stopped any interest in you kids the minute you came out of diapers."

Dad grinned at Mom who backhanded him in the stomach. I laughed because that was so off the mark it was untrue, and Dad knew it.

"I appreciate it, Mom," I replied, patting her hair which barely moved—my mom liked big hair.

"Hey everyone," it was Bronte.

She, Carter, Rett, Ellie and Hunter all trooped into the room.

"I didn't ask them to come too," I said pointing at Carter and Hunter.

"Hey douche canoe," my brother-in-law greeted me as he put Rett down so he could run to my mom.

"Hello, my little soldier," Mom gushed and landed kisses all over his face which he proffered up to her.

When she'd finished Rett held his arms out to Dad. "Orweo Ganpa."

Dad stood and took Rett from Mom. "Come on then, let's go get you a cookie." That was their thing; Rett came over and Dad gave him an Oreo from his 'special box of cookies just for Rett'.

As they walked off Mom followed. "I'll go and put coffee on and, Ellie, please put Shaw's mind at rest."

Ellie turned to me and smiled brightly. "Where is she?" she asked, clapping her hands. "I need to get my hands on her squishy little legs."

"Baby," Hunter groaned. "Do you have to get mushy over every kid you see?" Hunter's usual easy smile wasn't there. Instead, he looked concerned and flat out tired. It appeared that the baby making effort was getting to him.

Ellie snapped him a glare. "If I want to get mushy over a baby I will. You didn't have to come with me."

Hunter scrubbed a hand down his face. "I'm going to go talk to Jim about something." He then turned and left the living room.

"What the hell is going on?" Bronte asked.

"Lollipop," Carter warned. "Stay out of it."

My sister's eyes widened as she rounded on her husband. "What did you say?"

Carter shook his head. "I'm going to talk to Jim about something too."

"Great guys," I yelled. "Leave me alone with two women who look ready to cut someone's dick off."

"Shut up, Shaw. Now, Ellie what's going on with you and Hunter?"

Ellie glanced at me.

"Hey, don't mind me. I just want you to check on my daughter is all."

"He refused to have sex with me this morning. He said I'm too obsessed over getting pregnant and have taken the fun out of it."

Bronte's mouth dropped open and then closed. "Do you think that they have a pact?" she finally asked. "Because Carter said exactly the same thing."

"He did not. Damn it, the pair of sneaky bastards." Ellie started to pace. "Most men would like to have sex at least three times a day. But no, not my husband. He says he's tired." She threw her hands in the air. "He says he feels like a sex object."

"He did not," Bronte gasped.

Ellie nodded. "He also suggested that we stop trying to get pregnant and just see what happens."

"He did n… hey, wait a minute." Bronte's eyes brightened. "He may have a point. You know if you stopped trying to might just get pregnant."

My sister the sneaky little devil. She wanted to be the one to provide Henry and Melinda with grandchild number two, especially now I'd taken top spot on both counts from her with Mom and Dad. Ellie, however, was not stupid and I saw it dawn on her what my sister's plan was.

"Take me to the baby," she said, snapping her fingers and then pointing to the door. "I need to get Hunter home."

"I thought he'd withdrawn all sex?" Bronte asked with a hint of desperation in her tone.

"Yes," Ellie said, giving my sister a head wobble. "But I have a secret weapon." She started to walk out of the room.

Bronte gasped. "No. You're going to get your Belle costume out aren't you." She chased after Ellie. "Why you sneaky…"

"Damn it," I groaned. "Why can't I just live a normal life."

A little over thirty minutes later it was official. Tia was teething. She had a rubber chew ring and Ellie told me to go and get her some teething gel from the pharmacy when it opened in the morning but also to give her frozen carrot to bite down on. She then dragged Hunter out to his truck like a woman on a mission. I think the fact that Bronte and Carter left a couple of minutes before was what spurred her on. Especially as they'd left Rett with Mom and Dad for a couple of hours, and he was now watching cartoons with them and Tia. Mom had told me to grab some shut eye, but there was too much going on in my head.

That was why when my phone rang out, I was lying on my bed contemplating the next steps for me and Tia.

"Hey, Tate."

"Hey, Shaw, I need to speak to you on an urgent matter."

He sounded serious and I wondered if I'd fucked up at work. I'd already run past him how I'd dealt with the issue of Ruthie and how she'd managed to get the bank. He'd seen nothing wrong with the way I'd done it so wasn't sure why he could be sounding so off.

"Everything okay. Is there something you need me to come in for?"

I heard him let out a long exhale on the other end of the line. "I don't know how to tell you this, so I'm just going to come right out and say it."

My heart started to thunder, the noise of it pulsing in my ears. "W-what?"

"Mrs. Devonshire wants Tia back."

I jumped up and instantly felt a pain that ran from my stomach to chest. It took the wind from me, and I dropped back down to the edge of the bed.

"She didn't want her though."

"I know, Shaw. I'm so sorry. I have no idea what's changed but suddenly she's not going on her trip and wants Tia back."

Fuck. How can this hurt so damn much when she's only been in my life a week? I felt like I was going to be sick.

"What happens now? Do I have to give her back?" I couldn't do it. "How do I stop it? Why the fuck…?"

"I have no idea, buddy. I'm going to put another call in with her lawyer tomorrow now that I've spoken to you. I'm guessing the answer is you're going to fight it."

"Hell yes!" I pushed up from the bed and bent at the waist to try and ease the pain. "I just don't understand it."

"Me neither. The main thing is you're doing all the right things. Getting your name on the birth certificate is important because then you can assert parental rights including custody and visitation rights. You already logged it with the Department of Vital Records, right."

"Yeah," I breathed out. "It could take about a month."

"It's in the system though so that's a good thing. To be honest, Shaw I think you're good. She dumped Tia on your doorstep with a note. There is one thing though that might help your case."

"What?" I asked. "I'll do anything."

"Her lawyer may involve Child Services, so you need to make sure the family are all in on supporting you. Maybe get some sort of childcare plan drawn up, get her signed up to preschool now so that it shows you're committed to her future."

"Anything else?" I asked, the tightness in my chest starting to diminish.

"Get yourself a serious relationship."

He laughed but when an image of Nancy Andrews swam in front of my eyes, I was pretty sure that the pain was back.

CHAPTER 25

Nancy

It was the night of the big party at the Big D ranch, and I'd heard from Lily that there was going to be around a hundred people there. Jefferson had gone all out for it, determined that Kitty had a night to remember. The proposal would ensure that if nothing else did. As for the ring, well that sounded beyond amazing if Lily's description of it was anything to go by.

Talking of Lily, she'd taken it upon herself to get Bronte and Carter to give me a ride over to the ranch. I think that she knew I'd probably cry off otherwise. What with everything going on with the bank and Minnesota being there, I wasn't up for it. Don't get me wrong I knew it would be a great night, but I just wasn't feeling it.

"Okay," Bronte said as we pulled away from my apartment. "Tell me all about the bank. Shaw gave me a load a crap about client confidentiality, but like I told him, wasn't I the one who persuaded you it'd be a good idea."

"Lollipop, you wanna take a breath?" Carter looked at me in the rearview mirror and raised his eyebrows.

"I'm excited for Nancy is all," she said, smacking at his leg. "So, spill the beans."

Rett dropped his toy monkey on the seat next to me, so I handed it to him and got myself a smile and a giggle, while Bronte jumped impatiently up and down in the front passenger seat.

"It appears that Ruthie's bid on the property was sweetened by giving the contract for the rebuild to the guy selling it," I explained, unconsciously tickling Rett's leg. "It's called bidder something or other and Shaw got proof. He was going to speak to Ruthie's lawyer yesterday, but I haven't heard from him."

Bronte and Carter exchanged a glance

"He's been busy with stuff with Tia," Bronte sighed. She shifted in her seat so that she could see me better. "Tia's grandmother wants her back."

My heart stopped for a beat and then dropped to my stomach. An ache that I'd buried long ago spiked in my chest and surprised me. "Oh my god, how's he taken that? He's really bonding with her."

"He's pretty gutted," Carter said. "Like you said he's been bonding with her more and more each day."

"I feel so bad for him," Bronte added.

Shaw must have been feeling desperate and I just wanted to console him and support him as best I could. I hoped that he'd got Tate on the case.

"Tate will sort it," Carter said, as if reading my mind. "He's a good lawyer."

"Exactly," Bronte replied a little more brightly. "And Shaw said we're not even to think about it until it happens, especially not tonight. He wants us all to have fun and said tonight is all about Kitty."

My thoughts were that he might be saying that, but I doubted he had anything else but his daughter on his mind.

"I know but, even so," I replied, placing the hand that had been on Rett's leg against my tumbling stomach.

"Take his lead, Nancy," Carter said as he indicated to turn onto the main road out of town. "Because you know Shaw, he hates a fuss over nothing."

The problem was Shaw losing Tia wasn't nothing, it was huge.

***

"Hey, Kitty," I said, pulling her in for a hug. "Happy birthday."

The older woman squeezed me tight before pulling back to give me a huge smile. "Thank you, sweetheart, and I'm so glad you came." She leaned closer. "Lily said you may not, what with Minnesota being here. I feel awful, but I just told Jefferson to invite everyone we knew."

I shook my head. "Honestly, it's fine, things aren't that bad between us. I promise not to cause a scene."

"Oh Nancy, if a man needs putting in his place, then I'm all for it, no matter what the occasion."

"You look beautiful by the way."

And she did. Kitty was one of those women who owned their curves and the tight cobalt blue bandage dress that she was wearing accentuated every one of her assets.

"Thank you. It was one of my many gifts from Jefferson." Her eyes shone brightly as she looked over to the man in question. He was as usual looking handsome wearing grey dress pants and a shirt that was a shade lighter than Kitty's dress. "He's really spoiled me."

I smiled knowing that she was going to be getting another even bigger surprise later.

"He loves you," I stated.

Kitty's eyes went dreamy as she sighed. "He really does."

"Anyways, I'll let you go and mingle with your guests." I hugged her again. "Have a great evening."

Once I'd deposited Kitty's gift bag on the designated table, I made my way to the bar which Penny the owner of Stars & Stripes had set up on the edge of the paddock. It was the same paddock where Hunter and Ellie's wedding had been held, but there was no marquee this time. There were tables, chairs and hay bales laid out around the edges and a wooden dancefloor had been laid in the middle. Hundreds of white lights were crisscrossed overhead and at the opposite end to the bar was a small stage. Dewey Roberts the manager of the food market was currently showing some great DJ skills, but Lily had told me that later a Huey Lewis & The News tribute band were going to be playing as a surprise for Kitty. Jefferson really had thought of everything to spoil his woman.

"Hey Nancy," Pauly Jansen said as he wiped down the makeshift bar, "What can I get you? It's all on the house."

I blinked. "Really?"

He nodded. "Tate's contribution apparently."

God, I missed having a family who would want to do nice things for me.

I couldn't decide between vodka or beer. Then I spotted a tall, blond guy with a cute blonde toddler on his hip and made my mind up. "I'll have a beer please, Pauly."

Once he'd handed it to me, I looked around and felt that pull of loneliness again. Once we'd arrived, Carter and Bronte had disappeared to deposit Rett with the babysitting club, and Hunter and Ellie were chatting with Tate along with Ellie's parents. Alaska and Jennifer were sitting at one of the tables, with Jennifer looking about to burst seeing as she was only days away from having her baby. I could have gone over to them, but I saw Minnesota standing close by talking to his and Alaska's parents and I didn't want to risk it. So, as I looked around, I felt self-conscious and on the edge of everything, wondering how long I'd have to stay before it wasn't seen as rude to call an uber and get out of there.

After a few minutes of trying to melt into the background, I felt a hand grab a hold of mine and tug on it.

"Here you are." It was Lily. "I've been looking for you. I thought you'd come into the house with Bronte and Carter."

"Hey, Lily." We hugged and the relief of having company, if only for a few minutes was huge.

"You look pretty." She grinned and took a step back to examine the white broderie anglaise knee length dress and ankle boots that I was wearing. "I love this. How come I've never seen it before?"

I shrugged deciding not to say that I'd bought it for my trip with Minnesota and then never wanted to wear it because it made me feel mad. Tonight, though I'd decided that I'd done enough crying and complaining about the card that man had dealt me, and wearing the dress was my first fuck you to him.

"Anyway," Lily said excitedly. "Come on, we've got a table over there." She nodded to a couple of tables down from Jennifer and Alaska where Carter and Bronte were now sitting and giggling with each other. As we looked over Ellie and Hunter joined them and then I felt a swarm of butterflies in the pit of my stomach as Shaw appeared. He was talking to Austen, and they were laughing as they walked along.

"Hey, guys." Lily waved her hands at everyone. "I found her. I just need to go and speak to Jefferson about something." She ran off leaving me at the table.

"Where did you go?" Bronte asked, patting the chair next to her. "We thought that you were following us into the house."

I sat down. "Sorry, I didn't know you were waiting for me." As the chair next to me shifted, I turned to see Shaw and Austen sitting down. I smiled at them and got a grin from Shaw and a wink from Austen, the little shit.

"Looking lovely, ladies," Austen said to the group of us.

"For fuck's sake, Aust." Shaw rolled his eyes. "You're a dick."

I burst out laughing because Shaw and I seemingly had the same thoughts about his little brother.

"What?" Shaw asked.

"I think we're on the same wavelength about Austen."

Shaw gave a short laugh. "Well he is."

"Whatever," Austen replied. He looked around and when his eyebrows arched and his mouth turned up, I guessed a girl was responsible. I was right when he stood up and waved to us all. "Laters old folks."

"What the hell is going on with that kid?" Hunter appeared, clinging on to Ellie's hand.

"He's found his dick," Shaw grunted.

"Hey sweetie." Ellie leaned down and kissed my cheek. "You look lovely." She then turned to Bronte. "Have you had sex today?"

"Ellie, really?" Carter threw his hands in the air. "Do you have to be so fucking nosey?"

"At least if she's asking you questions then she's not begging me for sex…oof. Ellie that fucking hurt."

"Good but you do know that once you've impregnated me, I'm only going to be begging for more." She reached up on her tiptoes and kissed him hard on the lips and then dropped into the chair that Austen had vacated.

Lily appeared again and plonked herself in a free chair and heaved out a breath. "Oh my god, Hunter your dad is freaking out." She slapped a hand to her forehead. "He's nervous as hell."

Hunter grinned and put his arm around Lily, dragging her to him. "He'll be fine little sis."

Lily grinned and patted Hunter's chest and it was lovely to see them together. I knew that she already had Tate as a big brother, but from what I'd seen the three of them already had a great bond. And there was that loneliness again.

"You okay?" Shaw's mouth was right near my ear, and it made me jump.

"I'm great. How are you? Bronte told me about Tia."

His shoulders sagged. "Fucking bitch just decided that she wants her back."

"I'm sorry." I put a hand on his thigh and gave it a squeeze. "I know that you didn't want to talk about it. Bronte said you didn't. I'm sorry."

"Tonight is about Kitty and I don't want to bring the mood down." He forced a smile. "Anyways, I meant to call you to tell you that Ruthie's lawyer is going to get her to consider her options."

"Thank you but no work tonight, just try to enjoy yourself."

He tipped his beer bottle at me and both subjects were forgotten.

***

"You want a beer?" Shaw asked as we watched Hunter and Ellie doing some weird dance with Ellie's dad, Henry.

I looked at him and shook my head. "I was thinking maybe vodka."

He reared back and laughed, slapping his hand against his chest. "Woah, Nance. You know what happens when you drink vodka."

"Huh, as if," I said, feeling as if I just might, seeing as he looked so hot. Seeing as I was well on my way to being a little more than giggly drunk.

"Listen," he said, leaning in close. "We both know we can't stand each other, but for some reason we kinda like having sex with each other."

"And your point is?"

He cocked his head on one side and let his beautiful blue eyes slide over my face and then my body.

"You don't have a point," I prompted.

"No, I do, but I got a little distracted." He drew in a breath. "Do you have any idea how fucking sexy you are?"

"Is that the point that you wanted to make?"

My heartbeat notched up a level as Shaw took a step closer to me. I wanted him to kiss me and yet I hated the idea of it. If he kissed me then it would undoubtedly lead to sex because he was right, we did like having sex with each other. The problem was, while at first it had been all about the immense gratification that angry sex brought with it, each time chipped away at my intense dislike for Shaw. I'd already had my heart dented and my confidence annihilated by Minnesota, and I wasn't sure I could take another hit. Then again Shaw wasn't promising me a future like my ex-boyfriend had. He was just offering me really, really good sex.

"I'll get you that vodka in a few," Shaw said nodding toward the stage area. "I think Jefferson is about to do his stuff."

My head shot around to look in the same direction and immediately a stupid grin broke out on my face. Jefferson, the normally confident and sexy rancher, was wiping his palms on his pants as Kitty laughed at something that Melinda was saying to her off to the side of the stage.

I spotted Tate give Dewey a signal to stop the music and then my eyes went back to Jefferson who was taking a deep breath. Hunter ran up to him and slapped his back before rejoining Ellie and Lily who were giving him a thumbs up. God, I wanted what they all had. Family was everything and I didn't think I'd felt the loss of mine so deeply as I did at that moment. When the man of the moment cleared his throat, I shook my head of the memories.

"Hey everyone," Jefferson started tentatively as Kitty rushed to his side and wrapped an arm around his middle. "I want to thank you all for coming to celebrate Kitty's birthday, which," he said with a grin toward his woman, "isn't her fiftieth."

Kitty rolled her eyes. "I told you that word isn't to be mentioned ever again. Especially not this time next year."

"I know, and I promise it won't be." Jefferson kissed her temple before turning back to the crowd listening intently. "Anyways, we're glad you have you all here at *our* home."

My stomach swooped at his words and the way he said them; full of pride and love and gratitude that he was now sharing it with the woman he loved. I was beyond happy that both he and Kitty had been given a second chance at joy in their lives.

Jefferson blew out his cheeks and then continued. "There is another reason why you're here," he said, looking at Kitty. "Our kids and close friends know about this but not even Kitty is aware of what happens next."

Kitty looked over at the people watching and mouthed, 'what's going on?' to Tate who was beaming at her. He then nodded at Jefferson who hadn't dropped to his knee but was holding out a black box. Kitty gasped and placed her hand on her chest, exactly where her heart was.

"Baby?" She gazed at Jefferson and then at the box.

"Kitty," he started. "You came back into my life a little under a year ago and every day since then has been beyond amazing. You filled my heart with so much love I can't express what it's meant to me." Kitty's hands moved in front of her mouth, like she was praying, and I was sure I could see tears on her cheeks. "Everyone knows what I've been through, what Hunter and I lost, but you've done something that I never thought possible. You've made me feel happy and look forward to the future again." I looked over at Melinda and Darcy who were hugging each other and both swiping at tears as they watched their friend lay bare his heart and soul. "We first found each other when we were just fifteen and then over thirty years later you made your way back here and back into my heart." Jefferson looked up to the sky and then back to the woman he loved. "I kinda think someone had a hand in that, because she knew how much we needed you and how just how much you'd love us."

"Aww shit, Pop," I heard Hunter mutter, his voice breaking with emotion.

Jefferson looked at his son and smiled softly before continuing. "Katherine Louise Carmichael would you do me the honor of being my wife, and before you say no, I already checked with your dad, and he said yes, so that kinda means that you have to."

Kitty's head swiveled over to a table where her parents and her uncle Norm were sitting. There were two empty seats where Jefferson's sisters Lynn-Ann and Janice-Ann had been, but they were now both hanging on to Hunter's hands and gazing at their brother.

"Well?" Jefferson asked, regaining Kitty's attention. "What do you say, baby?"

"I say yes," she cried and practically jumped off the floor and into his arms, raining kisses all over his face.

"What about the ring," Henry, Ellie's dad yelled.

"Oh gosh, I forgot." Kitty pulled away and held out her left hand.

Jefferson took the ring from the box which he then coolly threw to Hunter, before placing the ring on Kitty's finger. Once it was securely on he took her into his arms and gave her one of the most romantic PG kisses that I'd ever seen. After what felt like was a real private moment in front of a hundred people, they pulled apart and Jefferson faced all the partygoers.

"Okay, folks, let's continue with the party."

Dewey started the music again and Jefferson and Kitty were suddenly surrounded by their families and friends. It truly was a beautiful moment and as I gazed at them, I was surprised to feel a warm, big hand take mine.

"Pretty cute, hey?"

Shaw's breath whispered against my skin, and everything went on high alert. The beer mixed with the emotion of the evening and the feelings of loneliness were enough for me to decide.

“Do you want to go somewhere quieter?” I asked, with my eyes still on the happy family tableaux in front of me.

“If you do.”

I turned to see Shaw’s blue eyes were dark and hungry and I didn’t think I’d wanted something so much in all of my life. Okay, so I was pretty sure I might regret it in the morning, but life was too damn short.

“I do.”

Shaw looked over to the table where we’d been sitting and everyone was occupied with either drinking, talking, or congratulating the happy couple.

His hand tightened around mine. “Let’s go.”

“Where to?” I asked as he pulled me behind him.

“There can only be one place,” he said. “The place that it all began.”

I giggled knowing that we were on our way to the back of the Delaney’s barn, and I couldn’t wait.

Nancy’s Bitch List for Shaw

☐ Maximus Douchimus
☐ Captain Shitsmear
☐ Shit Talking Cock Womble
☐ Dildohead
☐ Dipshit Cockhead
☐ Scrote Noggin
☐ ~~Assilicious~~ Fat Ass
☐ Fucknuckle
☐ Bronocchio
☐ Asshobbit
☐ Jerkass
☐ Studly McStudly

CHAPTER 26

Shaw

When I pushed Nancy against the barn wall, I was sure I'd combust with the need building up inside of me. Every day I seemed to want her more which wasn't right. We were supposed to hate one another. We had since high school and things weren't supposed to change now. The problem was with those long, tanned legs and that dark hair that fell down her back, almost touching her heart-shaped ass, she had me hooked. All that and her magical pussy.

I took her face in my hands and kissed her, relishing in the feel of her tongue on mine. Fire pulsed through my veins as she hooked her fingers in my belt loops and pulled me closer. Her body was soft and warm against mine in the gentle breeze of the evening and when she let out a soft moan, something changed inside of me. It was like I'd been hypnotized, and someone had snapped their fingers waking me up from my fuck buddy stupor. Sex against the wall of a barn suddenly didn't feel right. I wanted to be inside her, more than anything, but I wasn't sure that this was the way I wanted it. I couldn't comprehend the thought that was blowing around my head that I wanted more than this from her.

"Nancy, are you sure you're okay with this?" I asked, dropping my forehead to hers, not sure how to put into words what I was thinking. Not sure I wanted to. "We can go somewhere else… your apartment?"

She frowned and dropped her arms to her sides, the palms of her hands going flat against the wood of the barn. There was rejection in her eyes, and I felt like a shit for putting it there because that was the last thing I was trying to do. The total opposite in fact.

"I swear I want this, Nance. I just think you deserve something better." I ran my finger down the v on the neck of her white dress and then placed my palm over her heart. It was beating fast and hard, echoing mine. "Your heart is racing."

She placed her hand over mine and exhaled slowly.

"I thought that you hated me," she said. "So why would you care what I deserve?"

"I don't actually think that I *hate* you." I rolled my eyes and earned a giggle from her which broke the tension. "You definitely hate me though. You have for years, and why is that by the way?"

She pulled her head back and widened her eyes. "You are kidding, right?"

"But you have." I shrugged.

"No, I mean you have to know why I hate you. Which I actually don't." She folded her arms over her chest, creating a distance between us. "I mean I don't like you an awful lot, but I don't hate you."

"Okay." I gave a slow, single nod. "So why don't you like me an awful lot?"

"You really don't know?"

"No, I don't." I smirked. "I mean everyone else thinks I'm a wonderful human being. You're the only person who doesn't, and I have no idea why."

"Seriously?"

"Seriously."

"You don't remember prom?"

I frowned trying to recall something at prom that might have made her hate me. I remembered that we kinda danced around each other at middle school, a little too young and scared to do anything about our mutual attraction. Then around sixth grade, right after I'd taken her to our little sweetheart dance, she started to ignore me which gradually turned to disdain which moved on to hate.

"Did I feel you up at the little sweetheart dance?" I asked. "Because that's pretty much the last time that you spoke to me during school."

"You remember taking me to that?" She sounded surprised that I did but I wasn't sure why, it wasn't that long ago.

"You wore a cute little cream dress with black biker boots, a black leather jacket and a black Fedora." She stared at me open-mouthed. "So, you see, Nance, I do remember. I don't remember anything happening at prom though. In fact," I said, with a shrug. "I don't remember seeing you there."

"And that's because I wasn't," she snapped.

"And?"

"You really don't recall?"

"No, like I said." I had no clue how we'd gone from us almost having sex against the barn wall to us discussing our childhood, but suddenly I needed to know where our issues had stemmed from. It seemed like it was important to Nancy, so I wanted to know too.

She chewed on her lip and then leaned back against the wood with her eyes fluttering shut for a few seconds. When she opened them, she looked up at me and studied me.

"You do remember that you asked me to prom, don't you?"

I reared back and frowned. "No, I don't. I didn't. Why would I ask you to prom when you'd barely spoken to me for almost four years?"

"But you did." Nancy narrowed her eyes on me. "You sent me a note. It said you were sorry we hadn't hung out much since middle school, but you'd been an idiot, and could we be friends again and so would I go to prom with you."

I thought about what she said but it definitely wasn't me. Ruthie had pretty much told me that I was to ask her to go with me. She even bought her own corsage and then made me give her the money for it. Funny though, she wanted to keep us going to prom together on the downlow for some reason.

"Why would I send you a note?" I asked. "You know me, Nancy. When have I ever been the kind of guy who wouldn't have the cojones to ask you in person to something as important as our senior year prom?"

Nancy shrugged. Her shoulders almost coming up to her ears.

"I waited on the porch for you," she said in a quiet voice. "In the most disgusting yellow dress ever made."

"I swear Nan—"

"Ah so here you are?" Mrs. Callahan cried. She then turned and yelled. "I found him making out with Nancy Andrews against the barn."

"We were not making out," Nancy protested.

"What is it with you youngsters that can't treat your women right?" Mrs. Callahan sighed. "I mean, in the last five minutes I saw Carter's bare ass going up and down in the back seat of his truck and found Minnesota in a compromising position with some young woman who I'm pretty sure was—"

"Mrs. C," I interrupted not wanting to hear what Minnesota Michaels was doing. "What did you want me for?"

"That baby that you've acquired is crying for you. One of the babysitters has been looking for you."

Immediately I pulled away from Nancy and started toward the house. As I did one of the high school girls doing the babysitting appeared. Carly was blonde and perky and carrying my little girl.

"She wanted you." She handed Tia over to me.

"What's wrong baby?" I asked as Tia threw herself at me, grabbing at my shirt.

"I think she's tired," Carly said. She was almost eighteen and the sister of my old high school buddy Danny Sivantes and I knew she had a thing for my *sixteen-year-old* brother. That kid had some magic going on in his pants that was for sure.

"Hey, Tia." Nancy was by my side and stroking her hand down Tia's blonde head. "You tired sweetie?"

"I'm not going to ask where that child came from," Mrs. Callahan said with a little shake of her head. "All I'm saying is Shaw Jackson, you and Nancy ought to be gloving up. You do not want any other babies arriving out of wedlock."

"I'll take it on board, Mrs. C," I said, starting to walk away.

"Oh, we're not…" Nancy blustered.

I turned and looked at her over Tia's head and winked. "I think you'll find we are, Nancy. Not tonight maybe, but we are, and we will finish that conversation about prom."

I then walked away leaving her to think on my words, while I went to get my baby to sleep.

***

To say that I was the only one who wasn't hanging out the back of my ass, was an understatement. The birthday come engagement party had been a blast, particularly for my mom and dad who were currently groaning in their room with the drapes closed and the A/C on full blast while they lay like the dead on their bed. They weren't aware but even Austen was suffering with a hangover. I think he and his buddies pulled the old, distract the bartender and then steal some booze trick. We all had at some point in our lives. It was a rite of passage, wasn't it? It seemed though that my brother and his buddies were particularly good at it because he was an odd shade of green that only came with your first taste of spirits.

I on the other hand was fresh as a daisy. Once I'd settled Tia back down with the babysitters, she'd slept pretty much all night, even on the journey home on the school bus that Jefferson had hired to transport everyone. Because she'd been unsettled earlier and I also didn't think it was right being in charge of a toddler while inebriated, I'd gone onto soda for the rest of the night, hence why I was not hungover.

Once I went back to the party, I'd looked for Nancy, but she'd been nowhere to be seen. It was only after I'd done a second lap of the party that Lily told me she'd grabbed a lift home with Alaska and Jennifer as she wasn't feeling well. I didn't believe that and was pretty sure it was all to do with the stuff about prom, but I'd given her the space she clearly wanted. She'd had twelve hours of space though and now I was going to examine those feelings that I was starting to have about her.

Shaw: *I searched for you last night after I got Tia back down. Kinda wanted to finish the conversation that we were having, among other stuff.*

It took her almost five minutes to reply and I was getting a little impatient. I had approximately twenty before my daughter woke from her nap and then I would be too occupied to converse with Nancy. So, when my phone trilled with the text message, my heart had its own little dance party which surprised me.

Nancy: *What other stuff? Be specific!*

Okay, a flirty response, I could get down with that.

Shaw: *You really want me to say how I want to get you in a bed and then…*

Think about that one, Ms. Andrews! I grinned as I put my phone on the arm on the couch and waited. When it rang out with a call, I almost jumped a few feet in the air. I picked it up with a smile, thinking that Nancy evidently was as anxious as I was to finish things off. I was surprised to see it wasn't her.

"Hi John, what can I do for you?" It was Ruthie's lawyer and my optimism spiked.

"I'm sure you know, Shaw." He cleared his throat. "Miss. Grey, on my advice, has removed her interest in the property owned by Mr. Jennings."

"Is that so?" I asked with a smirk. "I'm sure that my client will be pleased to hear that. I assume Mr. Jennings will be expecting a call from

Miss. Andrews?"

"He's not my client, so I couldn't say."

Bullshit. He knew exactly what Jennings had said. Ruthie was only pulling out because Jennings was no longer getting her business and so had now rejected her bid. The whole thing stunk of the Delaney ranch's barn.

"Thanks for letting me know, John," I replied. "I'll contact my client and let her know to expect a call from her realtor."

The dick didn't even say goodbye before ending the call. Fucking rude. One thing I knew though, rude or not, he'd given the best news and I couldn't wait to tell Nancy.

***

Mom and Dad finally surfaced and after spending the day stuffing themselves with carbs and black coffee, they felt well enough to listen out for Tia for me. That gave me the opportunity to go and see Nancy and give her the good news in person.

She hadn't texted me back after my last one, but I figured she was over thinking it. That meant as well as giving her the good news I was also going to suggest we call a truce and actually start being nice to each other. Outside of the bedroom as well as inside.

Maybe it was becoming a father that had changed my feelings toward Nancy. Maybe it was being the father of a daughter. Because let's face it what father would want their daughter to be some douche's fuck buddy. The thing was I wasn't a douche, and she certainly was worthy of being much more.

When I got to her apartment block, I ignored the elevator and ran up the stairs, feeling energized by my day. Tia and I had played in the yard and then I'd taken her to the park at the end of our street and met up with Carter and Rhett. Apparently, my sister was lying with her feet in the air because it could help her to get pregnant. I had no damn clue what he was talking about so nodded, smiled and pushed Tia on the baby swing.

Smiling at the memory of the fun we'd had, when I reached the fire door to the Nancy's floor, I pulled it open with enthusiasm and was… immediately deflated.

Minnesota fucking Michaels was coming out of her apartment. My heart missed a beat when I saw him, but when he then turned and hugged her tightly and for too fucking long, I felt like it had dropped to my boots. Not wanting to watch their inevitable goodbye kiss I left, realizing that was why she hadn't texted me back. She'd been reconnecting with Minnesota, and I hated the thought of it more than I'd imagined possible.

CHAPTER 27

Nancy

It appeared that I had a lot to thank Shaw for because according to the call I'd had from Belinda, Mr. Jennings had reconsidered the bids and would like to go with me. I tried to call Shaw to find out what I should do, because a part of me wanted to lower my bid now that I knew how low Ruthie had bid. He didn't answer my calls or text messages though, which made me think we were back to hating each other. It kind of proved it when I got an email from him, *as my legal representative*. It pretty much told me what Belinda had but advised me to stick with the original bid which was competitive and fair. It said under no circumstances should I get into conversation with Mr. Jennings about the amount and not to go a cent higher, even if he asked.

I'd been excited about everything and wanted to share it with him and thank him, but clearly, he didn't have the same desire. So, I simply replied with a thank you and that I'd let him know once Mr. Jennings had contacted me in person and that I'd managed to secure a contractor as per Shaw's advice.

It was all so damn confusing. He was confusing what with his flirty messages which I admit I ducked out of because I got side-tracked. Once I was able to give them my attention again it felt a bit weird as almost five hours had passed. I just figured we'd get back to it in person when I next saw him. Plus, that lack of confidence that I suffered from kicked in. I was worried that he'd been messing with me and would laugh at me if I responded how I wanted to i.e., by telling him exactly what I wanted him to do to me in bed. And it appeared that I was right. He had been messing with me because there'd been nothing since.

Now, it was weekend again and Melinda and Henry had organized a cookout in their back yard and Ellie had invited me. When I pulled up on their driveway, I was beginning to second guess my outfit of cute jean shorts and a floaty boho blouse. I'd originally left enough buttons open on the blouse so that there was a great view of my cleavage, but as I turned off my car engine, I did a couple of them back up again. I'd dressed for Shaw, and I couldn't believe how stupid I'd been to do so.

When I walked around back clutching two bottles of wine, I found everyone else was already there making me feel a little self-conscious. I hated being the last to arrive, but it wasn't surprising since I'd only decided at the last moment that I was still going to come because 'damn Shaw Jackson, who cares if you hate me again.'. Yep, clearly, I did.

"Nancy," Henry called, as he spotted me. "Come on in."

I walked over to him trying not to let my eyes wander around the garden and look for Shaw.

"Hey, Henry." I offered him the two bottles and smiled. "I hope this is okay, I wasn't sure what to bring."

He took them from me. "You didn't need to bring anything. Didn't Ellie give you the message?"

"She did but I couldn't come empty handed."

"Well thank you." He leaned in and kissed my cheek. "Go grab a cold one from the kitchen. I think Ellie is in there with Bronte and Lily."

I nodded and wandered across the lawn to the house, waving to the group of family and friends gathered. There was a table of salads and other delicious looking stuff and one with a host of different uncooked meats, all covered in Saran wrap ready to be grilled. They'd certainly gone all out for a weekend family cookout. There were various chairs and a couple of bean bags dotted around and everyone seemed to be feeling relaxed. When I spotted Jefferson with Kitty sitting on his knee, I couldn't help but smile. They looked so in love, and it was just wonderful to see. What I could also see was how spectacular that engagement ring truly was in the daylight. I'd taken a good look at it when I'd said goodnight to them at the party, but the sun practically blinded me as it shone off the gorgeous emerald.

"Hey, guys," I greeted them as I passed them.

"Nancy, sweetheart." Darcy jumped up and hugged me tightly. "I'm so glad you came. I hear that the bank is back on."

"It is," I replied, trying not to look to my right where I'd spotted Shaw sitting talking to Carter and Hunter. "Thanks to Shaw."

What the hell was wrong with me? Just saying his name made me feel nervous and now I felt like I *had* to look at him. What sort of idiot was I?

"Hey, Shaw." Damn it. I looked and had to say hello. And oh shit, he looked hot in board shorts and a tight tee. And yes…damnit my eyes had to go there didn't they, right to his crotch where his beautiful penis lay bulging.

"Nancy." He nodded.

That was it. *He nodded.* He *fucking nodded.* I was admiring his penis and he *nodded.* I'd almost unbuttoned half my blouse for him, and he *nodded* like he'd never had his dick in my vagina. What was wrong with the man?

"Well, I for one am glad it's not going to be some strange bar with half-naked men," Darcy said, forcing me to tear my eyes away from her douchebag son.

"I don't know," Melinda sighed. "I'm glad for you, Nancy, but I quite liked the idea of some buff, topless young men serving me cocktails."

"Yeah, it was kind of an exciting thought." Kitty screeched and then started to giggle as Jefferson tickled her sides. "Okay, okay, it was a joke."

"Oh gosh," Darcy said with a roll of her eyes. "I think that means we're going to have to watch them making out again."

"For Pete's sake, Jefferson," Melinda added, slapping at his arm with the back of her hand. "Leave the woman alone."

When Jefferson then took Kitty's face in his hands and kissed her both Darcy and Melinda gave dreamy sighs.

"Pop, please," Hunter grumbled. "Children present."

I looked around but there was no sign of Tia or Rett, so I laughed when I realized he meant himself.

"I'd better go and get myself a drink," I said with a grin. "Looks like I might need it."

"Okay, honey," Darcy replied. "And again, congratulations."

"Yeah, great news, Nancy," Carter offered. "Can't wait to enroll Rett."

"Thanks, guys." Feeling a little more relaxed I moved inside the house and went in search of booze and the girls. When I found them in the kitchen, Bronte and Ellie were arguing about something while Lily looked to be the referee. She was stood in the middle of them her head whipping from side to side like she was watching a tennis match.

"Nancy, thank god," she said in a withering voice. "Will you sort this argument out between these two."

"What's going on?" I asked.

Ellie pouted like a toddler and said with her eyes on Bronte, "Tell *her* that you only have a real short time to get pregnant each month." She turned to me. "Because it's not like I'm the one who is medically trained or anything."

I shrugged. "She's right," I aimed at Bronte. "When do you think you can get pregnant?"

"She," Ellie said before Bronte had chance, "thinks that she and my brother need to have sex every day for the whole month, at least twice a day in order to get pregnant."

"You're only saying that because you want to scupper my chances of getting pregnant before you." Bronte raised a perfectly shaped brow and crossed her arms over her chest. "Because it's not like you and Hunter aren't at it at every opportunity."

"You know what, all this talk of sex is making me feel queasy," Lily offered with a sigh. "You're talking about having sex with my brother and it's not right."

Ellie gasped and pulled Lily into her arms. "Oh Lils, you think of Hunter as your brother."

"You know I do," she said, her voice muffled against Ellie's chest which weirdly looked huge. Then again so did Bronte's. They both did compared to my C cups which barely required a bra unless I was on my period and then they—

Ellie interrupted my thoughts. "That is so cute." She then burst into tears and sobbed about how happy she was.

"Oh God, don't cry," Bronte's voice broke. "You're going to start me off."

The next thing I knew both Bronte and Ellie were crying and hugging each other while poor Lily tried desperately to get out of the boob sandwich. I watched on in mild confusion. When she finally managed, she was breathing heavily and came to stand next to me.

"OMG, they've like been like this for the last hour, bursting into tears for no reason." She blew out a breath causing her pink hair to blow in the breeze. "Ellie hasn't stopped crying all week. It went to epic levels when she said Hunter had shrunk her silk blouse in the laundry. She came storming into the house from their house threw herself into Mom's arms and said he'd broken her heart. We all thought that he was leaving her, not doing the laundry."

As I watched the two best friends, I studied them both and then cleared my throat to get their attention. I'd seen a lot of hormonal moms come and go at the kindergarten and I thought I knew what the problem was.

"Hey, ladies," I said as they paused long enough to hear me. "Can I just run something past you?"

Their heads swiveled my way and they stared at me while they sniffed.

"I don't know how you've missed this, seeing as your sole pastime this last few months has been to have as much sex as possible to get pregnant."

"Missed what?" Bronte wiping her nose with her hand.

"Have either of you done a pregnancy test recently?"

Ellie frowned. "I think I'd know if I was late, Nancy. I have charts you know."

"Same." Bronte laughed and shook her head disdainfully. "And what do you mean you have charts? You never told me."

"Well unlike you, Bronte," Ellie said with a rapid blink and a head wobble. "I don't feel it necessary to advertise that I'm trying for a baby with my husband."

Lily snorted and I almost choked.

"I'm sorry, Ellie," I said around a cough. "But you and Hunt do nothing but advertise your sex life and have done so since the day you got together. The whole town has seen Hunter's bare ass or heard you screaming for Jesus at some point."

Narrowed eyes swung my way. "The point being, Nancy," she bit out. "Is that I would know."

"You are pretty distracted with sex," Lily added. "Mom said she's started calling ahead before she comes near to the house and seeing as you live like a few feet away from us it's a little annoying."

"So not true," Ellie grumbled.

"I would know anyways," Bronte said. "I have been pregnant before and my period isn't due…" She trailed off and then she mouthed fuck before rushing off. "Carter, we need to go to the mall real quick."

"No way," Ellie yelled. "She's not. She will not. Hunter, baby, start the truck." Then she ran off too.

"Thank god you're here," Lily said, laying her head on my shoulder. "They are so tiring to be around."

We both laughed and I just hoped that I hadn't got it wrong because imagine the tantrums there might be.

*

"Have you seen Bronte?" Austen asked, brushing a hand through his hair. "She promised me a ride into town an hour ago. I have someone to meet."

Lily snorted and I nudged her. "Leave him alone, Lily. When a boy has a date, he can get anxious."

"I'm not anxious," he protested.

"You've got a little vein just here." I pointed above my nose and between my eyes. "It's throbbing."

Austen's finger went to the same place on his own face and then glared at me. "I do not." Then he turned to Lily. "Do I Lil?"

She rolled her eyes. Closer to Austen's age she didn't feel the need to soften the blow. "Austen you look fine, but if you carry on the way you're going aren't you worried that either your dick will drop off or the very least your lips."

"Why is everyone giving me shit about girls. I bet no one gave Carter or Hunter crap, and what about Shaw he was banging Ruthie Grey when he was my age."

Something swooped in my stomach at the mention of Shaw and Ruthie banging. Banging at any age but talk of them banging at the age when he and I were supposed to go to prom together was worse.

"I don't want to think about anyone banging, thanks." Lily shuddered. "But all I'm saying is you have a lot of years of *banging* ahead of you."

"What you're saying is don't use all my love juice up now, before I get to college?"

"No!" we both cried in unison.

He shook his head. "You two are weird. I'm going to ask Mom or Dad if they'll take me."

I looked over to where the older members of the party were sitting. Each one of them was rolling drunk. They'd been getting louder and louder as the afternoon had worn on and we hadn't even eaten yet. Jim particularly seemed to have been distracted by the beer and shots.

"I'm not sure that will happen, Austen." I pointed to his dad who was now on his hands and knees and braying like a donkey.

"God, they're so embarrassing." He groaned and then suddenly his face lit up. "Shaw, are you drunk?"

My heart jumped a beat as Shaw's shadow loomed over us. I swallowed and gave myself a rapid talking to. I had no damn idea why I was so nervous around him all of a sudden. We'd know each other for years and we'd had sex. I'd seen his beautiful penis. His beautiful penis had been in my vagina.

"I've had a few, why?" Shaw's voice boomed into my senses.

"He wants a ride into town," Lily sighed. "He's got a hot date."

"Another?"

"What?" Austen gasped. "I've told you that the ladies love me."

"Well no, I can't give you a ride. I've had too much to drink."

I chanced a look up at him and almost jumped when I realized that his gaze was on me. Swallowing I smiled tentatively. I expected something back, but I didn't expect him to practically curl his lip in disdain and then turn away.

"What's eating him?" Lily asked.

I shrugged wishing I knew. I didn't think about it any longer though because Ellie and Bronte came running into the yard, jostling with each other. We all watched in rapt attention as they started to jog across the lawn toward the house, elbowing each other out of the way. When they got to the house, they both rushed inside yelling about bathrooms. As they disappeared, Hunter and Carter strolled into the yard. Rett immediately left the blanket that he and Tia were now playing on and ran to his daddy.

Carter bent down and picked him up and kissed each of his cheeks in turn and then blew a raspberry on his belly. Rett's laughter sounded out and that space in my heart twinged again.

Hunter sauntered over to us, rubbing a hand up and down his face. "Who got inside the house first?" he asked.

"Ellie by a nose I think," I replied. "Is it what I think it is?"

"I fucking hope so, Nance, because I'm tired as shit. I have to perform when we go to bed, perform when we wake up. Pretty much perform at any given time."

"Hunter," Lily protested. "Have we not had this conversation."

"Sorry, Lily but I need a break from sex." He rubbed his hands against his cheeks. "Who'd have thought it Hunter Delaney saying he needs a break from sex. I'm broken. Truly fucking broken. That woman has fucking broken me." He shook his head and muttered under his breath about his penis breaking off.

When I then looked over to Carter to see if he was just as tired, I saw that Shaw had joined him. He was holding Tia who was playing with Rett passing a ball between the two of them. When Rett dropped the ball Tia turned to Shaw and started playing with his chin. The smile that he gave to her was huge and if there hadn't already been bright sunshine it would have lit up the sky. God, I wanted him and was sick of the love/hate game that we were playing. It seemed though that Shaw was not on the same wavelength.

"Hunter!" I turned to see Ellie standing on the threshold of the patio door, beckoning her husband over. "*Hunter*."

Hunter turned and Lily and I watched as he looked at her. When she nodded and bit on her top lip the look that crossed his face was one of pure wonderment. The love between them was clear and brought tears to my eyes. When Bronte then came rushing up behind Ellie with a huge grin on her face, she made to move past her. She must have also seen the look on Hunter's face though because like the beautiful person she was, Bronte smiled softly and took a step back into the house.

Hunter rushed to Ellie and took her in his arms and held her tight. When he whispered the words, "God, I love you so fucking much," I didn't think that I'd seen anything more beautiful or anything that I'd wanted as much for myself.

"Looks like they get to steal the day then," Lily said, her gaze on the same place as mine.

"Looks like it."

The gate into the garden then burst open and Lynn-Ann and Janice-Ann, Jefferson's sisters burst in.

"Hey everyone," they cried together. "Guess what, we're getting married!"

"Oh shit," Lily groaned. "Jefferson is going to bust a nut."

When I looked over to their brother, I could see Lily had a point. He was now a deep shade of purple.

I looked over to Hunter and Ellie wondering whether they were upset that the twins had stolen their thunder. Looking at them though it didn't appear that it had even registered with them, they were so wrapped up in each other and their own news. Wanting them to keep their moment private I looked away and my gaze landed on Shaw. He was standing right next to me.

"Oh hey," I said, feeling a blush creep up my neck.

"Quite the day for announcements." He nodded to Carter. "He told me where he and Bronte got to. It seems it was quite the race with Hunter and Ellie."

I glanced over my shoulder to see that Hunter and Ellie had now disappeared, so they had probably gone inside the house to have their moment alone.

"Nothing you want to announce?" Shaw asked, surprising me. "To add to the day."

"Me?" I pointed at my chest. "I don't have anything I need to announce, no."

He shrugged and looked me up and down. "Funny that, I was sure you were going to tell us all you were back with Minnesota."

What the hell was he talking about?

"Why would I do that?"

This time the look he gave me had a curled lip and felt like he might hate me a little bit.

"Desperation, Nancy," he replied. "Because let's face it no one else seems to want you."

I'd been used to Shaw's comments before. We'd played the game for a long time, but never before had he made me want to cry. This time though, I could have sobbed.

Nancy's Bitch List for Shaw

- ☐ *Maximus Douchimus*
- ☐ *Captain Shitsmear*
- ☐ *Shit Talking Cock Womble*
- ☐ *Dildohead*
- ☐ *Dipshit Cockhead*
- ☐ *Scrote Noggin*
- ☐ *~~Assilicious~~ Fat Ass*
- ☐ *Fucknuckle*
- ☐ *Bronocchio*
- ☐ *Asshobbit*

☐ *Jerkass*
☐ ~~*Studly McStudly*~~
☐ *I have no name bad enough for how sad he's made me*

CHAPTER 28

Shaw

My head was all over the place.

My daughter could be about to be taken away from me. I was trying to study for when I went back to school after summer break and Nancy Andrews had me in knots.

I wasn't sure which of my problems to take on next in my ever-growing list of *Shaw's Shit List*. In order of importance, it was most definitely Tia first but what was worrying me was that Nancy was second. I'd worked hard to become a lawyer, but Nancy Fucking Andrews was currently more significant than that.

I couldn't sleep for thinking about either her or Tia. Sometimes it was both of them because I couldn't get out of my head what Tate had said about getting myself a serious relationship. It was something that I couldn't stop thinking about. I didn't think that I wanted to be with Nancy just for that reason, in fact I was sure of it. It was plain and simple. I wanted Nancy period. My feelings for her had been changing for a while and it suddenly didn't feel so much fun throwing her shade. Yet at Henry and Melinda's barbeque I hadn't been able to stop myself.

She'd looked so damn hurt the moment that I'd said it, I wanted to take it back. I wanted to get down on my knees and beg her to forgive me. I wanted to tell her I didn't mean a fucking word of it. It wasn't long after that she left. She told Lily that she had a headache, well she sure was getting a lot of those lately. Skipping Jefferson and Kitty's engagement party and then the barbeque with a headache. I was thinking that the headache she was leaving for was actually mine and was called Minnesota.

He was why I hadn't begged her to forgive me. He was why I'd said those words in the first place. She'd gone back to him after everything he'd done, and he damn well didn't deserve her. Not sure I did either but at least I knew I would treat her right if I got the opportunity. Which was funny as hell seeing as I talked shit to her on a regular basis and I'd hurt her with my shit talk.

"Hey Shaw."

I looked up to see Hunter grinning at me. Sighing I dropped my gaze down to the burger on my plate. All I'd wanted was to take a peaceful lunch break, but no, here was one half of Dayton's favorite comedy duo to brighten up my day.

"Hey, Hunt."

I waved a hand at him, hoping that he'd move on, but he didn't. He sat down at my table and poured some water from the jug into a glass. All the while grinning like an idiot.

"I heard your news," I said. "Congrats."

"Thanks, buddy." The grin got wider, and he straightened in his seat. "I am so fucking excited."

"That why you and Ellie left early on Saturday?"

"Yep, she did the test in the bathroom in her old room."

"I heard. I also heard that my sister did one in the family bathroom." I shook my head. "I thought those two were in a race to announce their pregnancy first yet they both ran home without telling anyone."

Hunter laughed and called to Delphine that he wanted his usual, before turning back to me. "I guess it wasn't so important who was first, just that they were. Carter is meeting me here for lunch actually."

"Great," I muttered. "Two for the price of one."

"They both saw the doc," Hunter continued. "He gave them both the same due date. Can you believe that?"

"Great. Now I have an image in my head of you both banging your wives at exactly the same time and seeing as one of them is my sister, I kinda feel sick."

A hand reached across to my plate. "Does that mean you're not finishing that burger?"

"No, it fucking doesn't." I whacked his hand with my knuckles. "What the hell are you doing here anyway? I thought you were busy branding this week."

"Nope, next week which is why Pop gave me some downtime this week. Carter and I are going to have some lunch and then go over to Jesse Connor's place in Bridge Vale. He's got a pony that he's selling, and I want to take a look at it. Carter is going to give his veterinary expertise."

"You're buying your kid a pony already?"

"Yep." He looked proud of himself.

"Does Ellie know?" The grin disappeared. "You are in so much fucking trouble my friend."

Hunter shook his head. "She's so damn happy at the moment nothing would piss on her grits, not even me getting our tiny little peanut a pony."

He looked pretty ecstatic himself and I felt a twinge of envy. I had a daughter but no one to share that joy with, and that was even if I got to keep her.

"Anyway," Hunter said. "What's up with you? You look like shit."

"Well, thank you. You're too damn kind." I sighed and pushed my unfinished burger away. "You know Tia's grandmother wants her back?"

He nodded. "Yeah, I heard. That's crap man."

"I'm waiting for a visit from Child Services, and they'll make the decision. I'm hoping that because I'm in the process of having my name added to her birth certificate and have applied to enroll her for childcare at college that they'll see I'm serious."

"You're going to take her to college with you?" Hunter blew out a breath and relaxed back in his chair. "That's a big commitment."

"I know and it might not come to that. Mom has offered to take care of her during the week if I'm at school, but I don't know." I shrugged. "It doesn't feel right just leaving her or asking Mom. Her and Dad should be enjoying almost having an empty nest, not starting again with my kid."

Hunter levelled me with serious look. "Shaw you know they wouldn't have offered if they didn't want to. That's why we're all going to be such great parents, because we have amazing ones of our own."

He was right, I knew that, but I still felt bad asking Mom and Dad to help out.

"You know what you need?" Hunter said, giving me a wink.

"What's that?" I sighed, expecting some remark about sex.

"A woman who wants to marry you and take your kid on as their own."

"And there he is, the neanderthal prick." I rolled my eyes and Hunter burst out laughing.

"I'm joking you idiot." He picked up my screwed-up napkin and threw it at me. "You've got this. If anyone can do it, you can."

I was saved from some emotional, less than manly reaction by the door opening and Carter calling hello to Delphine. I smiled and waved, but when I saw Minnesota was closely following behind, my hand went into a fist.

It was getting that I hated the sight of him. We'd never been particularly friendly, even though we were in the same class at school. He was always the cocky jock with model good looks while I was the cocky nerd with the boy next door good looks, and we seemed to clash a fair bit. Minnesota was the least likeable of the three Michaels brothers, not that I knew their older brother Tallahassee that well. Tally worked as a soccer coach in the UK and had done so for the last twelve years. He was now married with a couple of kids and Alaska always talked highly of him. I remembered he used to have a thing for Bronte when he was in college and she was in high school, but nothing ever came of it because after his first year he transferred to the UK and never came back except for a vacation every now and then.

It was just a pity that Minnesota hadn't been the one to go overseas—oh yeah wait, he did that and came back and took my woman.

Fuck. What the hell was I thinking? She was no more my woman than Taylor Swift would ever write a love song about me. Then again, I was no Jake Gyllenhaal.

"Hey, guys," Carter smiled, but it looked a little forced. "Look who invited himself to lunch."

Minnesota, without waiting to be invited, sat down next to Hunter and picked up a menu. He was still tanned from his travels, and he had a bunch of boho bracelets on his wrist and his hair was a little longer than it used to be. He was so good looking that I hated him a little bit more.

"Minnesota," Hunter said, with a tightness to his voice. "You still haven't left to finish your travels?"

"Nope." He didn't even look up, the arrogant bastard.

"Have you ordered?" Carter asked, sitting next to me. "I don't know what to have."

Hunter snorted. "We all know exactly what you'll have."

"I think that I might go healthy."

Hunter and I raised our eyebrows knowing that would never happen. When Delphine appeared at the table with her pad and pencil ready, my brother-in-law proved us right by ordering what he always had.

"All-day breakfast please, Delphine."

"Okay." She grinned undoubtedly thinking the same as us. "Minnesota?"

"Burger and coffee please Delphine." He didn't sound particularly happy, and I wondered if he'd had a fight with Nancy.

Damn it, I hoped he'd had a fight with Nancy.

"What's with your face?" I asked.

"Nothing." He shook his head. "What makes you say that?"

"You look like you lost fifty dollars and found a cent." I had to poke that bear. "You on the outs with Nancy or something?"

Carter's head shot up from looking at his phone and he made a strange sound in the back of his throat. By the look on his face my little shit of a brother had told my gossipy sister about Nance and me. She'd told Carter, who was now wondering where this conversation was going.

Minnesota folded his arms over his chest and studied me. "Well, you'd like that wouldn't you."

"I would?"

"We all know you've got a permanent hard on for her, Shaw. You've had it since high school and still do."

"You're a dick," I growled.

"You're not denying it then?" He snickered and then picked up the sugar dispenser, drawing a circle on the red and white check tablecloth.

Carter took it off him and slammed it down on the table. "Don't. Delphine doesn't want to have to clean up your shit."

Minnesota sighed and held his hands up in surrender. "You guys all get married and turn into boring old men. Even Alaska."

"We can't all go roaming around the world," Hunter replied. "Some of us don't even want to."

Minnesota looked at me and grinned. "Nancy did though, yet you think you're what she needs. Isn't that right, Shaw?"

What the fuck was with him? Why was he talking shit like that? No, we'd never been big buddies, but we'd never been openly hostile to each other before. Okay, maybe I'd started it, but he deserved it after what he'd done to Nancy.

"What the hell is your problem?" I asked.

He shook his head. "No problem. I have nothing but good memories of my time with Nancy, if you know what I mean." He winked and smirked and I wanted to punch him in the fucking face until he at least spat a tooth out.

"You disrespectful, dick," I hissed quietly as a woman walked past with her two small kids. "Don't you dare talk about her like that."

"Why's that Shaw because you've got similar memories? Wanna trade experiences?"

That was it. I stood up, toppling my chair to the floor and leaned over the table pointing in his face.

"Shut your fucking mouth." I looked over to the woman, who I didn't recognize. "Sorry ma'am but he's been discourteous about a lady that we know."

Minnesota snorted. "She may be a lady in public, but in the bedroom let's say she's less than that."

I grabbed his t-shirt and pulled him closer. "I told you to shut it. Do not say another word."

"Oh come on, Shaw," he sneered. "You do know she only wants you for your family, right?"

"Minnesota," Carter barked. "I suggest you do as Shaw says."

"Just go," Hunter added. "Before Shaw really lets loose on you."

"Shaw, buddy," Carter said his hand on my arm. "Let him go."

I dropped my hand from Minnesota's tee and watched as he stood up and then smoothed it down with his hands. He went to within a couple of steps from the door and then turned around.

"I mean it, Shaw," he said. "She only wants you for your family."

I shook my head. "What the hell are you talking about?"

"Family," he replied. "She fucking loves family. She hasn't got one of her own so yours will do. Little orphan Nancy just loves your mom and dad and wants them for her own and if that means latching on to you then so be it. And now you've got a kid as well, damn it, Shaw you've played right into Nancy's greedy little hands."

It was then that we heard the gasp and our gazes swung to the doorway. None of us had seen Nancy come in but I was sure she'd heard every word. When I saw the tears springing in her eyes, I knew I was right.

CHAPTER 29

Nancy

It felt like Minnesota had just turned around and punched me in the stomach. The air rushed from my lungs and pain radiated through me, from my gut up to my heart. He'd hurt me when he'd left me to go on *our* trip without me, but that had been nothing like this.

"Nancy." Shaw took a step toward me, but I shook my head and turned to Minnesota.

"How dare you?" I managed to get out with a strangled tone.

He mouthed, 'Oh fuck' and looked up at the ceiling but made no attempt to apologize or come to me. In that moment I didn't think I'd ever hated anyone more.

"You're a fucking bastard," Shaw growled at him and then moved to me.

"No," I said, holding up my hand. "Don't."

With my heart breaking, I turned and ran from Delphine's back down Main Street to where my car was parked.

All I wanted to do was get back to my apartment and be alone. It wasn't even like I had a job to go to. Mrs. Baker had pretty much fired me on the spot when I'd given her my notice earlier. It might have been premature but even if the bank didn't come off, I couldn't work for her any longer. She was a mean-spirited old buzzard who didn't deserve to work with the beautiful children that were in her care. I knew because of her I was more determined to help Mrs. Ranger get her kids at the custody hearing in a week's time.

I ran across Main Street, dodging a truck, and ignored Shaw shouting my name. I couldn't talk to him. What if he believed Minnesota? What if he really thought that I was going to try and trap him just because I loved his family. I mean I thought that they were great but that didn't mean I'd try and get with Shaw because of them.

What hurt was that I'd told Minnesota how I felt about family because we were getting closer, and I thought that I could trust him. Yet he thought it was okay to shout it out it in front of a load of people. It was like he'd never really understood how lonely it was having no one in the world. Like I'd just told him I had a headache, not constant heartache at losing my mom and dad at the same time.

I should have known at the time that he wasn't the right man for me. He'd given me a perfunctory hug and said, 'well I ain't that close to mine, so don't get your hopes up'. It was an out and out lie. A lie he'd told because even then what he really meant was don't pin your hopes on him being the man that I'd settle down with.

Reaching my car, I beeped the lock and opened the door, but Shaw's voice calling me wasn't far behind. I really didn't want to talk to him about it, it was too embarrassing. I wasn't quick enough though and before I had a chance to get in the car, he grabbed a hold of my arm and spun me around.

"Damn it, Nancy," he said, breathing a little heavy. "You sure can run fast when you want to."

"I don't want you here, Shaw. Just go away." Pushing a hand against his chest, I wasn't surprised when he didn't move even an inch. Instead, he reached for my hand and pulled me to him.

"Why are you embarrassed? He's the one who should be embarrassed."

"Why?" I said lowering my voice as Cindy Burbank who worked at the flower shop, passed us. "Because it's pathetic, yearning after other people's families just because I don't have one of my own."

"You really think that I'd believe that was the only reason you've had sex with me?" he lifted the corner of his mouth and grinned. "I mean it has to be because of my amazing penis, right."

He did have a point. "It's not for your humility, that's for sure." I dropped my face to my hands to hide the tears that were still threatening. "I told him that because I thought he cared. Because I thought I meant something to him."

"He's a dick," Shaw growled.

Then something struck me. "Do you think that's why he dumped me, because he thought I only wanted him for his family? Because I didn't." I shook my head. "I would never date anyone for any other reason than I liked them and wanted to be with them. I wouldn't have sex with you for your mom and dad, I swear."

Shaw shuddered. "Please don't talk about sex with me and my parents in the same breath, Nance. It's not pleasant."

That made me give a little laugh and suddenly I felt embarrassed for a whole different reason.

"I overreacted, didn't I?"

He shook his head and put a hand on my shoulder. "No, no way," he replied, his thumb grazing my neck and sending goosebumps all over my body. "Like you said, you told him because you thought you were close enough to share that."

"Still, it's not like it's the end of the world." I sagged, wanting to lean into his touch but it felt like it might be too needy, especially after what he'd just heard.

Shaw nodded and then removed his hand and rubbed it over his head. I missed him touching me, but I could see he was looking a little uncomfortable. Evidently, he was embarrassed at having touched me like that.

"Afternoon kids." It was Mr. Callahan, and he was looking particularly happy with himself.

"Hey, Mr. C," Shaw replied, giving him a quick nod of his head. When Mr. Callahan stopped walking, Shaw groaned under his breath. "Fuck."

"I believe Jacob has your trophy, young man," Mr. Callahan said, slapping Shaw on the back. "I can bring it around to the house if you'd like, or maybe we could have a presentation."

Taking advantage of Shaw being distracted by Mr. Callahan I put one foot inside the car. Shaw was on high alert though and grabbed my arm.

"Sorry Mr. C, can we do this another time?" he asked, his eyes on me. "Nancy and I have something important to discuss."

Mr. Callahan chuckled and shook his head. "No problem, but you take care that discussion doesn't lead to another baby."

"Oh my god," I groaned. "Can this day get any more embarrassing?"

"Only if you're caught with Shaw's bare ass in the air." Mr. Callahan laughed again and then carried on walking.

"I need to go."

"You don't," Shaw replied. "We need to talk."

"We don't," I said, with a heavy sigh. "And you didn't need to come running after me. And you certainly don't need to worry that I had sex with you for your folks."

He shrugged. "Well, I guess now that you're back with Minnesota, that'll be the end of it."

I took a step back and frowned, curious as to what he meant. "Sorry?"

"Now you're back with him. Unless you've changed your mind after that."

"I'm not back with him." I curled my lip at the thought of it. "Why would you think that?"

Shaw leaned his head closer to mine and peered at my eyes. "You're not?"

"No." I shook myself. "Not ever going to happen. Like you said, he's a dick."

"But I saw him coming out of your apartment."

"When were you at my apartment?" I leaned back against my car as I watched Shaw squirm a little.

"The day we were texting. The day after the engagement party."

I remembered when that was, of course I did. The day when I'd started to wonder if he actually liked me. The day before he turned back into a douche.

Wait! Was *that* why he'd turned back into a douche?

"Was that why you went back to being horrible to me?" I asked, my eyes wide with surprise. "You thought I was back with him. You were jealous?"

His eyebrows met in the middle, and he made some kind of mumbling sound. I was sure that the word no was not in there. Damn he *was* jealous.

"We'd been texting, and I thought I'd come and speak to you in person," Shaw said, holding his hands palms up in a shrug. "He was coming out of your apartment, and he hugged you. What was I supposed to think?"

"You could have asked me. I thought we'd made progress at the party. I thought we'd come to some sort of understanding." Okay, so that understanding had been he wasn't going to fuck me against a wall, and that he hadn't asked me to prom like I'd thought. It was enough for me to think that we were kind of friends though. "I felt like we were becoming friends and so you should have hung around and knocked on my door and asked me."

He looked at me through his lashes and grimaced. "I guess I should have, instead I acted like a dick and I'm sorry for that."

"If I was going to get back with him, and I promise you that I'm not, I would tell you."

Something passed over his face that I couldn't read. He almost looked shy, but this was Shaw Jackson. Mr. Confident.

"Why would you tell me?" he asked, pulling his shoulders back and taking a step closer.

My heart started to thud a fast beat at his nearness and tingles of electricity shot over my skin as I contemplated being honest. Of telling him how I really felt. When he lifted a finger and ran it down my cheek, I knew that this was my opportunity. For once I was going to be frank about what I wanted. Truth be known, the whole time I'd been with Minnesota I'd been the sort of girlfriend that he wanted me to be. One who didn't mind if he took weekend breaks with his buddies or went drinking with them for hours while I waited for him to come home. I was the sort of girlfriend who planned a long, overseas trip for us when what I really wanted to do was tell him he wasn't what I wanted or needed. That I really wanted a man who would commit to me.

I took a breath and licked my lips. "I'd tell you because I like you, Shaw," I breathed out. "I'd tell you because I want there to be more between us and telling you that would give you an opportunity to step up and be honest about how you feel too."

"You don't think I'm being honest with you?" He leaned in closer so that his body was flush with mine. His hips pushing against my stomach.

"I don't think so, no," I replied, and when I moved to lean back against the car Shaw came with me. "I think you like me more than you'd like to admit."

God, I hoped that I was right. I was going to look an idiot if I wasn't, but no one ever got what they wanted by sitting in the background. Better to be an idiot than disappointed.

"Maybe you're right," he whispered, his mouth close to my ear. "Maybe I do want more than just sex. I did say we needed to talk about all *the stuff.* Do you remember that?"

I nodded, conscious that my nipples were rubbing up and down his chest with each breath I took. The anticipation and desire made them sensitive to every brush and I wondered if anyone would care if we actually had sex on the hood of my car in the middle of town.

"So how about we go back to your place and talk about *the stuff*?" he asked, his fingers linking with mine.

"Aren't you on your lunch break?" I asked.

Shaw pulled out his phone and dialed a number. When he put it to his ear, his eyes grazed up and down me.

"Hey, Evie. It's Shaw…yep. Can you tell Tate something came up. I'll be back late and catch up the time…great. See you later." He smiled at me and with a glint in his eye said, "Okay, let's go."

Nancy's Bitch List for Shaw

☐ Maximus Douchimus
☐ Captain Shitsmear
☐ Shit Talking Cock Womble
☐ Dildohead
☐ Dipshit Cockhead
☐ Scrote Noggin
☐ ~~Assilicious~~ Fat Ass
☐ Fucknuckle
☐ Bronocchio
☐ Asshobbit
☐ Jerkass
☐ ~~Studly McStudly~~
☐ I have no name bad enough for how sad he's made me
☐ Hot Sizzle

CHAPTER 30

Shaw

When we got to Nancy's apartment the tension between us was high. The anticipation was high. Fuck *I* was feeling high at the thought of just spending time with her. I wanted it enough to skip work for a few hours and I loved my job and wanted to be good at my job. Being with Nancy though seemed to be more important. It felt like I might just lose my mind if I wasn't with her. Did I want to have sex with her? Of course I fucking did. She was gorgeous, and she was starting to mean something to me. If that didn't happen though, just spending time with her would be enough.

"I'm sorry about the mess," Nancy said as she turned the key in the lock.

"I don't care," I replied, and I really didn't.

When she got inside and turned to look at me, I'm not sure who moved to who first. Maybe we were so in tune with each other that we went for each other at the same time. Suddenly we were a tangle of limbs as we kissed and tugged at each other, with our hands roaming over each other.

I wasn't the sort of guy who got glassy eyed over a girl, or who fell head over heels. I'd had deep feelings for Monique and when she left me for the professor, I was angry. Angry enough to punch him. I wasn't heartbroken though. To me, if a girl didn't want me what was the point in drawing it out by thinking about it all the time? Trying to get someone to love or like you when they'd made it clear that they didn't want you any longer was pointless. Yet the thought that I might have blown it with Nancy had me going crazy.

"Nance, we don't have to do this," I groaned against her neck. "We need to talk about *the stuff*."

"I know, but I want this too. More than anything."

When her fingers gripped my hair and she pushed herself closer to my steel hard dick, I wasn't sure I'd ever felt such a rush as I did in that moment. My head was swimming like I was drunk. My heart was hammering and the blood in my veins was at boiling point.

"Nancy, I want you to know something," I gasped as my hand went up her shirt.

"What's that?" she asked, letting her head drop back and giving me more access to her neck.

"I really, really like you and I want us to be something."

There were so many more words that I could have said. Other things that I could have told her, but I was only just getting my head around the thoughts. How could I explain them to Nancy?

"Shaw." My name was whispered from Nancy's lips, sounding like a plea.

"I need to know, Nance."

"Yes," she replied. "Yes."

Her hands pushed under my shirt that she'd already pulled from my pants and when her nails scraped up my back it was ecstasy. I reached for the zipper on her dress and slowly pulled it down. As soon as I saw her tanned shoulders, I dropped a kiss and nipped at the smooth skin that tasted and smelled of sweet coconut.

“Why do you want this?” Nancy asked, as my mouth trailed a path across her skin.

“Because I like you, *a lot*.” I gently pulled her hair, giving me more access to her neck. Then as my dick went harder than I thought possible, something real stupid came out of my mouth. “Tate, also said being in a relationship would help my custody case.”

Instantly Nancy stiffened and I knew I’d said totally the wrong thing. It hadn’t even been necessary to say it because it hadn’t even entered my head to use her in that way. It would cheapen her and our relationship.

“Hey,” I said, grabbing her hand as she took a half-step away from me. “I was joking.”

Her expression was impassive as she stood with her hands dangling down to her sides. “Did he say that?”

“Well, yes, but that isn’t why I want us to be more than fuck buddies.” I winced because even to me that sounded lame. “I swear, Nancy.”

She sucked in both her lips and took a deep breath. “I think you should go.”

Damn it, I was an absolute idiot. Why the hell didn’t I just put my brain into gear before I said anything.

“Nancy, I swear.”

She held her hand up and shook her head. “No, Shaw, I don’t want to hear it.”

“I didn’t believe what Minnesota said about you,” I protested. “When he told me that you were only interested in me for my family, I didn’t believe him.”

She threw her hands into the air. “You just admitted it, Shaw. It came from your very mouth that Tate said it would help your cause with Tia if you had a girlfriend. And then guess what? Out of the blue you suddenly you decide that you want something more with me. Well, isn’t that a coincidence.”

“I was joking. Tate was joking.” I mean I think Tate was joking.

She exhaled and turned away from me. “Well, it didn’t really sound like that.”

“Nancy.”

"Just go, Shaw. Leave me alone."

Her posture was rigid, and it was clear that she wasn't going to budge. I took a step toward the door, not giving up but giving her some time to hopefully forgive me.

"For the record, Nance," I said, pausing. "I really do like you and even if I didn't have Tia then I'd want to be with you."

Then I left and when I got into the elevator, I spent the short journey down banging my head against the wall.

***

"*Shaw.*"

Tate's voice boomed out from his office and my belly flipped. I'd only ended up being forty minutes late back from lunch and worked like a demon all afternoon to make up for it. Surely, he wasn't going to yell at me for being late. That I could do without, particularly as I was still beating myself up about Nancy.

I heaved myself out of my chair and walked down to Tate's office, rapping on the open door once I got there.

"Did you want me?"

He beckoned me in without looking up from the papers on his desk. "Shut the door."

I did as he suggested and dropped into the chair on the opposite of the desk to him. "Anything wrong?"

He looked up and flashed me a smile. "No. I have news for you."

"Oh, okay." That was even more worrying than him ripping me a new one about being late.

"Did you manage to deal with whatever your issue was at lunch?"

"Kind of." I flashed him a half smile. "That was okay, right?"

"God, yeah. I don't micromanage people, Shaw. Get your work done and I don't care whether you come in for an hour or twenty a day." He took his glasses off and threw them onto his desk. "Okay, so I've heard from child services."

My heart dropped right down to my boots. In fact, I was sure it stopped on the way down.

"What have they said? Is it bad?"

"They're coming to see you tomorrow. It's just a meeting at your house with you and Tia. They may want to speak to your mom and dad too. Do you think they can be around?"

I nodded. "I mean I think so. They-they should be okay. I'll, erm." I pointed my thumb behind me. "I'll go and call them to check."

"It's not a major issue if they can't but Tia does need to be there."

"I figured." I nodded, feeling like a damn bobble head. "W-what time are they coming?"

Tate looked down at the paper on his desk. "Nine-thirty." He looked back up at me. "Is that okay? Does that fit in with Tia's routine?"

"Yes, sure. She wakes at about seven and Mom says she's been taking a nap at about nine until ten, so that will give them the opportunity to talk to me first."

"That sounds good. Now, if your mom and dad are there make sure that you are the one that does everything for Tia. Let them see that your mom and dad are all in, but make sure it's clear that you're the care giver."

"Do I tell them that Mom offered to care for her when I'm at school? I mean I've applied for childcare at school, but if we can't get her in…" I scrubbed a hand down my face. "Fuck, I'm petrified Tate. What if they decide to give her back to Mrs. Devonshire?"

Tate smiled. "This is a huge change from the guy who sat nervously on a plane to Wichita hoping to god he wasn't going to be a dad."

I shrugged. "I know, but she's kind of cute, you know. She has a way of getting you to fall in love with her."

"As it should be, Shaw. Exactly as it should be." He picked up his glasses and put them on to read through another paper in front of him. "You'll be meeting a Mrs. Shelby and a Mr. Alexander. I don't think you need me there; it might look a little too hostile."

"Yep, I agree."

"Excellent." He then took another file and opened it up. "The other thing I needed to touch base about was the custody hearing for Mrs. Ranger."

I blinked, having totally forgotten that it was a place of work and Tate wasn't just my personal lawyer.

"It looks like we're going to need Nancy's testimony," Tate said giving me a thin-lipped smile. "The father has brought in some child psychologist to testify that the kids, especially Eddie have suffered some form of PTSD while living with the mother."

"That's bullshit. Nancy told me the kid was only ever miserable when his dad picked him up."

"I know. He's throwing money at it, or rather his mommy's money. I'm pretty sure she's the driving force behind the case."

"Asshole."

"Exactly. The point is we need Nancy, so after the meeting with Child Services tomorrow I want you to concentrate on prepping her. Is that okay?"

It wasn't an ideal way to spend time with Nancy, but it was a way. She wouldn't be able to say no because it was for Eddie and Molly Ranger after all. Call me a dick, but I was going to use that time to persuade her to give me another chance. I was going to prove to her that I really did want her for her and not to be a mother to my daughter. Although, that was a thought that kind of excited me.

"Is it okay, Shaw?" Tate asked.

"Absolutely," I replied. "I'm looking forward to it."

CHAPTER 31

Nancy

Disappointment is a strange thing. It can range from, meh that was shit, to damnit I want to cry for weeks. The disappointment that I was feeling in Shaw was definitely at the higher end of the scale. It was hurtful to think that he might have considered wanting a relationship with me just to get custody of his daughter. I knew we'd had sex way before Tia arrived in his life, but it was no coincidence that he started to get interested in something more after her arrival.

I'd been a fool to think it was anything more. I'd wanted it and must have been blind. Well thank goodness he told me before I let him near me with that pretty penis of his. Even having the keys to the bank wasn't cheering me up from my misery.

"I think Don Jennings felt bad for messing you around," Belinda said as we stood in the middle of the main room and looked around. "Because you know it's not usual to have the keys before the deal has gone through."

"It's a cash sale and Mr. Jackson sent him the letter of intent and the proof of funds as my financial advisor."

Belinda grinned. "That was a great idea, sugar. This isn't Jim's first rodeo. I knew he'd do the right thing for you."

I'd agreed a couple of days ago to have Jim, Shaw's dad, be my financial advisor. I was now second guessing that decision since my conversation with his son the night before. This was business though and I wouldn't like the small matter of a dented heart spoil it.

"Whatcha going to do first?" Belinda asked, her eyes full of the excitement that I was sadly lacking.

"I need to get my apartment up for sale actually," I replied. "Is there a chance you can come over later and get the ball rolling?"

"Sure sugar. I have a two pm, but I can be with you by four. Does that fit in with you?"

I nodded, glad that I was finally getting things started. "The apartment here is good as is, so once the money is wired over and the contracts signed, I can move in. Will that make it easier for you to sell? It being empty."

"I won't make much difference. To be honest though," she said leaning in close. "I already have someone who I think might be interested. It's a much sought-after complex with the younger people in town."

"That's great news. Thank you, Belinda, I really appreciate everything that you've done on this."

I took out a notebook and tape measure from my bag, so I'd be ready to order furniture and equipment. I wasn't going to do anything until everything was finalized, but at least I'd have all the measurements. I didn't have a lot of money for that sort of thing anyway, not until I sold my apartment. It just felt a wasted opportunity to stand there and look around without doing anything productive.

"You want me to stay and help you?" Belinda asked.

"Not really." Then something struck me. "Are you okay leaving me here when I don't officially own it."

She waved a hand at me. "Oh, sure. It's not like you're going to take vacant possession." She looked at me wide-eyed and laughed. "Are you?"

"No, Belinda, I wouldn't do that to you." As much as Don Jennings didn't deserve it after the shit he tried to pull with Ruthie.

"Okay then." Belinda pulled me in for a hug. "Early congratulations, Nancy. I'll shoot and leave you to it."

We said our goodbyes and then I was left alone with my dream. It seemed a little empty and sad. I was sure though that the excitement would come, once I'd got over Shaw.

I'd been measuring the different rooms and making notes for about an hour when I heard footsteps in the main room.

"Hello," I shouted, moving back to the doorway and wishing I'd locked up after Belinda left. I wasn't one for the dramatic but whoever it was might be wanting to rob the place.

"Hey, Nancy."

I sighed with relief when I saw it was Bronte. "Oh hey, thank goodness it's you."

"I'm sorry, did you think that it was Shaw?"

I hadn't but now that she mentioned it. "Just worried it was someone wanting to rob me."

"I guess even that's better than my brother at the moment."

"You heard then?"

She nodded and putting her purse down on the floor came over to me. "He's so sorry, Nancy. He really didn't mean it you know."

"He said it though." I replied, feeling a tightness in my chest.

"I think he thought it was a joke of sorts." She reached for my hand and gave it a squeeze. "He's miserable."

I shrugged. "Well so am I."

"You don't have to be," she said with the corner of her mouth lifting into a smile. "You could give him another chance and then make him pay for the rest of his life."

I laughed quietly because she did have a point. I just wasn't sure I'd ever trust that Shaw truly liked me.

"This place is looking good though," Bronte said, looking around the room.

"It looks the same as when we viewed it." I rolled my eyes. "It is great though, Bronte, and I wouldn't have done this without you pushing me."

"I'm just glad you had faith in yourself. In any case," she said, nudging me. "I took Rett out of Mrs. Baker's, so you'll need to get up and running soon."

"Bronte, we haven't even finalized the contract yet."

"But you will. When you start signing kids up don't forget Ellie and I want to be the first ones."

"Is that going to be a race too."

"That is one I'm winning. You know we both got the same due date, right?"

"I heard. Lily told me." I pulled her in for a hug. "Whoever wins that race, I'm happy for you both."

She beamed at me and while Bronte was naturally beautiful all the time, she certainly was glowing.

"Anyways," she said stooping to pick up her purse. "I should go. I need to get to Mom and Dad's."

"Will you tell your dad that I'll go over to his office tomorrow to sort out the final paperwork."

Bronte nodded and then frowned. "He's working from home today and then having a few days off. It may be better if you go over to the house. I think he said he'd be free at about ten."

I wasn't sure about that. It might mean bumping into Shaw.

"You're going to have to speak to Shaw at some point, Nancy. He is your legal representative." She cleared her throat. "He's working today anyways."

I nodded. "Okay, maybe I'll pop over to the house."

"Don't forget, ten is when he's free."

Once Bronte had left, I realized that she was right, I would need to see Shaw at some point, so perhaps it was best to get it over and done with.

***

When I knocked on the Jackson's front door and Shaw answered, I wasn't totally surprised. I had no idea what it was, but on the drive over I'd had a feeling that he would be the first person that I saw.

"Nancy," he said, sounding surprised. "I thought you were someone else."

"Sorry." I looked behind me. "Are you expecting someone?"

He scratched his neck and seemed unsure on what to answer. Before he had a chance to open his mouth, Darcy appeared.

"Nancy, oh hey. Come on in."

"Mom," Shaw warned. "They're going to be here soon."

"They said they were running late; they could be hours yet."

I had no clue who 'they' were, but it seemed important. Then it struck me Shaw was home yet dressed in a button down and dress pants and Darcy had definitely had a blow out of her hair, seeing as it was particularly big today.

"Is it your Child Services visit today?"

Shaw's face colored but it was Darcy who answered. "It is, and you being here is perfect. You can tell them all about your new venture and how you've agreed to take Tia."

"Mom, no," Shaw growled. "I'm sorry, Nance. Just ignore her. If it's about the bank, can we talk later?"

I was going to respond when I heard a car behind me.

"They're here," Darcy hissed and reached out her hand to grab mine. "Quick Nancy come on in."

She dragged me into the hallway and when she did, I spotted Bronte and Jim both peering around the doorway of the lounge. Bronte had an impish grin on her face, and I realized then that I'd been played. I narrowed my eyes on her, but she didn't appear to care one bit that she'd been rumbled.

"Come on in, Nance," she said with the slight tinkle of laughter. "You're just who we need."

The people from Child Services introduced themselves to everyone and then asked who each of us were. The whole time that Bronte, Jim and Darcy spoke, I watched Shaw and noted how scared he looked. Tia was apparently taking a nap, but it didn't escape me that he kept lifting up the baby monitor to his ear, and then peering at the camera screen, double checking on her. He smiled at me a couple of times and while Darcy had made everyone some lemonade, he'd sidled up to me and told me I didn't need to stay. I couldn't walk now though, especially if talking about my preschool would help him to keep Tia.

"And who are you?" Mrs. Shelby a kindly looking lady with a sharp pixie cut asked.

"This is Nancy," Shaw said. "She's a family friend and owns the new preschool that we're hoping to send Tia to."

I frowned at him, wondering why he'd felt the need to answer on my behalf. Maybe he'd thought I'd tell them that he was a liar and would be a terrible father. That was far from the truth though. He was a great dad considering he had little to no experience.

"Ah okay," Mrs. Shelby said writing something on her pad. "So, when does your school open Nancy?"

"I have a three-month deadline," I lied. "I'm just about to start interviewing teachers." Damn I'd be going to hell for the lies I was telling. Well, they weren't exactly lies, more stretching the truth. I had the advertisement written up, I just needed to speak to the recruitment consultant in Middleton Ridge.

"That's excellent," Mr. Alexander added. "And you would help Shaw until then?" he asked Darcy.

She nodded and Bronte said, "Me too."

Then I had no clue why I said what I said, but the words just tumbled out of my mouth. "Obviously as Shaw's girlfriend I'll mostly be helping."

It was then that Shaw dropped the baby monitor, and I thought that I was most definitely going to hell.

Nancy's Bitch List for Shaw

- ☐ Maximus Douchimus
- ☐ Captain Shitsmear
- ☐ Shit Talking Cock Womble
- ☐ Dildohead

- ☐ Dipshit Cockhead
- ☐ Scrote Noggin
- ☐ ~~Assilicious~~ Fat Ass
- ☐ Fucknuckle
- ☐ Bronocchio
- ☐ Asshobbit
- ☐ Jerkass
- ☐ ~~Studly McStudly~~
- ☐ I have no name bad enough for how sad he's made me
- ☐ ~~Hot Sizzle~~
- ☐ Douche Canoe

CHAPTER 32

Shaw

What the hell was Nancy talking about? As my girlfriend?

Hadn't that been the exact reason why she'd thrown me out of her apartment?

"Oh, okay," Mrs. Shelby said, smiling at Nancy and then me. "I didn't realize that you were in a relationship Shaw. Is it a new one or is this long-standing."

"Eleven months, thirty-three days," Nancy answered with a cute little shrug.

Bronte coughed and Dad patted her on the back as Mom stared at me looking like she'd taken some crazy drug.

"It was a friend's wedding," Nancy added. "Although, we've known each other since kindergarten."

"How lovely." Mrs. Shelby turned to Mr. Alexander and evidently gave him some silent message because he nodded and wrote something down on his pad.

"All my checks should be up to date for the kindergarten that I work at." Nancy clearly knew what the secret message was. "Well, actually I don't work there any longer. I gave notice yesterday."

She did? I had no idea. Why the hell didn't she tell me? Oh, yes, because I'd been an idiot and said the wrong thing.

"You did?" Mom asked.

Nancy nodded. "Mrs. Baker was really sad to see me go."

It was at that moment that I saw movement on the baby monitor screen and heard Tia moving around.

"I'd better go and get her," I said, pointing to the monitor. "She's finished her nap."

Mrs. Shelby smiled and then immediately wrote something in her pad as I left the room. When I got to Tia's room, she was already sitting up in the bed and babbling away to her teddy bear. She let out a big yawn and stretched and damn she looked cute with her blonde hair all messy.

"Hey, sweetheart. You woke up."

Tia's head turned to me, and she gave me a huge smile. She certainly was starting to settle and had seemed much happier over the last week or so.

"Dada."

"Hello, baby girl. Did you have a nice sleep?"

She lifted up her arms for me and continued babbling away. She was getting good at waking up, not grumpy at all. I guessed she must take after Monique for that because it certainly wasn't me.

"Dada, biscy."

"Okay, sweetheart. We'll get you a biscuit." I lifted her and with a deep breath took her out to meet her public.

***

"Well, that went well," Mom said as she bounced Tia up and down on her knee after Mrs. Shelby and Mr. Alexander had left.

I glanced over at Nancy who was standing near the doorway, her eyes darting around the room, looking ready to bolt.

"Yeah, it did," I replied with a great sense of relief. "I think Nancy helped a lot."

Her gaze rested on me, and she gave me a small smile and I was aware that we needed to talk. I needed to know why she'd done what she'd done after our conversation the day before. "Do you have a minute, Nance?" I asked.

She nodded. "I guess so."

I walked past her and out toward the yard. I figured she was following me because I heard Mom ask someone, 'What do you think that was all about?'.

"You didn't have to do that," I said turning to face her once we were a safe distance from the house. I loved the women in my family, but they were so damn nosey. "But seeing as you did, why?"

She shrugged. "It just felt right."

"What if they find out?" I asked. "What if they discover you're not my girlfriend?"

"They won't, and I doubt it made that much difference to the result."

"I think it did." I scrubbed my hands down my face and groaned. "I don't want you to get into any trouble."

She dug her hands deep into the pocket so her jeans and shook her head. "I won't. Don't worry about it."

I did worry though because I didn't want her to get into trouble and potentially lose out on opening her preschool because of me.

She must have seen my worry because she said, "Honestly, Shaw, it'll be fine. It's not like I'm trying to get a green card or anything and I will help you out with Tia. Even if it's just as a friend."

Something stalled inside my chest at the thought of us being just friends, but I knew I'd blown it for anything else.

"Well, I appreciate what you did," I said taking a step closer to her.

It was only small, but I saw it, the tiny step back she took, so I forced myself not to move any closer. I had to accept that she was hurt, and I just had to bide my time until the time was right to get her to change her mind.

“I’d better go,” Nancy said, glancing over her shoulder. “I need to get the keys to the bank back to Belinda.”

“You got the keys already? How come?” There was no way the contracts could have gone through so quickly

“I think Mr. Jennings feels bad for what happened with Ruthie, so he said I could go in and measure up.”

“Figures,” I said with an empty laugh. “He clearly knows that he fucked up.”

Nancy smiled. “Is that a legal term?”

“Yes, kind of.” I grinned. “Anyways, the main thing is everything is going along smoothly now. It shouldn’t be too long before the contracts are complete.”

Nancy smiled, crinkling her eyes and a whole host of regret reared its head again. If only I’d just kept my mouth shut and not tried to be funny, things might have been different.

“Good luck with the custody case, Shaw.” She lifted her hand and gave me a quick wave. “See you around.”

“Yep, catch you later, Nancy.”

Then she was gone, slipping out through the side gate and leaving me wanting to punch myself in the balls.

“Hey, Shaw.” Bronte lifted her hand to shield her eyes against the sun. “Mom wants to know if you want some lunch. She’s going to make some sandwiches.”

She walked closer to me and poked me in the stomach with her index finger.

“What was that for?” I asked, rubbing at the spot.

“For saying what you did to Nancy and then letting her go again.”

“What do you mean? Letting her go again? She left Bronte, what am I supposed to do, force her to stay like some creeper?”

“You are so clueless.” She looked up to the sky and then back to me. “Do you not see why she did that for you today?”

“Because she’s my friend and wants me to keep Tia.” I got that strange feeling again at the thought of us just being friends. No more sex with Nancy was a kind of shitty thought.

"Friends," my sister scoffed. "I'm friends with Ellie and Hunter, but I'm not just friends with Carter."

"Mom always says you should be best friends with your partner." Hah, so take that, Bronte and stop with whatever shit advice you were about to come out with.

"I know. And Carter is my best friend, he's also the man who gives me amazing orgasms, who drives me crazier than anyone that I know and the man who I'd actually perjure myself for."

"She did not perjure herself," I replied, with a roll of my eyes.

"Pretty much." Bronte grinned. "Surely even you with a brain full of cotton candy understood why she did that."

"No, I didn't, because she didn't." I shrugged, not at all sure what Bronte was talking about. "It was a little white lie."

"Whatever, Shaw." She turned and pointed at the house. "That in there was so much more than a little white lie or even perjury. Now, come on before Mom comes looking for you. Oh, and FYI, we're all going out tonight to celebrate the babies, and Mrs. Dalhousie from two doors down is sitting Rett and Tia."

"Stinky Dalhousie? Are you insane?"

"She's much better these days since she gave up playing Dodgeball. Dad says you don't have a choice anyway."

"What if Tia needs me?" I was happy for my sister and Ellie, but I was not in the mood for celebrating babies. Especially as I could lose my own.

"Then there's this thing called a cell phone and it will ring, and Mrs. Dalhousie will say, 'hey Shaw, Tia needs you'. Then there's this great invention called a car which will bring you back here in, oh let me see." She put her finger to her lip and frowned like she thinking, although it looked more like constipation. "Ten minutes, tops." Bronte then landed me with a pretty scary stare. "So, you're coming with, no arguments."

"Bronte," I protested.

"No, Shaw, no arguments and just as a sweetener, you'll be pleased to know Dad is making Austen stay home with her too."

Wow, sometimes my sister was great at persuasion, and this was most definitely one of those times.

“I’m in,” I said, jogging up beside her. “As long as I get to be the one to tell him.”

Her steps faltered for a second but then she held up her hand and I high fived her.

“You’re on,” she replied and then sashayed back into the house, leaving me feeling just a little better and wondering whether I should just tell Nancy how I felt.

CHAPTER 33

Nancy

Stars & Stripes was not where I wanted to be. I'd tried crying off with a headache and Bronte sent Ellie round with a doctor colleague to check me out. Apparently, I'd been slipping off a lot lately with a headache, so she felt I should get a physical. I have no idea whether the guy was a real doctor, but I gave in and said I'd come when he pushed a thermometer in my face and told me to bend over.

Come to think of it his stethoscope didn't look real and how many ER doctors do house calls wearing scrubs and Crocs? Ultimately, I knew that Bronte had possibly tricked me twice in one day.

When I walked in and saw that Lily was there, talking to her mom, I felt a little better. I wouldn't have to talk babies all night with Bronte and Ellie or avoid looking into Shaw's eyes in case he realized I had grown the biggest of crushes on him. I stopped at the bar to get myself a drink and then made my way over to the cluster of tables and stools that had been pushed close to each other.

The usual crowd were there including, I was surprised to see, Jacob Crowne looking miserable nursing a bottle of beer. He was in his early thirties and so a little older than Ellie, Hunter and crowd. That, along with being a single dad meant that he didn't really hang with us. To be fair he didn't get out much at all unless Lily sat with his son JJ for him. Seeing as she was there, I wondered how he'd managed it. He didn't look particularly happy that he had though. The fact that he kept looking at his watch made me think he was ready to make his own getaway.

"Hi Nancy," Melinda said as I approached. "Good to see you again."

"Hi Melinda. Where are the two guests of honors?" I looked around but couldn't see either Bronte or Ellie.

"They're in the bathroom making sure that they look okay." Melinda rolled her eyes. "Seriously, who needs a special outfit to celebrate getting pregnant?"

"I'm guessing Ellie and Bronte do."

Melinda nodded. "They went shopping together and both bought from the same collection." She leaned closer to me. "Seriously they look like a younger version of the Lynn-Ann and Janice-Ann."

I burst out laughing starting to feel glad that I'd made the effort to come out. "No way. They're wearing the same outfit?"

"No. The same color and fabric pattern but different outfits. You'll soon see."

"Oh my god, they're becoming a nightmare." I held up my hand in apology. "Sorry I know that they're your daughter and daughter in law, but I think this race to get pregnant and now being pregnant has sent them a little crazy."

"Sweetheart, don't apologize," Melinda replied. "I'm with you one hundred percent. Ellie even bought one of those donut cushions with her tonight, just in case she had hemorrhoids."

"She doesn't though?"

"Nope. But like I said, just in case."

As Melinda and I looked at each other in wonderment, I felt someone pull up a stool beside me. I turned to see Darcy who looked a little frazzled.

"You okay, Darc?" Melinda asked.

"Sure." She took a huge drink of the wine that she was holding and then wiped her mouth. "I'm not sure I can stay okay for the next seven months though. Bronte is driving me crazy. This is not her first baby, yet you'd think she was pregnant with the next Messiah."

Melinda held up her hand for a high-five. "Tell me about it. Ellie is so precious now that by the time the baby comes, I'm sure Hunter will have her in bubble wrap twenty-four hours a day."

"Whatever made us think it would be lovely for them to be pregnant at the same time?" Darcy sighed and took another long slug of her drink.

I told them both I'd seem them later and made my way over to Lily who was now sitting alone and nursing what I thought was a glass of soda. She looked pretty miserable too, even though I knew she'd love the fact that she'd been allowed to join the party for once.

"Hey you," I said, pulling her in for a side hug. "You okay?"

"Yeah," she sighed, flipping one of the beer mats.

"You don't look it. What's wrong?" I pushed her pink hair from her eyes and then flicked her long braid over her shoulder.

"Jennifer is thinking of leasing out Cake Heaven." She stared up at me with a slight pout to her lips. "And she thinks the guy who is interested wants his daughters and wife to work there."

"Which means you'd be surplus to requirements?"

"Yep. I love working there you know." She looked over in the direction of Jacob who was now looking happier as he chatted to Jefferson and Henry. "JJ won't need me for much longer. In fact, Jacob has already said it might be best if I find myself something else."

"Wow, bummer. You potentially lost two jobs in one day, huh?"

"Yeah." Lily's gaze snapped back to mine. "Real bummer."

"Okay," I said, pulling out the stool next to her and sitting down. "How would you feel about coming to work for me?"

Her mouth gaped and her palms slammed hard on the table. "For real?"

"Yep, for real. It would only be part-time, so you'd still need to find something else."

"Anything, Nancy," she cried, throwing her arms around me. "That would be like, awesome."

"Okay then." I hugged her and then held her at arm's length. "It won't be for a few months, because I need to get the place ready and maybe if you like it you could go to community college and get some qualifications."

She nodded. "I've been thinking about doing a business course you know. Jennifer made me realize that if I was older maybe I could have leased Cake Heaven from her."

"Well that's great, Lil. See how you do at my place and then decide which course you want to take."

She grinned. "My mom is going to pee her pants when she finds out. She's been trying to persuade me to go to college for like forever." She hugged me again. "I'm going to go and tell her." She paused. "If he needs to would you let Jacob enroll JJ for after school?"

"I don't know what I'm going to offer yet, but maybe with you on board we can do breakfast and after school activities." It was a great idea to be honest and would certainly help to boost the funds until I could get an actual teacher or qualify myself.

"Mom's back from the bathroom. I'll tell her now." I looked over in the direction that Lily was headed and there was Kitty watching with everyone else as Ellie and Bronte walked in wearing similar outfits in red and cobalt blue fabric. Ellie's was a cute romper suit while Bronte's was a tight button through shirt dress which was nipped in at the waist with a belt. Weird though it was it kind of worked.

"I do believe my sister may well have lost her marbles."

I turned to see Shaw with a bottle of beer and a glass of clear liquid in his hand. He put the glass on the table in front of me.

"You could be right," I said and then nodded to the glass. "For me?"

"Yep. It's vodka." He grinned and the meaning behind it was clear.

As I looked at him, the breath was stolen from my lungs. All handsome and sexy, wearing a black t-shirt that stretched nicely across his chest. He also smelled delicious and there was cute little smile on his face that made me want to jump him right there and then.

Throwing any caution that I had to the wind, I picked it up and knocked it back, hoping that he understood what *that* meant. I was done with being mad with him. Watching Jefferson and Kitty and seeing how happy they were made me realize that life was too damn short. Okay, they hadn't been torn apart and I doubted Jefferson would have wanted a life without his wife Sondra in it, but the point was Sondra had died too soon. What if she hadn't taken a chance with Jefferson? What if Ellie hadn't seen Hunter in a different light after years of being friends? What if Carter and Bronte hadn't decided to stop arguing long enough to have sex? There certainly wouldn't be any Rett, or a second baby on the way. I'd gone over to the house earlier with every intent of telling Shaw that I believed him and would like to try and be something more than fuck buddies. After the people for child services had gone though, he only seemed intent on thanking me for the favor. He didn't seem to understand what I'd meant by doing that favor.

"I probably should buy you the bottle," Shaw said. "After the solid you did me today."

"And get me drunk? Are you sure, because you know what happens when I get drunk on vodka."

He nodded. "I certainly do." He took a breath and then moved closer. His arm brushed mine, making my heart thud faster than was probably healthy. "I'm so sorry for what I said. I was only joking, and I would never use you to keep my daughter."

I shrugged. "The funny thing is, if you'd asked me, I'd have done it anyway. You're a great dad, Shaw, and you should be allowed to keep her."

"I also know that Minnesota was talking shit when he said you only wanted me for my family."

"And how do you know that?" I asked, a small giggle escaping.

"You fucking love my dick, Nancy. As if my mom and dad would be a bigger draw than that."

I couldn't help the giggle turning into a full-on laugh at his usual cockiness. A cockiness that in the past I'd been irritated by—or had I? Who the hell knew?

"How do you know?" I asked, nudging him with my hip. "It might be the worst dick that I've ever seen."

He raised an eyebrow. "Yeah, and your pussy isn't magical. Now, are you going to kiss me or what?"

"Here, in front of everyone?"

"Why not? They all know that you're crazy about me."

"Do they though?" I tilted my head to one side and smiled at him. "I'm not even sure that I like you very much."

Shaw's mouth was close to my ear, and when he reached up to gently hold my earlobe between his thumb and forefinger, I thought my heart might punch its way out of my chest.

"I think you like me very much, Nancy Andrews. Because," he licked his lips, "I really like you. An awful lot. So much so that I can honestly say that you're mostly all I think about."

"Mostly?"

"Yeah," he whispered. "There's this cute little blonde who takes up a lot of my headspace too. She's not got much conversation but when she smiles at me my heart just about melts."

Wow, I was a puddle of need in the middle of the bar. That there, those sort of words were why I'd never really be able to truly hate him. He was too swoony at times to constantly want to cause him physical pain.

"Do you want to leave?" I asked.

He didn't hesitate. "Yes, I do," he whispered. His mouth came to mine and then he pulled back. "Nope. Not fucking happening."

My blood stopped running for a second and my heart sank.

"He can just fuck off," he said over my shoulder.

I turned to see where he was looking, and I groaned when I saw a smirking Minnesota walking toward us.

"What the hell is he coming over to us for?" I asked. "I told him, the other day at my apartment we are over. Done. Never to go back again."

"He clearly didn't get the message," Shaw growled and gently pulled me behind him. "He better not think he can touch you."

His arm went in front of me, his hand resting on the table, clearly to keep Minnesota away from me. It felt strange that he was protecting me, and instinctively my hands rested on his waist.

"What do you want?" Shaw asked, as Minnesota stood in front of us.

"I need to talk to Nancy."

Shaw shook his head. "Not happening." He turned to look at me. "Do you want to speak to him Nance?" I shook my head. "There you go, now fuck off."

Minnesota laughed and put his hands to his hips. "What the hell is your problem? What do you think I'm going to do to her?" He leaned the top half of his body closer to Shaw. "Steal her from you?"

"You want to go back to him, Nance?"

"Never."

"There you go." Shaw sighed heavily and placed his hands on top of mine. "You couldn't steal her from me if you tried. Besides which she doesn't belong to me, Nancy is her own person."

"Wow," Minnesota gave a hollow laugh. "That hard on you had for her in high school really never did go away, did it? I told Ruthie she would never truly have you while you were hot for Nancy."

"What?" I asked. "What does she have to do with it?"

He looked around Shaw to me. "Don't tell me you didn't know she set out to take him from you, right from her first day at school." He tapped the side of his nose. "I could see though that he liked you a lot and I never thought she'd do it, but she did."

"Can you just go," I said, stepping forward coming along side of Shaw, with one arm still around his waist. "I have nothing else to say to you. I told you at my apartment that we were over. Just because you got dumped, Minnesota, it doesn't mean you can come running back to me. As for Ruthie I have no interest in her petty games from when we were fourteen years old."

"You don't even care that she was the one who spoiled prom for you?"

Shaw looked at me and then turned his intense stare back to Minnesota and I instantly knew what he was thinking.

"What do you know about prom?" Shaw asked.

"You know exactly what I know, Shaw. I'm guessing Nancy told you about her standing on her porch in her yellow dress looking all lost and alone."

My hands clenched into fists. "I so wish I'd never told you half the things that I did."

He shrugged. "You painted such a sad picture Nancy." He cleared his throat and muttered, "About so many fucking things."

"What does Ruthie have to do with it?" Shaw asked. "Apart from the fact that I went to prom with her."

"The note to Nancy. Ruthie sent it." He shrugged. "Well, I wrote it for her and delivered it, but it was all her idea. She always hated Nancy because she knew that you still had a hankering for her."

"You wrote it?" Shaw asked. "And you delivered it to Nancy? For Ruthie?"

Minnesota nodded with a smirk on his face. The next thing I knew an arm came out with a clenched fist on the end. Minnesota went down on the floor like a stack of cards.

Nancy's Bitch List for Shaw

☐ Maximus Douchimus
☐ Captain Shitsmear
☐ Shit Talking Cock Womble
☐ Dildohead
☐ Dipshit Cockhead
☐ Scrote Noggin
☐ ~~Assilicious~~ Fat Ass
☐ Fucknuckle
☐ Bronocchio
☐ Asshobbit
☐ Jerkass
☐ ~~Studly McStudly~~
☐ I have no name bad enough for how sad he's made me
☐ ~~Hot Sizzle~~
☐ Douche Canoe
☐ My hero

CHAPTER 34

Shaw

Minnesota Michaels was a dick, a douche, a dipshit. He was a lot of things that I didn't have time to think of in that moment. All I knew was that he'd hurt Nancy on several occasions. Not least prom which should have been one of the best nights of her life.

As he sat on the floor, holding his bleeding nose, I could easily have gone at him again, but Nancy was gripping tight of my arm.

"Shaw, don't," she said, trying to pull me back. "He's so not worth it."

"You fucking dipshit," Minnesota groaned, his hand cupped under his nose to catch the blood. "What the fuck did you do that for?"

I leaned down and got in his face. "What the hell do you think I did it for?"

"It was years ago." He looked around me to Nancy. "She should be over it by now, but no, she's a damn drama queen."

I shook my head in disbelief. This idiot was seriously cruising for me to give him two black eyes to match his bloody nose. I didn't need to even think about it though because Nancy appeared from by my side, marched over to him and emptied my bottle of beer over his head.

"How's that for being a drama queen, you…" She paused, looked up at the ceiling and then leaned back down. "You *needle dick*."

I busted out laughing but when Nancy looked back to the table clearly for something to hit him with, I decided to show him some mercy. I wrapped an arm around her waist and pulled her back to me.

"Nance, seriously gorgeous, you were right, he's not worth it."

"I changed my mind, he is," she hissed.

"No, he's not." I kissed her neck, just below her ear. "Let's go and leave him and his needle dick to dry off."

"I have no idea what I saw in you," Minnesota yelled as he pushed to his feet with beer dripping from him.

"Yeah, well that's mutual," Nancy snapped, before grabbing my hand. "I'm going home to have sex with someone who knows what to do and not a gnome with a tickle dick."

God my girl was good with the insults. I certainly wouldn't want to be on the end of one of them, again.

We were just about out the door when Nancy gasped and pulled me to a stop.

"What?" I asked, turning around to see what was wrong.

"She's here," she said it like she was one of those psychics who reckon you have your dead loved ones looking over your shoulder. "I can smell her."

She sniffed the air and then started scanning the room. Lord knew what smell Ruthie gave off because she evidently did because Nancy pointed at her. Pulling her hand from mine she stormed off to the high table in the corner where Ruthie was standing with Bronte's nemesis, Mindy Parkinson. They both had long, blue colored drinks in front of them and Ruthie was wearing a white, almost-there strapless dress. It didn't take a law student with a 3.9 GPA to know what was going to happen next.

"You, bitch," Nancy yelled, striding straight for Ruthie. "You absolute bitch."

Ruthie must have known what was going to happen too, because she pulled Mindy in front of her and peered over her shoulder.

"Don't you come near me, Nancy Andrews," Ruthie whimpered.

I got a hold of Nancy's hand, but she glared at me. Being a man who wanted to have more children in the future I let it go. "Have at it, gorgeous."

Nancy didn't respond but turned back to Ruthie. "You ruined prom for me. You and Minnesota, you ruined one of the last memories I have of doing something with my mom."

Woah, I hadn't expected that and by the way Nancy's eyes had gone wide, I didn't think she did either. She looked heartbroken and hurt, crestfallen; every word I could think of to describe the worst possible feeling in the world. Not caring about my balls any longer, I took her hand. She didn't pull away, but she didn't let up on Ruthie either.

"I went shopping with my mom and then she died a few months later and all I can remember is the shitty yellow dress that she bought for me." She shook her head and took a deep breath, plainly sucking back the tears. "And you know what, it wasn't shitty, it was pretty, but you tainted that memory because of what you did."

Ruthie straightened her shoulders from behind Mindy and sneered at Nancy. "You can't blame me for that."

"I can," Nancy spat back. "And I do. You did a mean thing, Ruthie, a real mean thing. I hope no daughter of yours ever has the misfortune to have someone like you in her class, or even her airspace. You are a class A bitch and so much worse, but I'm a lady and won't use that word for you."

My brows rose on that one—I'd had sex with Nancy Andrews and there were times when she was no lady. That girl had a dirty mouth on her.

"Well it looks like you got what you want," Ruthie said, nodding toward me. "If you want my sloppy seconds then you can have them."

"Hey," I said, stepping forward and pointing at Ruthie. "There is nothing sloppy about me."

Nancy snorted and patted my arm. "Okay, baby, leave this one to me."

Reverting to being the man who wanted more children in the future, I stepped back and let Nancy take control again.

“I don’t care what you say, Ruthie,” Nancy continued. “Because I’m pretty sure Shaw will agree he saved the best ‘til last.”

“Yep,” I said, raising my hand. “I agree.”

“Oh whatever, he was a crap lay anyway.”

Now that was a damn lie! Thankfully Nancy agreed with me. She burst out laughing. “Bullshit and you know it.”

“Well if you like mediocre, Nancy, then you’re welcome to him and that stupid bank. I’ve found a much better building.”

It was this point that Mindy found her voice, clearly sick of just being a human barricade. “You have not. You told me that you couldn’t find anything for the money.”

Ruthie smacked her arm and hissed at her to be quiet.

“What a pity,” Nancy replied. “A topless karaoke bar is exactly what we’re missing here in Dayton.”

If it had been female waitresses, I might have agreed. Not in Nancy’s hearing distance though obviously.

“Oh shove it, Nancy,” Ruthie said, with a sneer. “Go talk to someone who doesn’t have narcolepsy.”

I looked at Nancy and she looked at me and I think we both silently agreed that wasn’t the insult that Ruthie was looking for and we both grinned. It was then, out of the corner of my eye, I saw Ruthie’s hand go for one of the drinks on the table. I tried to push Nancy behind me, but I should have known she was a step ahead of me. Nancy’s hand grabbed the drink first and in one swift movement threw it over Ruthie who screamed like a newborn baby.

“Oops,” Nancy said as we watched blue liquid drip down Ruthie’s face and onto her white dress, which now had patches of murky purple on it. “I must have tripped.”

Mindy, clearly the sensible one, made a quick exit and then her hand snaked back into vision as she picked up her drink before slinking away.

“I think you need to go home and change, Ruthie,” I said, looking her up and down. “It appears Nancy’s clumsiness has created a bit of an issue for you.”

Whimpering, she swiped at her face with her hands and glared at both of us, opening her mouth to speak but then thinking better of it. She knew better than to mess with us. We were one awesome team now.

As Ruthie ran from Stars & Stripes, dripping what I'm sure was Blue Bomber over the floor, I turned to Nancy and grinned.

"Wow, you're my hero."

She preened and wiggled her eyebrows. "I know. I'm so good it's unbelievable."

"I'm so in awe of you. Do you think you'd let me kiss you?"

She thought about it for a second and then shook her head. We were joking around but my heart did still stop for a second. Then she smiled and stood on tiptoe to whisper in my ear.

"I will let you fuck me though."

That was it we were out of there faster than a sneeze through a screen door!

***

When we got back to Nancy's place, I walked us to the bedroom at the back of the apartment, my mouth not leaving hers for a single second. I'd only been in her room once before, but I remembered every single moment of it. Every single gasp that had whispered from Nancy's lips, every touch and every wave of pleasure that had swelled through my body. Now I was ready to relive it.

Nancy was clearly on my wavelength because as soon as we were through the bedroom door, she pushed me away and scrambled to get naked, dropping her dress to the floor and kicking off her shoes.

"Get your clothes off, Shaw."

I didn't need much coercion and pulled my t-shirt over my head and then went straight for my belt buckle to get rid of my jeans. We were quick and frenetic as we undressed, never taking our eyes off each other, both knowing what we were about to do was going to be amazing.

Dropping her red bra to the floor, Nancy watched me carefully as I slowly lowered my boxer briefs. When they joined the rest of my clothes, she took a sharp intake of breath.

"I forgot how beautiful your penis actually was," she said, catching the corner of her bottom lip with her teeth.

"Yeah?"

She nodded, laying her palm flat against the swell of her breast as color spread over them and up her neck. "Oh yeah." She then bent and pushed her panties down her legs and stepped out of them.

"Maybe it's time I reminded you properly." I took the two steps toward her and gently pushed her onto the bed. When she lying down looking up at me, I didn't think I'd seen anything more beautiful. I truly hadn't appreciated this woman enough.

"I'm sorry that I've been an idiot, Nance." I dropped my forehead to hers and linked our hands together. "I should have opened my eyes."

"It's fine," she whispered and then grinned. "I had great fun coming up with names for you."

"You did, hey?"

She nodded. "Yep. I'll show you after you've fucked me."

How the hell could I refuse that offer. I got onto the bed and got ready to devour every single inch of her. Flashing her a grin, I dropped my head down and began my amazing journey. First, I kissed up the instep of her foot, along the inside of her leg, past her knee all the way up to the apex of her thigh. They were quick, soft kisses, little nips, soothing licks all while my hands played with her amazing tits and hard, dark brown nipples. She moaned beneath me, and my dick was as hard as steel, my balls aching. She tasted of coconut and sunshine and smelled like summer. Her skin was soft and tanned and covered in tiny little goosebumps.

Moving up the bed my mouth was level with her flat belly, and I licked either side of the thin strip of hair on her pussy, up her sternum and along her collar bone. My tongue flicking out teasingly as I linked our hands, holding them down against the pillow, keeping her captive as I worshipped her. Her perky round tits heaved as she breathed deeply, her flat stomach going in and out in time with her hips that lifted to offer her beautiful pussy to me. I could smell her desire and without even touching her, I knew that she was soaking wet. She was perfect and as much as I was ready to be inside of her, the feeling of Nancy writhing beneath me caused my heart to beat faster. That I was enough for her made me feel powerful. I could give her what she needed.

When I sucked one of her nipples into my mouth she gasped and pushed her hips up higher.

"Shaw…I…think…I…might…come…oh…my…god." She breathed heavily between each word, emphasizing the pleasure that she was feeling.

Never had I brought a woman to orgasm just through foreplay and I was glad that Nancy was the first. It proved that we were good together and that I was on this earth to pleasure her. When I circled my tongue around her nipple she started to shudder and her legs stretched, her toes curled over. Her orgasm was so strong that I could feel the ripples of it against my skin. When her hands wrestled to be free of mine, I held them strong and moved my mouth to her other nipple. She must have been right on the edge because as soon as my lips locked around it, she practically levitated off the bed and screamed her release. With a pop I moved my mouth away from her nipple and watched as she came apart.

"You still need me to fuck you?" I said right against her ear as she continued to buck under my body.

She shook her head but kept repeating the word "Yes." I smiled and opened the top drawer of her nightstand, knowing that was where she kept condoms and pulled a handful from the open box. Who knew how many I'd use, but if I had my way, I'd be fucking her all night, proving that she was mine.

As Nancy buried her face into the pillow, relishing in the aftershocks, I put the condom on, squeezing my dick to try and relieve some of the pain and pressure. Once it was on, I put my hands on Nancy's hips and flipped her over.

"Hands and knees, Nance," I commanded.

She was still a little floppy from the orgasm, but when I slapped her ass just once, it brought her to life, and she soon got into position. I put my hands under her hips and lifted her ass up, and pumped my dick a couple of times, ready to push inside.

Nancy looked at me over her shoulder and gave me a lazy smile. "Fuck me, Shaw."

I didn't need any further invitation, I thrust inside of her and pumped in and out like my life depended on it. I was right, she was soaking. I drove in and out so hard and so fast that Nancy was shifted up the bed and had to put one of her hands out against the headboard to brace herself.

"Fucking perfect," I ground out. "So perfect."

"Shaw, I'm going to come again." Nancy's voice cracked, as if she was going to burst into tears. Of fucking joy.

I wrapped her hair around my hand and pulled her head back so that I could kiss her. I needed to feel her lips on mine. Our tongues met and I felt the familiar pull in my balls.

"Mine, Nancy," I growled. "You're all fucking mine."

It was then that I shot my load and came with a roar, knowing that I wanted this with her for as long as I had breath in my lungs.

***

Lying in Nancy's bed with her in my arms, I felt at peace. The noise in my head around everything going on in my life had subsided. I felt confident that I would get to keep Tia. I had proved to child services that I was going to be a good dad. I had that confidence in myself. Of course school with a toddler was going to be hard, but something told me that I'd do it. Maybe it was the endorphins that were still buzzing around my body after great sex, or maybe it was simply being with Nancy that gave all that to me.

"Do you think we should go back to the party." I sighed as my fingers traced patterns on Nancy's shoulder.

She didn't answer but exhaled slowly and then moved to rest her chin on my chest. "Are you sure you want us to be more?" she asked. "You said you want us to be something. Do you?"

I lifted my head from the pillow so that she could see my eyes. "Yes, I do. That was so much more than fucking Nance and you know it." I kissed her softly. "Do you want us to be something more?"

"I do. I have for a while now." She smiled and looked coyly at me through her lashes.

"Yeah, well, we might have sorted this sooner had I not said that shit about needing a girlfriend."

"Let's forget about it," Nancy replied. "I know you didn't mean it. Otherwise, you'd have asked Bronte to tell me about the meeting and persuade me to pretend. You didn't do any of that. I was shocked when I turned up and realized that they were there. I'd come to see your dad."

"I was a little shocked," I replied, dropping a gentle kiss to the top of her head.

"Yeah, you looked it. That's how I knew that you hadn't sent Bronte to see me."

I then thought back to the bar and the run in with Ruthie. "Do you want to talk about your mom, Nance? How what Ruthie did upset you for more reasons than missing the prom?"

She was silent for a few moments, and I thought I'd upset her, but then she sighed. "No, I'm good. I didn't realize that was what upset me the most and I know saying it out loud once won't make it go away, but I feel better for it. I feel like saying it eases the pain a little."

"You know you can talk to me anytime about your parents, don't you?" I turned to look at her and she was smiling.

"I do and thank you. You know, it's your mom and dad that I really want to talk to." She started to giggle and when I tickled her side it developed into a full on laugh.

"You know it's me and my dick that holds your attention. Admit it." I tickled her some more until she gasped.

"Yes, okay, it's you I want."

"Good. We're on the same page now." Pulling her closer I sighed. "Plus, I think Minnesota seems to have got the message too."

She rolled her eyes. "Is it me or has he become an even bigger douchebag over the last few days."

"Tell me about it." I felt my jaw clench. "He's decided he hates me suddenly. Not that we were ever really friends."

She ran a finger over my eyebrows and sighed. "I think that might be my fault. I told him that I had feelings for you."

"What?" I blinked not sure I'd heard her properly.

"I told him that I had feelings for you, it was when you saw him leaving my apartment. I told him that we'd kind of been seeing each other and that I wanted to move things to a different level." She looked at me through one eye. "Are you mad?"

"The only thing I'm mad about is him thinking he can treat you like that." Wrapping my arm around her back, I pulled her closer. "It does explain why he was a douche in Delphine's."

"I shouldn't have said it though," she said warily. "I mean we weren't actually seeing each other. Not really."

"Did you say it just to get rid of him?" I asked.

"No. Maybe. I don't think so."

I laughed. "Which is it?"

"I know it's what I wanted to happen, so maybe it was my subconscious' decision to say it."

"Maybe." I winked. "And they reckon that saying your wishes out loud means they don't come true."

Nancy rolled her eyes and huffed. "It was hardly a wish, Shaw."

"More like a dream come true?" My smirk earned me a playful slap to the chest.

"I could change my mind you know."

"But you won't. I'm your biggest wish, remember?"

"Oh my god, now I see where Austen gets it from." She shifted and dropped a kiss to my chest. "Anyway, I thought you wanted to get back to Stars & Stripes."

"What and watch my sister and Ellie vie for Miss. Most Pregnant of Dayton Valley? No thanks."

We fell silent and watched each other for a few seconds and as I considered how damn beautiful that she was I wondered how stupid I'd been not to have asked her for a chance before now.

"Do you think anyone saw us leave together?" Nancy asked after a few minutes.

I laughed. "I don't know Nancy, what do you think?"

"They may have seen me throw a drink over Ruthie, and they may not. Either way we've only been gone a little over an hour."

I lifted my head to look at her. "And?"

"We could always fit another round in."

I grinned, liking that idea, but then I was reminded of something. "Okay," I said. "But one other thing."

"What's that?"

I rolled on top of her and pinned her hands above her head. "I give you an orgasm and you show me that damn list of names you have for me."

You know I don't think I'd ever seen Nancy Andrews go pale before.

CHAPTER 35

Nancy

Four months later

We'd finally done it. We'd finally finished my preschool and it looked amazing. Craig, my contractor, had performed nothing short of miracles to get everything that I'd wanted done. It hadn't helped that there'd been a huge hole in the roof of the apartment upstairs and any rain leaked in right where my bed was going to be. A new roof had been an extra expense, but thankfully I'd sold my apartment quickly so had the money available. Tate had bought the apartment as an investment, as he lived in Kitty's house that she'd bought before she moved in with Jefferson. As soon as Tate had possession of my apartment Evie had moved in leaving the apartment above Cake Heaven. It was all wheels within wheels in Dayton Valley that was for sure.

Top and bottom of it was, I was more than pleased with KidsZone, my new business venture. I knew it was going to be hard work, but I was going to love it. Particularly as I had the support of my gorgeous, lawyer boyfriend.

Yep, Shaw and I were official. To the point that I'd stayed at his folk's place for the last six weeks until my new apartment was ready. Tate had said I could stay at my old apartment, but funnily enough Shaw was adamant that I let Evie move in. Things were going good for us, especially as he'd been given custody of Tia. Child services had liked what they'd seen and had made their minds up quickly. They were going to keep a check on Tia for the next year, but they didn't think anything would change. It seemed that the guy Mrs. Devonshire was supposed to be marrying had dumped her, which was why she'd suddenly wanted Tia back. When she didn't get custody, she'd admitted it to Shaw. She thought Tia would stop her from being lonely. Since then, however, the guy was back on the scene, and they'd gone on a world cruise instead of getting married. As for Tia, well Mrs. Devonshire hadn't once enquired after her. Proof that the right decision had been made to leave Tia with her daddy. Tia had grown fond of me too, which I loved. Maybe it was because I'd done what I'd said and helped a lot when Shaw went back to school, or maybe because I'd lived with her for the last month and a half. I didn't really care because I loved her like she was my own. In fact, I was going to talk to Shaw about him and Tia moving in with me. Not yet, because maybe it was too soon, or maybe I'd miss them too much and do it anyway. Who knew?

There'd also been a good result for Mrs. Ranger in her custody case. I hadn't had to take the stand because Tate had been amazing. He'd pretty much annihilated Mr. Ranger's case through questioning him, getting him to admit that he hired a sitter for most of the time, even when he was home. Lily had found out that information through the babysitter's club who had looked after the kids at Kitty's party. That meant Eddie and Molly were now back with their mom and would soon be enrolling into KidZone. Mrs. Baker wasn't happy about the number of kids that were moving to me, but then she shouldn't have been such an old bitch.

Another bonus, Minnesota had gone back to London. Apparently, he called his fiancée and groveled a lot and she said they could try again. He'd been gone just over two months, but Jennifer told me that he was already calling his mom and complaining about the weather and the warm beer. I'd smiled, cooed over Jennifer and Alaska's baby girl Montana and then put Minnesota Michaels out of my mind. He was of no interest to me whatsoever.

"Hey, gorgeous," the sound of Shaw's voice interrupted my thoughts and made my stomach swoop.

I turned to see him striding toward me, looking sexy and a little disheveled. If there weren't other people hanging around, I might well have jumped him.

"What's up?" I asked, as he pulled me into his arms.

"All the stuff in the main room has been put away and Mom asked if you want her to make up your bed in the apartment or are you going to stay with us one more night?"

I laughed, noticing the pout as he said it.

"I have to move upstairs sometime," I replied, not really liking the idea any more than he did. "But I guess one more night won't hurt if your mom is okay with that."

"She's fine with it," Shaw replied, a huge smile spreading across his face. "Although, you're looking so sexy today I really could do with making you scream tonight."

I slapped him playfully against his chest. "Maybe we go gentle tonight, baby, and tomorrow night you make me scream."

"You want me to stay here tomorrow?" His eyes lit up with anticipation.

Ah shoot, life was too damn short. "Shaw, I'd love you and Tia to stay here every night. You know I've painted my guest bedroom pink with yellow balloons on the wall. You really think I'd do that if I didn't think that you both might spend a lot of time here."

He let out a breath and took my mouth in the hottest of kisses, threading his fingers through my ponytail with one hand as he cupped my face with the other.

"I didn't think you were going to ask," he breathed out when he finally let me go.

"You don't think it's too soon?"

He grinned. "Damn it, Nance, we've been dancing around each other since we were fourteen years old. I think if we leave it any longer and we could end up in the history books as the longest session of foreplay of all time."

"Foreplay comes before sex, and we've had plenty of that."

"Isn't that the truth." He smacked my ass and then dropped another kiss to my lips. "Me and Tia would love to move in, although I think Mom may kidnap my daughter a couple of nights a week."

I knew he wasn't wrong there. Darcy and Jim adored Tia and Rett and spoiled them rotten and would continue to do so with the new baby due in a few months' time.

As I thought about the new grandchild, they were about to have I heard voices shouting from the main entranceway. Shaw groaned and dropped his head to my shoulder.

"Here we go."

In marched Bronte, Carter, Ellie and Hunter with the girls squabbling about gender reveal parties. Both were pretty big now although Ellie's bump was neat and compact compared to Bronte's which was considerably bigger. She claimed it was because she was further along, but the doctor had re-confirmed that they both had the same due date. The current argument was all about the gender and who was going to give the Maples' their first granddaughter. Ellie insisted it should be her, but for a pediatric nurse you'd think she'd know that the sex of your baby wasn't decided on what you felt you should or shouldn't have.

"I want my party first," Ellie said. "You've already had a baby shower."

"And don't we know that you're jealous of that fact," Bronte sighed.

"Why don't you just have a joint one," Hunter said, his hand rubbing up and down Ellie's back. "We can have those gender reveal balloons and burst them at the same time. How does that sound?"

The girls looked at each other like it wasn't the most logical solution ever and high-fived each other.

"That's the best idea yet," Bronte said. "We are so clever."

"Don't," Carter quickly warned Hunter who had opened his mouth to speak. "It's not worth it, if you value your balls."

"What are you doing here?" Shaw asked. "You can see we're all pretty busy getting everything set up for Nance."

Bronte startled and then looked at Shaw. "Oh yeah. We've come to get Rett."

I shook my head and laughed. "He's with Henry and Melinda. They've taken Tia too."

"I did tell you, Lollipop," Carter groaned.

"No, you did not." Bronte flashed him a snarl. "You said no such thing." Then without another word she stormed out with Carter trailing behind.

"Thank goodness," Ellie sighed. "She's so dramatic since she's been pregnant."

I thought Hunter was going to speak but then he evidently considered Carter's warning about his balls because he closed his mouth again and covered his crotch with his hand.

"What can we do?" he asked instead.

Shaw slapped him on the back. "Well, your dad and my dad are trying to put some bookcases together in the toddler room, so maybe they could do with your help."

"Is it not going so well?" he asked with a grin.

Shaw shook his head. "Nope."

Hunter chuckled and walked off to help leaving me, Shaw and Ellie.

"What about me?" Ellie asked with a huge grin.

I looked at her swollen belly. "A coffee and pastry run would be good." I winced wondering whether she'd burst into tears and rant about not being given something more hands on to do, but she didn't. All cute and joyful she clapped her hands and said, "Leave it to me".

Then there was just the two of us again with a whole load of noise going on in the rooms around us. I sighed contentedly and allowed Shaw to pull me back into his arms.

"This place is going to be amazing. You know that, right?"

"I do," I said through a grin. "And I couldn't have done it without you."

"That's my pleasure." He kissed me and then laughed. "So, as a matter of interest if in theory you were still compiling that bitch list about me, what would today's entry be?"

I looked up at him and thought about it for a second or two and then smiled.

"Todays would be Best Boyfriend Ever."

"I thought that was yesterdays?" he asked with a playful frown.

"It was," I sighed. "And the day before and the day before that and the one before that. And you know what?"

"What's that?"

"It'll be tomorrow's too."

And that earned me a sexy kiss up against the wall.

Nancy's Bitch List for Shaw

☐ ~~Maximus Douchimus~~
☐ ~~Captain Shitsmear~~
☐ ~~Shit Talking Cock Womble~~
☐ ~~Dildohead~~
☐ ~~Dipshit Cockhead~~
☐ ~~Scrote Noggin~~
☐ ~~Assilicious~~ ~~Fat Ass~~
☐ ~~Fucknuckle~~
☐ ~~Bronocchio~~
☐ ~~Asshobbit~~
☐ ~~Jerkass~~
☐ ~~Studly McStudly~~
☐ ~~I have no name bad enough for how sad he's made me~~
☐ ~~Hot Sizzle~~
☐ ~~Douche Canoe~~
☐ My hero
☐ Best Boyfriend Ever
☐ Mr. Hot Stuff
☐ Best Boyfriend Ever

- ☐ *Best Boyfriend Ever*
- ☐ *DILF*
- ☐ *Best Boyfriend Ever*

EPILOGUE

Tate

I scrubbed my hand down my face and wondered how the hell I was going to help Evie. This was one problem that I'd never encountered before. As a lawyer in San Francisco, I'd faced all manner of weird and wonderful problems. Nothing like this though.

"And this cult that your parents are a part of, you're sure that they're coming for you?"

Pale grey eyes stared up at me, and not for the first time I marveled at the combination of them with yet black hair, so black it was almost blue.

"It's a church," Evie replied with her bottom lip trembling. "Pastor Michael is the church leader, and he is the one who takes a wife from each family."

I shook my head. "It's a cult, Evie. No recognized church would let an old man… you said he's seventy-eight… yep, an old man, make young girls be his wife. I think you'll find it's illegal."

"They're not real marriages. Mother Josephine is his real wife. The other girls they're just called his wives."

"Yes, so he can have sex with them when he likes no doubt."

Evie's gaze dropped to look at the floor of my office, so I knew that I was right.

"You're positive that they're coming for you?"

"Yes. This is the third place I've lived in since I ran away at eighteen. I have a friend, Jerome who services their vehicles and he messages me on a burner phone that I have. He said he'd heard that they'd found me again."

"You can't keep running, Evie." I laid my hand on her shoulder and stooped to look her in the eye. "They can't force you to go back with them."

"I know that, but I know what my daddy is like. How persuasive he can be."

"Why the hell would any father want this for his daughter?" I asked, moving away to pace my office. "It's prehistoric, inhumane. It's practically slavery."

Evie took in a shuddering breath. "He wants me to do it as his only daughter because he doesn't get to eat at the big table if I don't. Literally."

I swung around to face her and laughed. "You're kidding, right?"

She shook her head. "It's that simple, Tate. He wants to become one of the elders who eats at the big table during celebrations. Plus, they get a new car and a kitchen re-fit."

I looked around for the cameras sure that I was being punked or something. Was this some elaborate joke by my soon-to-be stepbrother, Hunter?

"You are joking?"

"I'm not Tate. The only way I'd be exempt was if dad had another daughter who would be willing to take my place."

"This is not the fucking *Hunger Games*, Evie. No one needs to volunteer as tribute."

"You don't understand, Tate. No one does. My mama and daddy were born into the life. My grandma was one of the previous leader's wives, my aunt is one of Pastor Michael's wives. It's all they know."

Shit, I thought my dad was sick getting an underage girl pregnant. At least he provided for her even if he wasn't in her life, which was a bonus in my book. My four-year-old half-sister, Daisy, lived in Portland with her mom, and new stepdad, who seemed like a good guy. Lily and I had met her a couple of times, but it seemed like it confused her, so we'd agreed with Daisy's mom that we'd send cards for her birthday and meet again when Daisy was old enough to understand who we were. I think to be honest it was more her mom who found it difficult. We were older than her and the kids of the man who'd she thought would love her forever—she really didn't know my dad at all.

"You don't think if you run, they'll find you again?" I asked. "Because they will. How are you ever going to settle down to a good life?"

She shrugged. "I probably won't. I don't stay anywhere long enough to find someone to have that life with."

"Someone to protect you, you mean."

She sniffed and wiped her nose with the tissue I'd given to her when she'd come into my office to say she was leaving.

"Yes, but someone to marry me and have a family with. There was this one guy in the last town that I lived in. I thought he might be the one. We were real serious and he asked me to move in with him, but then I heard from Jerome that they'd discovered I'd changed my name and knew where I was. There's only one way to stop them, so I asked Robert if we could get married, but he was horrified at the idea. He kind of backed off a little after that, so I left town and came here."

"Wait, you changed your name?" Evie nodded. "So, what is your real name if it's not Evie Walker?"

"Yvette Nicholls. I've also been Vetty Larouso. I figured with my coloring I could pull off being of Italian or Spanish descent, but I couldn't keep up with the accent."

I burst out laughing, realizing this shy, young woman who apparently had more balls than most men I knew, was also a little ditzy and cute.

"I'm sorry but you don't have to have the accent Evie to be of foreign descent."

Her eyes flashed wide, and her mouth gaped open. "Really? So I could be Vetty Larouso again in my next place?"

"No." I shook my head and moved back to stand in front of her. "You're not going anywhere. If they come, they come, but you're not leaving with them."

She let out a whimper. "But Tate you have no idea, you really don't. If they can't persuade me then they'll kidnap me or something. I have to leave. I just have to."

This was the most ridiculous thing I've ever heard. It was like something from a shitty 80's made for TV movie. There was no way she was leaving town. The poor girl deserved a break and besides which she was the best receptionist/assistant that I'd ever had. She worked damn hard. She was smart and efficient, and she was getting a pay raise.

"You said that there was one way to stop them."

She nodded as she played with the tissue in her hand. "If I was married then they can't make me be his wife." She paused and looked at me with a tentative gaze. "I'd be tainted. That's why a few of the girls from the group have ended up marrying local boys who were wholly unsuitable."

"Other girls have run away?" I asked, still unable to get my head around things.

"Julie Osmon got all the way to Vegas and was just about to marry a drag queen from Ohio when they found her. I just thought it best to run. I didn't have a boyfriend and I'm a little shy so would feel bad asking someone I didn't know to marry me."

Yep, this was definitely a prank put on by Hunter and Lily. It was a trick for my birthday seeing as they got me a shit present. They both thought it was funny to get me tickets to see Undefendable a tribute band of my dad's band, Defender. This was just something else that the pair of shits had cooked up between them.

"Evie, you're not lying to me, are you? This isn't a joke, right?"

"No, Tate. I swear I've been on the run for eight years, so I don't have to be the wife of a great big fat guy who wears white robes and a crown and calls himself Pastor Michael."

Fuck me. This was…I had no words.

"And you don't just trust us, your friends and colleagues, the people in this town to protect you if they show up?"

"I know y'all try but I can't risk it, Tate."

I thought about what she was saying. About the kind of life that she'd have if they found her and made her go back. I couldn't let that happen. I was an advocate for women's rights and for women to feel safe and protected. I had to do something.

God help me I'd done some stupid shit when I'd been a coke head, but what I was about to do was probably the worst, most stupid. I just hated the idea of this woman being alone and, on the run, again.

"Okay," I said taking a deep breath. "There's only one thing for it."

"You'll help me get a new life?" she asked, not sounding particularly enthusiastic.

"No," I replied. "We're going to get married."

THE Groom MATE

Coming 2023

THE BITCH LIST PLAYLIST

Spotify Link: shorturl.at/io257

River	Bishop Briggs
Dependent	Mac Muller
Hurts 2 Hate Somebody	Elio
I Found	Amber Run
Fav Boy	Ricky Reed, John Robert & Alessia Cara
Troublemaker	Olly Murs feat. Flo Rida
Nobody	Dylan Scott
Can't Stand the Rain	Lady A
A Little Less Conversation	Elvis Presley
When I Was Your Man	Bruno Mars

NIKKI'S LINKS

If you'd like to know more about me or my books, then all my links are listed below.

Website:
www.nikkiashtonbooks.co.uk

Instagram
www.instagram.com/nikkiashtonauthor

Facebook
www.facebook.com/nikki.ashton.982

Ashton's Amorous Angels Facebook Group
www.facebook.com/groups/1039480929500429

Amazon
viewAuthor.at/NAPage

Audio Books
preview.tinyurl.com/NikkiAshtonAudio

nikki
ashton

Printed in Great Britain
by Amazon